RED RAIN

Gill Wendel

RED RAIN

TIM WENDEL

The Writer's Lair Books
www.writerslairbooks.com

Nottingham, Maryland

Published by
THE WRITER'S LAIR BOOKS
P.O. Box 44286
Nottingham, MD 21236
www.writerslairbooks.com

Book designed: s.k.y. designs

ISBN: 9780975440216
LCCN: 2008937273

PRINTED IN THE UNITED STATES OF AMERICA

Disclaimer: This is a work of fiction based on historical facts of World War II. All characters and events portrayed in this novel are products of the author's opinion.

For my parents,
who taught me to look to the morning sky.

For my children, Chris and Sarah,
who keep me laughing.

And for my wife, Jacqueline,
who always believes.

"Historians have tended to make light of this use of man's oldest air vehicle, seemingly a pathetic last-ditch effort to retaliate against the United States. It was, however, a significant development in military concept, and it preceded today's intercontinental ballistic missiles launched from land or submarines. Had this balloon weapon been further exploited by using germ or gas bombs, the results could have been disastrous to the American people."

Robert C. Mikesh,
Japan's World War II
Balloon Bomb Attacks on North America

"I know it's a secret, for it's whispered everywhere."

William Congreve,
Love for Love

PREFACE

By late 1943, the tide of war had turned against the Japanese. Only a few years before, the empire of the rising sun had extended far into Asia and encompassed much of the Pacific. From the borderlands of India to the islands of Alaska, half of the globe went to sleep fearful about what the darkness could bring. After the battles of Midway and Guadalcanal such concerns began to diminish in the United States. The yellow hordes were no longer on the horizon, the politicians proclaimed. But the fear of another surprise attack, the long shadow of Pearl Harbor, would remain a nightmare for a generation in America. As the B-29 bombers began to pound Tokyo and most of the other major Japanese cities to rubble, the Japanese military became desperate to find a way to once again instill fear in its enemies. Out of such efforts was born the fire balloon.

Able to reach heights of nearly forty thousand feet above

the earth, carried eastward by the jet stream, these inventions may have been constructed out of paper, but they were strong enough to transport small bombs all the way across the Pacific Ocean to North America. That such a contraption could travel a distance of six thousand miles or more remains impressive to this day. The goal was to deliver, in some small measure, a hint of the fire and destruction that poured down upon Japan. The fact that these successful calculations of material and weather were made at a time when the sky burned red from the nightly bombing runs on Japan remains as remarkable as the balloons themselves. Even though security was tight for every launch, soldiers often slipped *samhara*—slips of paper with their personal prayers to the Shinto gods—into the folds of the balloons before liftoff.

From a modern point of view, the Japanese fire balloons would appear to be as effective as Don Quixote tilting at windmills. At first, the U.S. command in Washington and the Pacific was confused and then increasingly concerned about such attacks. The fire balloons, elegant though primitive, would not reverse the Allies' methodical campaign across the Pacific toward Tokyo. However, General Douglas MacArthur and many in the White House soon realized that for a nation weary of war, alarm about a new attack could lead to a lack of resolve. The Allies' goal was to win an unconditional surrender from Japan, the same terms that appeared imminent in Germany. Perseverance was sorely needed to finish the job.

So, the order was given to keep the fire balloons secret. Only the top levels of the U.S. military and the White House would truly know what kind of foe this was. A news blackout was evoked. Elite fire crews were formed throughout the Western states to fight the blazes resulting from such strikes. In most cases, only their commanders knew what they were combating. Meanwhile, in the Pacific, a fledgling spy network had taken root. It would never have the numbers or success of its counterpart in Europe. After all, there were more obstacles —time, language and culture—in this theater of espionage. Still, Japanese-American agents had been employed with success in the retaking of the Philippines. Perhaps they would work closer to Tokyo too.

OFF THE COAST
OF JAPAN

Here, beneath the waves, Yoshi Minagi found that any noise, no matter how faint or inconsequential, carried a life of its own. The ripples of whatever happened swept through the submarine, with everyone knowing everybody else's business. It was so unlike Manzanar, where the high desert winds took away anything of hope and consequence and carried it over the snow-capped mountains. That's what her brother had once said and Yoshi couldn't disagree. The jagged line of mountains, the heat in the summer, the cold in the winter—they all combined to separate them from the sea and how life had been before the surprise attack on Pearl Harbor.

But here, beneath the shimmering blue surface of the Pacific, any sound was precious and often acknowledged. Yoshi had been aboard the submarine for only four days. Her time with them was almost at an end. Still, she couldn't understand how these men, these American sailors, kept themselves from going crazy. Even though Yoshi had her own small room, a luxury aboard such a small vessel, she often had difficulty falling asleep. And when she did sleep she often awoke with a start, her forehead damp with sweat. She felt the anxiety well up inside her as she inhaled ragged breaths of the damp, stale air. She almost always dreamed of Manzanar and her family that so needed her to succeed. For a few agonizing moments she was uncertain about where her nightmares ended and where her new fortunes began.

Yoshi arose from the steel berth with its thin mattress that folded into the wall. She walked on tiptoe to her doorway and peered out. No wonder they all spoke in hushed tones, like they were in a church or a courtroom. Even from here she could understand much of what was said. It floated like music above the dull throb of the engines and the whir of the periscope going up. Only yesterday they had allowed her to sit with the boy at the sonar table. He was a proud one, trying to act like a man in his creased khakis and white tank top. She noticed the sheen of perspiration on his forearms as he let her listen for a few moments to his precious headphones. That strange language of pings and clicks belonged to the adverse world that surrounded them. Yoshi gazed at the screen and its revolving bar of light and listened, listened hard, but she could make no sense of it, and too soon the boy asked for his headphones back. She knew he was afraid that he would miss something if he allowed her to listen for too long. After all they were approaching the coast of Japan.

On this day, her last one scheduled aboard the submarine, the crew soon realized that she was awake and watching them.

"Don't be shy," Butch Allen said as he stepped back from

the periscope. "Come take a look at what you're heading into."

Yoshi walked down the corridor and the men paused in their work as she entered the control room. Most of them worked in their shirt sleeves, and Yoshi couldn't understand how they did that. Here, far beneath the sea, Yoshi never felt warm enough.

Lieutenant Neil Starling stood next to Allen. He was nervous, on edge, while Allen, commander of the U.S.S. Stephen Crane, simply smiled and nodded in her direction. Allen was so happy that he was nearly rid of her.

"It looks pretty quiet, doesn't it?" said Allen as Yoshi peered into the viewfinder and saw the dark outline of the coast. Quickly she scanned to the left and now the right. The metal of the scope felt cold to the touch. "But don't you worry your sweet little head," Allen added. "It'll be burning soon. The B-29s will make sure of it."

"That's enough," Starling said and Allen started to reply but then stopped, perhaps thinking better of it.

"All right, scope down," Allen said. "Ahead slow."

Be burning again soon. The phrase rattled around inside Yoshi's head after she returned to her cabin to prepare for her departure. The small room with steel walls was located adjacent to the aft bulkhead. This room had been part sanctuary, part cage for her during their four days at sea. About all Yoshi had been able to see through the periscope was the twisted wreckage of a factory, probably the Osaka textile mills. Farther over to the right, where she was scheduled to land a few hours from now, stood the hazy outline of trees. The towering cedars intermixed with cypress. That's where the rendezvous was scheduled to take place. In an odd way it reminded her of home, a place that she sometimes pretended was still out there, waiting for her to return. It was a small farm south of Monterey, where her family had once lived, back in that time when everything seemed so simple and perfect.

"You ready?"

It was Starling, the one who had accompanied her from the Manzanar Internment Camp. He had convinced her to enlist and then recommended her for this mission. Some would say that she should hold this against him. But she didn't. In an odd way he had done her a great favor. Starling had gotten her out of the internment camp and out of witnessing the slow collapse of her family and her people. It wasn't his fault that all he could offer was substituting one form of lunacy for another.

"Yoshi, it's time," Starling said when she didn't answer.

He stepped into the room and Yoshi instinctively leaned forward, momentarily shielding him from seeing the two photographs lying on the small table next to the cot bed. But then she realized that this was ridiculous. If anybody knew about her past, where she had come from, it was Starling. So, she turned toward him, allowing him to peer over her shoulder at the photos. The larger one had been taken on her parents' wedding day. Neither of them smiled in the sepia-tone image, but their dark eyes appeared so hopeful, filled with expectations. In the old photograph, her mother wore a long dress with a small strand of pearls around her neck. Her father appeared almost regal in his dark suit. They had decided to wear Western clothes, not traditional Japanese attire, because they lived in the United States now. They were proud to be Americans. That's what they considered themselves—Americans. That's why being taken away from their farm and forced to live in the desert beyond the Sierra Nevada mountains had broken their hearts. Her father had tried to farm on the patch of desert where they had been told to grow their food. He went out with the men every morning while Mother stayed in what was supposed to pass for a home, the small barracks they had been assigned. Every morning her mother swept the small room clean of sand and dirt, and every morning she needed to do it again.

The other photo, the smaller one, was of the farmhouse that had once been theirs. In the far left-hand corner of the photograph were the artichoke fields that led down to the sea, the vast and simmering Pacific.

"You can't take those with you," Starling said, his face clouding over, always attentive to any detail.

"I know," Yoshi replied.

Until that moment she had thought she would simply throw the photographs away when the time came. That's what her mother had done. Anything that could trace them back to the old country had been burned before they left the farm. Yoshi remembered how Mrs. Hamada, who lived down the road from them, threw her fine dishes against the wall the day before the buses came to take them to Bay Meadows. Mrs. Hamada broke every single one instead of selling them for pennies to the vultures that were their Caucasian neighbors.

"You'll take care of them for me?" Yoshi asked.

Surprised, Starling tried to smile at this and Yoshi watched him closely. His face was framed by brownish-red hair, closely cropped like all the men did these days. His crooked smile erupted for a moment, a passing fascination, only to quickly subside. Those blue-gray eyes soon regained their seriousness.

"All right," Starling said. "If you'd like me to."

"Please," she replied, happy to see him smile again, shy for a moment in his presence.

"It's going to be OK," Starling added, even though Yoshi

knew this was another one of his sweet lies. Sometimes, especially when he was nervous, such words tumbled out without much thinking. Sweet, sweet lies. Just something to say to help move things along.

Yoshi picked up the photographs and held them out for him. As he reached for them, she moved her hand forward so their fingertips briefly touched. She was acting crazy. She knew that. But with the time of her departure nearly at hand, she found herself hungry for any memory she could store away and take with her.

"We've gone over everything repeatedly," Starling said. "But do you have any questions?"

More than you can imagine, Yoshi thought to herself. How did you convince me to do this? What was it you saw in me that could be transformed into a spy?

After Starling had brought her down from Manzanar, Yoshi had studied for three months at the huge military base in the Presidio. Even though the men in uniform routinely worked such raw recruits twelve, fourteen hours a day, it felt good just to be close to the sea again. Hearing the seagulls chatter in the morning, smelling the eucalyptus trees and the salt air at night, had somehow strengthened her for whatever the Navy people asked of her. While three-quarters of her class had flunked out, Yoshi surprised herself by not only surviving the training period at the Presidio, but being one of the handful selected to go into the field. It helped that Starling had been there too, that he seemed to have a vested interest in her success.

"Once you get ashore," Starling said, "our people will be there to help you."

Yoshi nodded. They had gone over this many times before.

"Just get to Kyoto. That could be the toughest part."

Yoshi doubted that, but still she found herself nodding her head.

"I will," she said.

"Once you get in touch with our people there, find out what you can," Starling said, his voice picking up speed. "Anything, any detail will help."

Turning away for a moment, Yoshi nodded again. They had been all through this so many times before. These military men hated the realization that there was something out there that they couldn't control, that they had to turn to one as inexperienced as she was. Yoshi almost smiled at the silliness of it all—how such circumstances had become as fickled as the winds of Manzanar. Two and a half years ago, they had banished her family to the lonely lands where nobody wanted to live. They sent them to Manzanar because they were of Japanese descent and living in California. Her cousin, Yero, and his family were still living in their home in Kansas City. But any person of Japanese descent in California, Oregon or the state of Washington was sent to the camp because of the Civilian Exclusion Order. That damn piece of paper was posted in stores, restaurants and telephone poles four months after the attack on Pearl Harbor. There was no place to hide. To make sure they were sent away, their Caucasian neighbors had told the authorities that the Minagi Family could speak Japanese fluently, even though it wasn't necessarily true. Yoshi and her mother were the only ones who could really speak in the old tongue. Still, there was no denying it. In such times, rumor took root and quickly blossomed into fact. They went to the camp and later were told that the military needed people like her. Somehow they went from being outcasts to the only hope the U.S. forces had in this particular situation.

"Good luck," Starling said, and he came to attention and briefly saluted her. Instead of returning his salute, Yoshi took her time gathering up her things and then slipped close to kiss him once on the cheek. Again she found herself too daring, always ready for any experience she can hang onto and perhaps transform into a pleasant memory.

"Good-bye," she whispered and brushed past him, eager now to go, to get on with it.

Topside, the seas were choppy, rougher than either of them had expected. Two sailors held her raft as Yoshi waited between Allen and Starling and listened to the instructions she had memorized weeks before.

"You keep bearing for that big stand of trees," Starling said and pointed toward the shore. It was dusk. "Go as hard as you can. It will be darker soon."

There was hardly any wind and the angry waves slapped the hull of the submarine, sounding like distant gunfire.

A head appeared in the hatchway. "Captain, activity to the west," he said. "Betcha it's that patrol boat we picked up earlier on radar."

"Time's a wasting, folks," Allen said. "Jensen, lower her on down."

Yoshi took the sailor's hand and half-tumbled into the gray-black raft. Down here she was surprised by how much the craft pitched and rolled. She tried to look high, toward the horizon, to keep her stomach settled, just the way Starling had once told her back at the Presidio.

"It would be good to bring her in closer to shore," she heard Starling say high above her.

"The hell we are," Allen replied. "We've got the bombers coming in. Their patrol boats are on our tail. This is as good as it gets, lieutenant. Take it or we scrub the mission."

"I'll take it," Starling said reluctantly.

"Then let's get moving," Allen said. "Cast her off, men."

Two sailors pushed the raft away from the submarine and scrambled for the hatch.

"C'mon," Allen told Starling.

"Go," Starling said and Yoshi couldn't tell if he was speaking to Allen or her.

Still, she did as she was told and began to paddle, fighting the first of many waves that lay between her and the shoreline. But then Yoshi turned and saw that Starling was still watching her.

"Go," he repeated. "Go as hard as you can."

The other men had already disappeared below deck. Yet, for some reason, Starling stayed. His face, even from this distance, was filled with concern. For a moment Yoshi wished that the lines of protocol hadn't extended into every minute of every hour that they had been together since Manzanar. When she looked at him, her mind sometimes ran away from her. She had dreamed of him in the nights leading up to this departure, and she vowed that she would dream of him again.

Starling moved his entire arm forward, as if he could magically propel her forward to the distant beach, as if everything he hoped and prayed for somehow rode upon her shoulders now. It wouldn't be the touch or the impromptu kiss that she would remember. It would be the memory of him standing there on the deck of the submarine and the concern that had somehow crept across his face.

Yoshi dug her paddle back into the black sea and pulled hard for the shadow land far out in front of her. After a long while, when she glanced back again, the submarine was gone.

STRICTLY
HUSH-HUSH

"Sounds like a dicey exit, lieutenant," McCeney said.

"I wanted to get her farther into shore," Starling replied. "But Allen wasn't buying it."

McCeney took a deep drag off his cigarette.

"You did what you could, Neil" he said. "That's enough."

At times like this the war seemed far away to Starling. He stood with McCeney along the rail of the U.S.S. Renegade. The destroyer raced to catch up with the rest of the fleet. His transfer from the sub had gone off without a hitch. The men stared at him like he was some kind of god or a damn fool when the launch brought him alongside. Now he and McCeney gazed across the wide expanse of blue water and open sky. No enemy activity had been reported in the area for weeks. Here was a moment or two for a guy to rest easy, perhaps smoke a Lucky Strike with somebody who could pass as a pal in such turbulent times.

McCeney was right. There was nothing more he could have done. But for some reason Starling still worried about her—about this Yoshi Minagi. That had never happened before. Maybe he was getting soft.

The Kempei Tai had increased their patrols in the Osaka-Kyoto corridor. Recent reports confirmed it. Now that the Japs had lost the war in the Pacific, they were determined to win the home front—anything to put them in a better position to repel an invading force.

He could still remember her oval face with those dark eyes. He could still remember the way she peered back at him from the raft.

McCeney cleared his throat. "Neil, you've got a new posting. This one's straight from the top."

Starling nodded. He had been expecting this. Since the invasion of the Philippines, MacArthur was making good on his promise to return. The only path left led to Japan. The battle for Okinawa was on. After that it was on to Tokyo, where they needed more intelligence and resistance in place. Perhaps, he could find a way to help Yoshi Minagi in the process.

"You're a lucky man," McCeney went on. "You're heading stateside."

Starling stared at McCeney.

"Don't joke with me," Starling said. "It's been a long couple of days."

"No joke, Neil. Mac's sending you back to California and then to Arizona. There are matters there that need your attention."

Far below them the ocean swells softly rocked the vessel, and McCeney swayed deftly on the balls of his feet to such movements. Starling knew that McCeney had been with Douglas MacArthur's command since the beginning of the war and was always a step ahead of everyone.

"What the hell's so important state-side?" Starling asked.

McCeney took another drag of his cigarette and then in a lower voice he added, "This ties in with the package you dropped off, that Yoshi Minagi."

McCeney said her name like it was almost too much for him. The syllables clanging together like trains in a switch-yard. Yet the sound of somebody else speaking her name stopped Starling in his tracks. Silently, he waited for McCeney to continue.

"Everything becomes a race against time in this damn war, doesn't it?" McCeney said. "How fast can a force take the next island? How fast can we get to Tokyo now that Germany is about to fall? That's always what you hear from the suits and brass back in Washington. A bunch of nervous Nellies if you ask me. Not much concern about how many lads have just laid down their lives. It's always how fast can you get the next impossible job done."

Starling nodded patiently, determined to hear McCeney out.

"Last week another fleet of those fire balloons hit the West Coast," McCeney continued. "This weapon is more of a nuisance than anything. But the old man is getting worried. The President, too, for that matter. Near as we can tell what's left of the empire is letting them loose from various locations inside Japan. Soil samples confirm it. They hook a few incendiaries, the odd explosive, on a balloon that's thirty-some feet in diameter. The boys in Washington are certain that they're floating them across the Pacific Ocean."

Starling nodded. "We've know that for months. That's why we're smuggling Yoshi Minagi and god knows how many others into Japan. To see what they can find out about these devices."

"But in the last few weeks the situation has become worse. Our newest race against time," McCeney said.

He paused and gazed out at the sparkling Pacific. The war was coming to an end. Anybody in uniform could sense it, and Starling wanted to be there to see it finally put out of its misery.

"You see, Neil, our country's been blessed," McCeney said. "Except for a few isolated incidents along the West Coast immediately following Pearl Harbor, a few U-boats off New Jersey, our populace hasn't come under fire. We'd like to finish the war with people believing that they were safe and sound in their beds almost all the way through. But in the last month or so, these fire balloons have reached Arizona, Washington, Oregon, Utah and California. One's even floated as far east as Detroit, believe it or not. We've got a detail of Corsairs north of San Francisco on twenty-four hour patrol. But I'll be honest with you, Neil, you can count their kills on one hand. Mac's concerned, as is the Administration— "

"So what are we going to do?"

"We've got the makings of new panic on our hands. The same rumor mill that got churning after Pearl could happen now. Mac's afraid that people back home will get wobbly. That they will keep us from finishing the job here in the Pacific."

Starling didn't know where McCeney was leading him with all of this. They had nearly caught up with the rest of the fleet. How could anything float over all of this vastness? More importantly, how could a weapon, a balloon for God's sake, inflict any real damage after such a long journey?

"Bob, you and I know the real war's out here," Starling said. "It's just about Japan and nothing else right now."

"There are fronts everywhere in a war," McCeney said. "Last week Washington was ready to issue an APB throughout the West. It would have instructed common folk about what to do if a fire balloon came down in their back forty, what the weapons look like, how they're rigged, etc."

"Sounds like the right thing to do."

McCeney took a last drag on his cigarette and flicked it over the side.

"Neil, the old man rescinded that order."

"Why?" Starling said, glancing back at McCeney. "Why would MacArthur do that?"

"Because he's the first one who realizes that's playing right into the Japs' hands. That's what they want us to do. Get tongues to wagging right when we're trying to force them into an unconditional surrender like we'll soon have with Germany. Mac raised the issue and the President agreed with him."

"So, they've decided to keep it a secret."

"That's right," McCeney nodded. "Strictly hush-hush. But like anything it comes down to time. The boys in Washington aren't going to sit on that APB forever. At some point it'll get too political and somebody will get all concerned about warning their constituency and the word will be on the street. Also, MacArthur is convinced that the Japs will start hanging nerve gas, god knows what else off these balloons, instead of two-pound incendiary bombs. Then we'll surely have a full-fledged panic on our hands back home."

Starling shook his head. "I still don't understand what this has to do with me?"

"In an odd way, you and your Yoshi Minagi are working together. We've got to pray that she and her kind find out something more about these balloons. Where they're being made, who's doing it, so we can take immediate action. Set the bomb coordinates in Tokyo and wherever. Finish the job. Meanwhile, you and about a dozen other unfortunate souls are being stationed throughout the West. With your experience in espionage and explosives you're a natural. You'll be heading up a fire crew, fighting forest fires. The fires these damn balloons are starting."

"And I'm supposed to keep it all a secret?"

"Afraid so," McCeney replied. "Like I said, we'll have an unconditional surrender soon with Germany. We need the same thing from Japan. If they remain too strong after all of this, if we can't take the island, then who knows? Maybe we have to fight them again a generation from now. That's why Mac's concerned about anything that could push things off the tracks. That's why he's sending you to Arizona. To keep everything strictly hush-hush."

LUI

Yoshi was soaked through by the time she reached the shore. Wave after wave had broken over the snub-nose of the raft, spraying her with water as she pulled toward the trees. It had taken much longer than she had expected to complete the journey. The waves and current seemed to be always going against her.

She pulled the raft ashore and used her pocketknife to cut two-inch gashes in it, then kneeled on it to squeeze as much of the air out of it as she could. When it was lifeless, bearing no resemblance to the beast that had carried her across the black waters, Yoshi gathered rocks to anchor it. She rolled the rocks into a misshapen load that she tied together with twine that Starling had given her for the purpose. Only then did she push the whole mess back into the Kii Channel, watching it disappear below the surface.

Yoshi shivered and looked across the water. Two large shadows were moving back and forth, far away from the shore, from where she had come. She crouched close to the ground. But their searchlights remained locked on the patch of water where the U.S. submarine had been. The patrol boats had no interest in her—not yet.

She knew she should leave—move as quickly as she could toward the rendezvous in the forest of cedar and cypress. But she couldn't help but stare and pray as the Japanese patrol boats moved back and forth across the dark waters. One and then the other slowed, drifting in place where the submarine had been. No, Yoshi prayed as she watched them load the metal canisters, the depth charges, into place. Even though she knew what to expect, the explosion of water and sound still shocked her. Wide-eyed she rose, wanting to cry out, anxious to do anything she could to help. But there was nothing to be done, except pray that the submarine, with Starling aboard, had somehow evaded the wolves now on its tail.

"You fool," a voice said in Japanese. At first Yoshi thought she was babbling out loud. But when she turned toward the trees, she saw the figure. "Come with me. Now."

After a final glance back toward the sea, Yoshi began to run toward the trees.

"We don't have time for this," the voice said.

Yoshi saw it was a woman, perhaps a bit younger than herself. The girl had a black woolen cap pulled over her head and was dressed in a black long-sleeve shirt and pants. From a distance she could pass for a man. Yet standing so close, there was no doubt, in the eyes and voice, that she was a woman.

"You're soaked."

"I'm sorry," Yoshi said.

"Take this," the girl said, stripping away her long-sleeve shirt. Underneath she wore a black T-shirt.

Yoshi shook her head.

"Start following orders," the younger woman said, "or I'm leaving you. I mean it. You didn't reach the rendezvous point in time. You're crying over people you cannot help. Put this on. Do it now."

Yoshi did as she was told as the girl took Yoshi's old sweatshirt and dug into the sandy ground with both hands, burying the garment in a shallow hole. Then the two of them began to hurry back into the woods.

Behind them came the drone of the B-29s and soon the far side of the inlet burst into light and flame. Yoshi turned to see if the first wave of bombers had scared away the patrol boats. It was as if the other one could read her mind.

"Don't look back," she said. "Stay with me."

They had just moved farther into the forest when the sound of the engines overhead grew louder. More planes were coming in at a lower altitude. It was another wave of bombers, moving in from over the water. Next came a loud hissing sound—incendiary bombs. Against the dark sky, the incendiaries began to sparkle like fireworks—clusters of fire falling down from every angle. New constellations briefly overshadowed the old. Yoshi and her guide tumbled to the ground. The voice warned Yoshi to keep her head down, but the sight was too captivating to completely ignore.

As the bombers swept over them, the forest to their right was flooded with light. As the noise diminished, they scrambled back to their feet and moved cautiously into the clearing, nearer the glow. There a stray incendiary lay embedded in the ground, still spurting fire. It was a petroleum bomb. Yoshi recognized it from Starling's books. He knew everything about bombs and explosives, and during their time at sea he had come to her cabin several times to tell her about what she might encounter. The two of them had sat side by side on her bunk, with him trying to tell her about every potential danger on this mission. She remembered the soft reassurance in his voice. How she longed to hear his voice now. Yoshi watched this lone petrol still spraying a bit of oil trying to spread the fire. It was nearly extinguished.

"Come," the voice said. She took Yoshi by the hand. "We must get as far away as we can."

"How far do we have to go?"

The taller one gripped Yoshi's hand hard and then let it drop in exasperation.

"My name is Lui," she said. "That's all you need to know for now. No more questions, please. We have a long ways to go to reach Kyoto, and I fear that they've already sounded the alarm about you."

As they ran farther into the woods, all Yoshi could see was the whites of Lui's long arms. Thank God she had given me that sweatshirt, Yoshi thought. If not, I would have lost her in the darkness by now.

In single file, with Yoshi trailing, the two of them ran until they reached a road pocketed with craters.

"It's still passable," Lui muttered. They were crouched in the ditch that ran alongside the road. "The bombers didn't do the job. See?"

Indeed, far down the road Yoshi could make out the lights of the military transports.

"We need to keep going," Lui said. "Before they seal this area off and trap us."

Crouched at the waist, they scurried across the ravaged surface. As they neared the far side, Lui stumbled in the darkness and came up clutching her left arm.

"Are you OK?" Yoshi whispered as Lui rolled onto her back in pain. Beyond them, the transports rolled closer.

"Help me down," Lui gasped and Yoshi led her into the ditch. A deep gash ran along the inside of Lui's left forearm.

"We need time to get away," she told Yoshi, reaching into the small pack that was tied snugly to her waist. "Here, take this." Lui held a small bottle out to Yoshi.

Yoshi took the glass bottle from her and looked at it dumbly.

"Please tell me that at least you can do this correctly," Lui said.

"It's a Molotov cocktail?"

"That's right. Now you must light it," Lui said, rummaging through the pouch until she found two matches. "They're all I have, so be careful."

"I'll try," Yoshi said.

"Light the rag wick," Lui said. "Once you're sure it's going, throw it to the other side of the road, as far as you can. If we're lucky, it will distract them."

Yoshi fumbled with the first match. Lui cut away the tail of her T-shirt with a pocket knife and bound her cut with the fabric. When she was finished, she again turned her attention to Yoshi.

"You have it lit?"

"Not yet," Yoshi said, dropping the first match to the ground.

"C'mon here. You have a lot to learn."

Yoshi leaned close to Lui, heard her impatient breathing, and saw the blood already soaking through the fabric wrapped around her arm.

"I'll light it, but you need to throw it."

"I'll try," Yoshi said as the wick flared to life.

"Now," Lui said, "before they see us."

Yoshi took the small bottle of flammable liquid and crawled to the edge of the road. The trucks were converging on their position. Searchlights fanned across the dark woods from where they had come. In one motion, Yoshi rose and flung the bottle as far as she could. She watched as it quickly burst into flame, igniting the surrounding undergrowth.

"Come," said Lui, who was back on her feet. "We must go."

Behind them, Yoshi heard the shouts of men and several rounds of gunfire. This time she didn't turn around to look.

Yoshi and Lui slept during the day hidden in the bamboo trees, back from the Kamo River, which was the last in the thread of waterways they had followed inland from the coast near Osaka.

"You're still dreaming about that submarine, whoever was on it, aren't you?" Lui said.

Yoshi didn't reply. The two of them lay close together back in the bamboo forest, where they could whisper and remain undetected to anyone passing by on the riverbank. Lui was lanky, all arms and legs. Her narrow face was framed by shocks of brown hair that she made no effort to keep in line. Back home, in the United States, she would have been called a tomboy.

The cut on the inside of Lui's arm had grown infected in the days since they had escaped the coastline near Osaka. The angry slash began below the elbow and ran toward the wrist, and was now yellow with pus.

"You need to see a doctor," Yoshi said.

"I'll see one when we get to Kyoto."

"How far is that?"

"We're getting closer."

"But we're also slowing down."

Lui looked at her and shook her head. "You worry too much. You worry about things you have no control over. That's so foolish."

She took Yoshi's hand and held it against her belly.

"Tell me about yourself," Lui said in a softer voice. "How did you end up here? With me?"

How indeed? How could she explain to anyone that they had been given only five days to leave the farm? It may have been months and months ago now, but Yoshi would never forget it.

On March 31, 1942, the notice warning that all residents of Japanese descent along the West Coast of the United States would need to move from their homes was posted for the lands south of San Jose. Heads of families were directed to report to the local 'control stations.' At that point there was no mention of where her people would need to go.

But nobody in Yoshi's family had gone to town that day— not father or mother or her brother. She was home from the university on break. They didn't find out until their neighbor, Mr. Gaskill, came by, asking what they were ready to sell. That's how it began.

Yoshi closed her eyes and tried to calm herself by listening to Lui's measured breathing as both of them drifted off. They had to be a ways from Kyoto, out in the country, for Yoshi could smell the manure in the air. That's how Bay Meadows had smelled, especially after it rained.

At Bay Meadows, the stink seeped up through the newly cut floorboards and fresh whitewash and permeated everything about them. That's where her father's heart broke. She was certain of it. Others in the family might claim it was later at Manzanar, during the first long winter that was followed by the hot summer when hardly anything would grow. But Yoshi knew it was at Bay Meadows, the race course down the Peninsula, south of the City. They soon learned that this was one of the temporary assembly centers, along with Stockton, Turlock, Merced, Pinedale, Fresno, Tulare and Santa Anita. No Japs were allowed within two hundred miles of the coast without supervision. That's what the new notices read.

School was held in the glass-enclosed grandstand overlooking the muddy racetrack. The youngest children were down at the far end, with the upper grade school and junior high in the middle and the senior high students at the opposite end. Yoshi didn't need to go to the makeshift school. She was supposed to be entering her senior year at the University in Berkeley. Her father had worked hard to cobble together the money for that. She was the first from their family to go to a U.S. college, even though it was expected that her younger brother would follow her.

Those first few days Yoshi stayed in the stables and helped her mother. She had brought a few books with her, a chemistry textbook, Don Quixote and Homer. There was also the family Bible. Her plan was to keep her mind sharp, as father suggested. She could read after she finished helping mother hand-wash the family laundry in the large steel buckets the government had issued them. The wet clothes were hung on a line to dry.

"You go," mother would say before they were half done with the chores. "I can manage the rest."

At first Yoshi wouldn't hear of it. But soon she was walking around the muddy track, happy to see the morning fog on the soft green hills that rose to the West. Up in the grandstand, the young children smiled when they saw her come in. Out in front of them, sparkling like broken glass on the road, was the San Francisco Bay. Throughout the afternoon, as she walked among the various study groups, Yoshi would gaze out at those waters and the straw-colored hills that rose on the far side.

The smaller children would giggle when they caught her closing her eyes and reopening them upon the water and the hills of the East Bay. What they didn't know was that Yoshi was studying this view as intently as she had ever done anything in her life. Time after time during the first few weeks away from the family farm, she would test herself. When the sun broke through the morning fog, the water sparkled and danced with light. She remembered that there were two hump-like hills and then one more on the far side, separated by a notch that was almost as wide as her thumb.

The afternoon of their last day at Bay Meadows, Yoshi walked up the track grandstand. The doors were locked. There was no school today because everyone needed to pack, to go to this new place called Manzanar. One last time she looked out at the hills they needed to cross and she knew there were steeper ones between here and where they were going. Once more she tried with all her might to memorize this particular view of the world. But as she hurried down to the stables, to help mother pack up everything once again, Yoshi knew it was already slipping away from her.

Lui held Yoshi's hand until nightfall. Only then did they arise and walk again in the long shadows of the riverbank. They ran when they could, but they were much weaker than three nights ago when their journey had begun. Overhead the night sky was clear and a half-moon illuminated the land like a distant searchlight. Finally, that evening, they reached the outskirts of Kyoto—mostly single-story structures with gated entranceways. Every now and then they heard dogs barking. It was if they were re-entering civilization after days lost in the wilderness. They appeared to be safe, walking into the glowing city, the yellow light reflecting off the Kamo River's shallow rushing waters. Yoshi thought the worst was over until Lui looked behind them and began to walk faster.

"They've found us again," she said and Yoshi turned to see the flickering orange lights, torches being held aloft, and the echo of more dogs—dogs that were tracking them.

"We need to split up," Lui decided. "At the next bridge I'll try to draw them away."

"No, please," Yoshi said. "Let's stay together."

"Then they will surely catch both of us," Lui said. "No, there's a better way. You need to run two more bridges farther upriver. It's a quarter-mile. No more. You can do that, right?"

"But what about you?"

"You need to stop worrying about everybody around you. How many times do I need to tell you the world isn't that way anymore?"

Lui began to run and Yoshi forced herself to keep up.

"The next street is Shichijo," Lui said. "I'm going to cross to the other side of the river. I'll make some noise. Draw them off. You go up two more blocks. They're long blocks, but you can do it. First to Gojo and then to Shijo. Stay on this side. Keep moving."

"But where am I going?" Yoshi asked. Inside she felt as if everything was falling apart. She had been a fool to volunteer for this assignment. She should have stayed in the internment camp and waited until the war was finally over. She should have waited no matter how much her family needed her help.

"In two blocks, at Shijo, go up the embankment to the street," Lui told her. "There you'll see the Kabuki House. Go to the back. Up the outside stairs to the top floor. Now here's Shichijo. This is where we need to split up. Don't worry, sweet Yoshi. Nobody knows their way around Kyoto better than I do. If I can reach one of the temples, I'll hide there. The monks are good to us."

At the base of the stone bridge, Lui began to scramble up the embankment to the sleeping city of Kyoto above them. Yoshi stood in the shadows, watching her.

"Hurry," Lui hissed down at her. "They're getting closer."

Yoshi glanced back and saw that the men holding the torches aloft were bearing down upon them. The baying of the dogs was growing louder. When she looked back for Lui, she was gone. With that Yoshi began to run as fast as she could. The sound of her feet upon the wide dirt path along the river echoed in the darkness underneath the Shichijo Street Bridge. Behind her she heard Lui running across the bridge for the other side of the Kamo River and somebody shouting for her to stop. At the bridge for Gojo Street, Yoshi briefly looked back, but Lui was no longer in sight and the men with the torches had disappeared around the last gentle curve of the Kamo River. Out of breath, she soon reached Shijo and scrambled up the embankment, away from the river to the street.

It was quiet and only a few lights were on, Kyoto's belated acknowledgment of the war. Everyone knew that the holy city was never bombed. It had little industry and was home to the Golden Pavilion and hordes of other temples. How much better to take possession of the country without destroying such treasures. Instead the B-29s concentrated on Tokyo to the north, and Osaka and Kobe to the south.

Across the street was the Kabuki Theater, a four-story building with a clay tile roof. Even in the shadows, Yoshi could see that it was an impressive sight. The clay tiles made the roof appear to roll and ripple, like small waves on a distant sea, and the corners of the building swept out over the street as if they had a mind of their own. She looked up and down the street one last time and then ran for the rear of the building.

A wooden staircase led up from the street and she followed it. At the top landing, she reached a door. It was shut but wasn't locked. Yoshi put her shoulder to the heavy wood, cracking it open wide enough to wedge herself inside. After closing the door behind her, she froze, allowing her eyes to adjust to the newfound darkness. At first it appeared to be pitch-black, but in a few moments Yoshi was able to make out a flickering light, a candle, far down the hall. Slowly she began to walk across the planked floor. Yoshi moved on tiptoe, trying to stay quiet, but it was no use. With every step, the corridor awoke with squeaks and titters, sounding as if a flock of strange birds was mocking her every effort. Even when she tried to stay absolutely still, the strange floor moved and shifted beneath her. Its squeaking and clattering loudly announced her arrival.

In a panic, Yoshi began to run, which only made the squawking noise louder. Somewhere in the shadows she heard laughter. It roared forth deep and guttural, mixing with the high pitched cries of the birds, taunting her. Yoshi collapsed onto the floor.

"The nightingale floor claims another victim," the voice said from the shadows.

An older woman dressed in a dark flowing robe moved toward her. She held a samurai sword in both hands, and it flashed silver in the half-light as she replaced it in the scabbard.

"The floor has saved my neck many a time," she said. "Just as it once did for the shogun."

Yoshi could only stare at this old warrior woman, wondering what kind of crazy world she had entered.

"Now, now, my child," the woman said. As she crept closer, the floor chirped faintly with every step she took. "I'm Madame Isobe. I've been expecting you."

Yoshi let the old woman help her to her feet.

"It's all right, sweet Yoshi," Madame Isobe said. "You're safe here. You and Lui did well. That's a long distance to traverse in such troubled times."

"Lui isn't with me," Yoshi said. "Not anymore. We had to separate down along the river. The men were coming for us."

A look of concern stole across the older woman's face.

"Our Lui is a resourceful one," she said and tried to smile. "There's nothing we can do, not at this hour. In the morning, I'll send others around to see what they can find out. If she made it to Tijo Temple she'll be all right. The monks there are enthralled with her."

Isobe led Yoshi down the dark hallway, away from the door.

"For now you need to rest," she said. "Come with me." And with an arm across Yoshi's back, Madame Isobe led her deeper into the theater. Faint squeaks and squawks—a man-made duplication of the sweet nocturnal song of the nightingales—accompanied their every step.

IN DREAMS

"Did you sleep well, my dear?"

Madame Isobe stood in the doorway with a bamboo tray and two steaming clay cups of green tea.

"We don't have much, but we always share at the Kabuki Theater."

Yoshi rose to a sitting position and Madame Isobe knelt with the tray alongside her.

"Lui?" Yoshi asked as she sipped her tea too quickly, burning the tip of her tongue.

"Slower, child," Madame Isobe said. "They were right. Your Japanese is very good. But you are too much in a hurry. Too much like an American. Too much like a *moga*."

"*Moga?*"

"A modern girl. The kind that used to smoke cigarettes and drink cocktails in the English hotels before the war," Madame

Isobe said. "I remember when I was much younger how the *mogas* danced in the jazz clubs. They bobbed their hair and showed off their bared arms and put on red lipstick. You'll have to be careful not to remind anyone of them. Don't ever be too American in this land, my dear."

Tiring of the old lady's lecture, Yoshi asked, "But Lui? Is she okay?"

"See, that's just like *moga*," the old woman sighed. She paused before continuing, "All right, for today, I'll indulge your Western ways. But after this, no more questions, please. You must learn to be quiet. To simply listen. To be obedient and therefore wise."

Madame Isobe blew upon her tea but didn't try to take a sip. When she glanced up to see how crestfallen Yoshi was, she smiled with thin lips.

"I take it as a good sign that we have heard nothing," Madame Isobe said. "If she had been caught, word would already be going around. Yoshi, let's be patient and see what happens."

Yoshi did as she was told and sipped her tea, feeling the warmth seep through her.

After awhile, Madame Isobe asked, "What did you dream about last night?"

"A question?" Yoshi replied.

"Ah, you are a sharp one. For this one time, we'll break my rule."

For a moment, Yoshi couldn't remember anything from the night.

"Who is Starling?" Madame Isobe said.

"Starling?"

"Yes, you said his name several times in your sleep, child. At first I thought you were speaking of my nightingale floor. But this means something else, right?"

Yoshi sipped her tea and tried to be as slow and as thoughtful as the old woman wanted her to be.

"He's a commander," she said. "The one who convinced me to do this."

Madame Isobe considered this and then said, "He must be quite a commander for you to whisper his name in the night."

Yoshi blushed slightly and Madame Isobe added. "No, child, that's good. I won't mislead you. This task isn't going to be easy for you. Hang onto anything that helps."

Later, after Madame Isobe left with the bamboo tray, Yoshi began to remember her strange dream. In it, Starling was standing on a hill, looking back at something behind him. By the look on his face, Yoshi could tell he wasn't happy.

Starling stopped near the ridge line and gazed down the trail at his crew. They weren't ready for this—not by a long shot. It was only early afternoon and already they were spent. He would have to slow his pace or else they would be scattered across this forest, easy pickings whenever the flames arrived.

"Move it up," he yelled, and heard Leo Webb repeat his command like an echo from the back of the cutting order.

As fire boss Starling was at the head of the line, leading the way, while Leo was in the rear, trying to hurry them along. The king was in front and the prince was in back. That's what the others whispered about the arrangement back at base camp, and Starling always made sure he knew what others were whispering. But Leo was loyal, and that's all that mattered. Starling knew that the only thing a kid like him wanted was to belong to a world larger than he could imagine. After all, that's how it had begun with him.

Starling had been raised to be a dynamiter. He had told Yoshi that much. His grandfather and father had worked the rivers that flowed into Lake Michigan. When the lake ice melted in the spring on through to the following winter their task had been to keep the logs flowing downstream toward the cities and mills. Throughout the north woods, the Starling family had a reputation for doing whatever was necessary to break up a logjam. When the charge was needed far offshore, in the matchstick tangle of floating tree trunks, his father would grease himself down with crankcase oil. A line was tied around his waist and his uncle would ply out the thin rope with his crooked fingers. Uncle Les never wore gloves for this part of the procedure. "I need to know the feel of it, boy," he explained to Neil way back when. And Starling had never questioned the wisdom of those words.

On this afternoon, in northern Arizona, Starling's crew was stretched along the ridge deep in the woods, a bit south of Mormon Lake, in the high country between Butch and Horse Knoll mountains. There were good-sized blackjack pines intermixed with Douglas firs and plenty of brush. The locals had been right. It was plenty dry enough for things to burn up here—not that he was going to tell them that. It seemed that the thunderstorm that had passed through the previous evening hadn't made a dent. It must have been nothing but dry lightning—not a piss of rain.

As Starling watched, the crew did pick up its pace, moving faster, more concentrated with their strokes. He had found fighting fire a simple enough job. Put down a trail, a scratch line through the forest and then widen it, improve upon it, as you went. An eight-foot-wide trench would stop most blazes. It sounded easy, but it was hard, dirty work.

Overhead daylight filtered through a hazy light smoke. Starling saw pieces of white ash high up, floating on the slight breeze that was beginning to grow in strength. Out there, maybe beyond the next side of the stand of pine and red cedar juniper, was the fire. Sometimes, when the breeze shifted in the right direction, he could hear it. The sound was a distant roar, something like a waterfall or a rushing river, or maybe a fleet of B-29s passing way overhead. From a distance, the noise could be called beautiful, perhaps even seductive. But soon the wind would slacken and the distant roar would fade until all that was left was the sound of his crew's handtools striking against the hard ground. Just behind him came the Cunninghams, a father and son, with their double-handed crosscut. They followed the markings he had made with his brushhook—gashes into the trunks of the trees that stood too close to their planned fireline, ones that had to be taken down if the flames were to be contained.

Eli Cunningham and his fifteen-year-old, J.C. Jr., manned the crosscut saw. The noise they made when they went about their work was airy, almost graceful compared to what followed. Pulaskis were savage-looking tools with ax-hoe heads. Flip the tool one way and it could chop away branches, roots, and even a fair-sized tree trunk. Turn the shaft one hundred and eighty degrees and it could grub and tear at the ground. Koch, Fugery, Pierce and Riddle wielded the Pulaskis. Behind them came the shovels: the Mexican, Perez, the two girls, Genie Holahan and Taylor Webb, and, finally, Taylor's baby brother, Leo.

At times like this Starling felt like he had become a champion of lost causes. Somehow between Pearl and Midway he had gained the reputation for doing the dirty jobs—the ones that everybody else knew to avoid. Perhaps he embraced details too readily. He had been the only one to complete the entire tour of the internment camps: Manzanar, Granda, Poston, Rohwer, Jerome, Minidoka, Gila River, Heart Mountain, Topaz and Tule Lake, where the hard cases were sent. They had pleasant enough sounding names, but to this day Starling couldn't believe that they had made people live like that—locked up behind fences of barbed wire, two hundred people lining up to use a single latrine, a fine dust covering everything. It was like the world was trying to bury these people, Americans by all rights, before they had a chance to live a life. Into that world he had come with the recruiting agents. What a crock. For all their trouble, you could count on one hand the viable candidates they had found. One of them had been Yoshi. The whole situation was about as sorry as a Navy man being stationed miles away from the sea, the last real front of this god-awful war. He had been sent to a town that seemed determined to hate his guts.

They waited until night to take on the main flank of the fire. As they followed the switchback trail down from the ridge, their miner's lamps shone from atop their silver helmets and the small beams of light danced crazily in the darkness. Once more they were in cutting order, with Starling in front, followed by the Cunninghams with the crosscut, Koch and the other Pulaskis, and finally the shovels, the Mexican, the two girls and Leo.

To their left, the Teague Fire roiled and hissed like a strange ocean. It glowed red-orange, outlined in darkness and shadows. Occasionally flames shot up the side of a ponderosa pine or one of the smaller evergreens and more of their world was briefly illuminated as if a giant hand had lit a match. For a few moments, Starling could see the whole crew stretched out behind him. They looked like a primitive army. They were all bent over at the waist as if they were paying homage to some fierce god—hurriedly trying to finish their new task before the blaze reached them.

Starling worked as hard as he ever had that evening, but out of the corner of his eye he saw revelations. Directly in front of him was the safe, honest dirt of the trail, the fire-line his crew was set to work on and improve and widen. But down to the left, farther into the valley, the land had become fluid with color and heat. He tried not to stare. It was if he had been lied to for so many years, taught that the world was one way when underneath it was as wild and as dangerous as any nightmare he had ever known. Pieces of white ash began to fall from the sky. They settled like snow upon their helmets and shoulders. To stare too long at such things was to risk going insane.

Starling's walkie-talkie buzzed alive. It was Leo. Spot fires had erupted on the hillsides behind them. The fire boss stopped his crew and told them to buddy up. They had to control the spot fires or else the blaze was lost.

Starling joined Koch and Leo around a ponderosa pine that was already half consumed with flames. The tree's resin bubbled through the bark, evaporating in the growing heat.

"Fan back," Starling shouted. "Watch for any sparks flying off it."

They walked slowly backward—their handtools at the ready. At first the fire crept down the sides of the twenty-foot tree and Starling thought they could manage it. It looked just like the way they explained it back in the classrooms at the Presidio. But then the top section exploded into a shower of flying embers. Bits of glowing wood were spit into the air and the crew fanned out in the twilight, thinking they could do the impossible, thinking they could stop every spot fire that would allow the Teague Fire to escape.

"Go on," Leo shouted. "I'll finish this one."

"Where are the girls?" Starling shouted.

His number two looked confused and shook his head.

"Get everyone back to the trail, you understand?" Starling said and Leo nodded. "We need to pull out of here. I'll find them."

He guessed that Taylor and Genie had gotten carried away—run headlong after the farthest spot fire, thinking this was just like any other blaze in these parts. Nothing could have been further from the truth.

Behind them something exploded in the high canopy.

"How can it be crowning already?" Leo exclaimed, but the fire boss realized their situation was deteriorating faster than the boy could imagine. Only an incendiary bomb made that loud a noise. This area had to be pocketed with fire balloons.

"Get the rest of the crew out of here," Starling said. "I'll find Genie and Taylor and catch up."

"But, sir, we can still get this."

"Do it!" Starling ordered. "We're pulling out, understand?"

"Yes, sir."

Thick gray smoke rode the night breeze, causing Starling's eyes to well as he headed off the trail toward the spot fires. He found the girls near one of the new blazes. They were digging single-mindedly at the ground with their shovels, flinging dirt at the base of the flames. Starling fell in beside them and together they beat down the ribbons of light that crept along the ground with the back of their shovels and sometimes their boots. In the gap between his leather gloves and fire shirt, a small sliver of skin tingled from exposure to the flames. Behind them Starling saw that the fire-line, which once looked as perfect as a good stretch of highway, was pocketed with eruptions of light and smoke. The spot fires had linked up, eager to force their way through the canyon.

"Stop," Starling shouted. "We've got to get out of here."

He had to wait a few moments for the words to sink in. That's how caught up these two were in the task at hand. They were willing to labor until everything swept over top of them.

Starling led them through the growing smoke, trying to find a way back to the trail and the ridge. Up ahead, several spot fires had joined, and in the shifting breeze, a wall of orange and red began to advance toward them.

"This way," Starling said and headed away from the flames.

But the newer fire seemed to hear him and it moved adeptly to cut them off. Behind them was the larger blaze, the Teague Fire, the one that they had almost stopped by moving down from the ridge. Ahead of them were the spot fires, glowing bright clusters that were merging and growing larger.

"We have to go through it," he told them. "Go into the smaller burn."

"No," Taylor began to protest, but Starling had already locked his arm with hers and switched hands with his long handle shovel so he could do the same with Genie. The steady roar of the bigger fire, the Teague, was behind them and gaining.

"It's our only option," the fire boss said. "We've got to keep angling away from the bigger one. That's the one that could kill us."

Taylor shook her head. "I'm not going."

"The flame wall is two-foot thick, three feet at most," Starling said. The spot fire hissed and glowed only a few yards ahead of them. "Put your shovel up, up in front of your face to protect yourself. Don't breathe until we get through to the other side."

Without giving them another moment to think, Starling led them forward. Together the three of them raced toward a small break in the flames. For an instant they felt suspended in mid-air, held briefly in that space between the elements, before falling back to earth, rolling onto the smoking black, safe ground that the fire had just consumed. The flames had been small enough, his guesswork accurate enough, for all of them to be spared this time.

THE NIGHT OF
RED BATON

Yoshi and Madame Isobe knelt on either side of a small table and ate the meager helpings of fried fish and burloak root. How Yoshi longed for a bowl of rice, but there was none to be had. Even back at Manzanar they hadn't been lacking for such basics. They made sure of that by becoming the most productive farm in the Inyo County. The Caucasians couldn't bring forth much abundance from the dry, cracked earth. It was said to be almost impossible until her people, the Nisei, had done so. "Remember that, my daughter," her father often told her when he returned from the fields. "We have a way with the world. When we first came here, we had one plow, but now we have rows of corn, melons, radishes, turnips, tomatoes, cucumbers, even watermelons."

Yoshi would smile and pretend that what her father said would somehow put everything right. In many ways he was one of the lucky ones. He was allowed to venture beyond the inner rectangle of barbed wire and help with the growing farm. Water had been siphoned from the nearby Symmons Creek and the fields had grown from a few hundred acres to nearly two thousand. Work was done in three shifts, enough to revive and then triple the yield from the old orchards that gave Manzanar its name. Six hundred lugs of apples and five thousand boxes of pears were picked that first summer. The growing patch of green beyond the barbed wire, however, still wasn't enough to hold down the dust. Yoshi soon lost track of how many days she returned from her job, covering her eyes with her hand from the dust, her dark hair tied back under a kerchief.

Yoshi worked as a secretary to the director. She had gained Mr. Ogden's trust because she could fully translate anything for him.

"I'd be lost without you," he often joked to Yoshi. "Completely and utterly lost."

What was just as important in Yoshi's estimation, even though she never told Mr. Ogden, was her ability to communicate his latest directive to as many in the camp as she could. Most of them at Manzanar may have been Nisei, born and educated in the United States (as American as anyone else as her little brother liked to say), but there were many in camp more comfortable with the old tongue. One was her mother, who was classified on Mr. Ogden's roster as an alien because she was born in Japan. She had come to this country as a mail-order bride to marry her father. Yoshi thought it important that those who preferred the old tongue be told the latest news in Japanese, and she eventually convinced Mr. Ogden of such merits as well.

So, every other afternoon, even when the dust storms did their worst, she walked among the five hundred and four barrack buildings that made up Manzanar. A family of four was allotted a space of twenty by twenty-five feet. They brought only what they could carry, what had fit on the buses from Bay Meadows. The only heat in the winter came from small oil-burning furnaces. After that first winter, Yoshi found written in Mr. Ogden's papers that the military had officially called Manzanar "theater of operations" housing—meaning that it was only suitable for combat-trained soldiers, and then only on a temporary basis. She never told anybody else that.

In the afternoons, Yoshi spoke with Mrs. Sugahara, Mrs. Hamasaki, Mr. Yamagata—all the old ones that she could find. Speaking Japanese made her happy in the heart, but such gladness often faded when she returned to her family's small unit. Almost always she found her mother sweeping away the dust that came through the cracks in the tar-paper walls and up between the planks in the floor. That's what her father never saw, what he would never understand.

But here, in Japan, the shortages were more acute than anything Yoshi had experienced back in Manzanar. Madame Isobe had inspected the clothes Yoshi had worn—clipping away the metal buttons with a small knife. Anything metal had long ago been turned over to the government to make bullets. The metal buttons had been replaced with ceramic ones. Even the bronze statue of Ninomiya Kinjiro that had once stood in the schoolyard down the street had been taken away, Madame Isobe said. Before the one-meter-high statue of the boy in a kimono, his hair in the old-fashioned topknot, disappeared for good, the schoolchildren had stepped up, one by one, to say goodbye to him. Most schools in Japan had a statue of Ninomiya Kinjiro,

Madame Isobe told her. He was the model of an ideal student. Now all such statues had been turned into bullets or shells.

Yoshi quickly cleaned her plate. Bored, she tried once again to strike up a conversation with the older woman.

"Is there a way to walk across the floor without it squeaking?" Yoshi asked. She had been at Madame Isobe's for several weeks now.

"Your accent is very good," the old woman replied, "for a moga."

Yoshi sighed. She was growing impatient with her host's ways. For the first time since she had arrived she concentrated on Madame Isobe's face. The network of wrinkles spread back from the eyes and knotted the skin from the eyebrows on up to the forehead. Her gray hair was pulled into a tight bun. The old woman sat back on her knees with the tranquility of a Buddha. Yoshi couldn't determine how old she really was. The skin was crinkled and ravaged, but her shadow that passed along the curtain walls at night could have belonged to a far younger woman.

"I wonder if I can trust you, dear Yoshi?" Madame Isobe said. "Or are you really an assassin sent to hunt me down? To grow like a weed inside my house until everyone overlooks you. Then do you strike?"

"You know where I came from," Yoshi said, looking with resignation at her wooden bowl with nothing left in it and hearing the rumble of protest in her belly. "How I got here."

"But do I know you? No. One can never be too careful. Not now."

Yoshi tried to remain still.

"Did you ever hear of a man called Richard Sorge?" Madame Isobe asked.

Yoshi shook her head.

"He was a good Nazi," Madame Isobe said. "Or that's what he pretended to be. In the early years of the war, he rose to the highest levels of society here. A dashing, charming man. But he wasn't as he seemed. All along he was sending information back to Russia, back to Stalin. Our hopes were that some of it would find its way to Churchill and Roosevelt, too."

"You worked for him?"

Madame Isobe shook her head. "You are too direct, so American."

"I'm sorry."

"Like I said he was a charming man, but he knew when to stay quiet, how to listen. Sorge discovered from our leaders that Hitler planned to invade Russia. He warned his superiors a month before the German tanks started rolling eastward. He learned such things because he was still and he didn't draw attention to himself."

With that Madame Isobe stopped speaking and folded her hands together in her lap. This time Yoshi vowed to stay quiet, too, and wait the old woman out. Madame Isobe sat with an impassive face, eyes closed, for how long? Five, ten minutes? Then her eyes reopened and she gazed again upon Yoshi.

"Good, you're learning," she said. "Patience may be the greatest virtue. When Sorge was caught, a few of us escaped. That's when I came here, to Japan's holy city. It had become too dangerous for me in Tokyo. Sorge was the one who told me about the shogun's nightingale floor. He was always interested in history, how those who had preceded him had done things. When I took over the theater, I had the top floor renovated into my living quarters. That's when I remembered what Sorge had told me about the nightingale floor. The shogun built it to warn him whenever somebody was approaching. It's very simple really. In Japanese, it's called the uguis-bari. You set the planks atop the joints with a clamp and then a nail. The floor isn't set firmly in place. It's strong, as strong as the cypress tree by the water, but when one walks upon it, the clamp moves into a small hole, rubbing against the nail. That's what causes the squeaking sound. The sweet sound of the nightingale."

"Everyone makes that sound except you," Yoshi said.

"If you think of it as a carpenter would, that would mean the occasional floorboard has actually been nailed down in place. No holes, no clamps, no sound. But which ones are firmly anchored and which boards are ready to sing? Some would say it's as easy as, how do they like to say it in the United States? I know—one, two, three."

After they finished eating, Madame Isobe stood up and stretched her arms out wide. "It is a pleasant evening," she said. "We should go and enjoy it."

Yoshi looked at her with curiosity. Since her arrival she had been allowed outside of the theater only a few times, and never for very long.

Madame Isobe laughed. "What, my child? Did you think I was going to keep you under lock and key until you began your work? That would be silly of me, wouldn't it? We need to get you out, see the city, or you will be like a moga bumpkin from the country, doing nothing but gawking at ancient Kyoto. You see, I have your best interests in heart. Come, there's a festival, a very famous celebration, tonight at Toji Temple. Everyone should see it once in their lives."

When they came down the rear staircase, a rickshaw was waiting for them by the stage entrance. It was an hour or so past sunset and the narrow streets around the theater were alive with activity. From the theater they took a circuitous route to Toji, first heading north through the alleyways of the Gion District, where the geisha girls, in their wooden clogs, once trotted about. From there they swept over the Kamo River, down through the small downtown toward the southwestern perimeter of the city. From several blocks away they could see the towering spire of Toji.

"Legend says it marks the boundary of Kyoto," Madame Isobe said. "It was built to protect us from any evil gods. So far it's done its job."

As the rickshaw drew closer, they heard yelling and chanting, and Yoshi bit her tongue, trying not to ask anymore questions. Outside the temple, the streets became too crowded for any vehicle to move through, so the two of them got out. Madame Isobe paid the driver and held out her elbow for Yoshi. Arm in arm, like a mother and daughter on a nightly walk, they strode into the swirl of faces, letting the crowd carry them toward the temple grounds.

Once inside the main gates, Madame Isobe led Yoshi through the masses until they came to the back of a grandstand, where monks dressed in golden-colored robes guarded the wooden steps up to a temporary placing of bleachers. Several of the monks nodded at Madame Isobe and they were allowed to pass. They found seats near the top and peered down at packs of people dressed only in loincloths. A few also wore tight-fitting tunics over the top half of their torsos. These strange competitors ran back and forth in front of the stone steps that led up to the temple gates.

"It's a sight, isn't it?" Madame Isobe said, clearly excited by the chanting and the various teams of half-naked people charging about.

Yoshi only nodded and Madame Isobe smiled.

"Good," she said. "You're learning to be still. What you see before you, my dear, is the Festival of the Spring Moon, the last full moon before summer. The Festival of the Spring Moon dates back to the time of the shogun."

Inside the long sleeves of her evening kimono, Yoshi found herself pinching her fingertips, running up and down either hand like a maestro would play a piano. She had so many questions about what she saw, but she knew none of them would be answered if she didn't stay silent.

"Watch, my child," Madame Isobe finally said. "At the stroke of midnight, from the temple eaves, four batons will fall. Three are counterfeit—of no worth whatsoever. But the fourth is the red baton, the lucky bamboo baton. Anybody who touches it will have luck for the year. That is the belief. The one who secures it, takes it home—well, such good fortune can be without measure. Neighborhoods form teams and devise strategies to capture the baton."

Below them the first of the several groups charged up the temple steps and began to jump and yell outside the gates.

"Where those ones stand," Madame Isobe said. "That's where they'll drop the baton. So everyone will want to be there. But it won't be easy to hold one's position."

With that, water fell onto the ones under the temple eaves. It hit the warm naked skin, forming clouds of condensation.

"That's the temple priests, doing their dirty work," she explained. "They won't make it easy for whoever wins."

From the sides several new groups of half-naked competitors charged those on the top landing and pushed several down the slick stone stairs to the laughter and cheers of the growing crowd.

"For centuries, the competition has been all men. But, with the war, it was decreed that women could try their luck. Look carefully and you'll see them."

Yoshi did find a few. They were the ones with tight-fitting tunics over their breasts. But like their male peers, they too only wore a loincloth from the waist down. Their buttocks glistened with sweat and temple water.

As the minutes crept toward midnight, the top platform became so packed that more contestants slid and fell down the stone steps. Some were injured, too battered to continue. They stood and clapped, edging back from the fray. But most of them got up and tried to mount the steps again, eager to find a place while those already in position were determined to keep them at bay.

The mass of people, the arms outstretched, the cries of bemusement and anguish—it could have been the world as the gods on high once saw it. That's what Yoshi decided as she watched the spectacle, and she almost whispered such visions to Madame Isobe.

Time after time groups charged those atop the gray-stone steps, trying to move the others from the cherished position beneath the temple eaves. Various factions wore headbands or wrist wraps, marking their side in hues of golden yellow, mint green or truce white. Here were the armies of the world in miniature, Yoshi decided, as idiotic and misguided as the real ones that ravaged the world far beyond these temple grounds.

As the crowd counted down the seconds to minutes to midnight, the torches immediately above the arena were extinguished. One last bucket of water was dropped on those directly under the temple roof and then the batons—one, two, three, and four—were dropped onto the crowd of heaving bodies, and the battle began anew.

After a few more minutes Madame Isobe said, "Come," and the two of them left the bleachers, once again arm in arm, and hurried past the cheering faces and through the temple grounds to the street.

Their rickshaw was waiting for them. The driver took them a few blocks away from the temple and then stopped, still running in place. Behind them there were more cheers and the streets again began to fill. Yoshi looked around, wondering why they had stopped here. She didn't say anything. They waited until there was a great commotion behind them.

Madame Isobe glanced back and then told the driver to move ahead, slowly. The noise behind them grew louder and the old woman slid over, falling against Yoshi.

"Bear with me, child. We have a visitor."

With that Lui leapt into the seat alongside her. Immediately the driver began to run as fast as he could and on either side of the rickshaw several competitors appeared, their faces red with exertion. A few tried to hang onto the rickshaw as it picked up speed. Madame Isobe brought out a switch from beneath the seat and deftly struck their desperate fingers. The intruders fell like pine cones from a tree, hitting the cobblestone street hard. Wide-eyed, Yoshi stared at Lui, who was nearly naked, only ribbons of white clothing hanging from her torso. She was cut and bleeding in many places. Lui smiled, revealing a bloody lip and several loose teeth. Then she held up the red baton, the beacon of good fortune for the rest of the year, for all of them to see.

"You are the lucky one, child," Madame Isobe said.

Lui could only nod and try to catch her breath. As she snuggled down among them, her skin cool with sweat, Yoshi found herself running an arm over her shoulders and briefly pulling her close.

Once they returned to the theater, Madame Isobe helped Lui begin a hot bath. Yoshi lingered in the doorway, amazed by the cuts and scraps that peppered Lui's tomboy yet lovely torso. From a distance Lui could have been a marble statue found in some museum. That's how perfect she appeared to be in the shadows as she eased herself into the steaming tub.

"She is a wonder, isn't she?" Madame Isobe said as she stopped in the doorway.

"Yes, ma'am. She is."

In a whisper, Madame Isobe said, "The day after tomorrow, you'll begin. I've secured you a job in a factory not far from here. There aren't many factories in Kyoto, so this could lead to something. There have been rumors about this place."

"The fire balloons?"

"Hush, child. Never say those words again. You become so excited sometimes. That's what worries me about you. You become so caught up with things. Just go to this factory and work and watch and listen. If it's important, sooner or later it will make itself know. Good night."

"Good night," Yoshi replied and Madame Isobe brushed past her and disappeared into the shadows. Yoshi listened for the nightingale floor to announce her departure, but no sound echoed forth.

Yoshi stayed in the doorway, admiring Lui. How beautiful and confident she was. Yoshi decided Madame Isobe was right. She did become too excited, lost in the moment. How Yoshi wished she could be more like Lui—always knowing when to act and when to stay in the shadows.

Caught up in such admiration, Yoshi stepped farther into

the room. Lui turned, the hot waters gurgling about her.

"Oh, Yoshi, it's you."

"Yes."

"Please, help me. The cuts on my back – I can't reach them."

"I'll do it," Yoshi said, eager to please.

For a long time, Yoshi cleaned away the gashes with soap and clean water. When Lui arose from the hot tub, Yoshi was there with a large towel to cover her nakedness. Then once Lui was dry, Yoshi pulled the towel down to the waist and dabbed at the cuts once more with antiseptic. Attentive and careful, Yoshi paused every time Lui took a deep breath because of the sharp pain. When they were finally done, Yoshi pulled the towel back up to Lui's shoulders and rested her chin lightly upon her guide's shoulder. When Lui turned toward her, Yoshi kissed her lightly on the cheek, happy to feel Lui's arms envelop her once again.

Early the following morning, Yoshi awoke first. The southern sky, in the direction of Osaka, was red. The B-29s must have bombed that area again. For the first time since the night she left the submarine, Yoshi felt brittle with apprehension. How she wished Madame Isobe would tell her more about this factory where she was to work.

"You worrying again?" Lui asked.

Lui was curled up on one side, her cut arm nestled under her head, studying Yoshi.

"Is that what they teach you to do in your land? To always worry?"

Yoshi tried to smile. "Yes, they are good teachers of worry in the land I come from."

Lui yawned and rolled back over and appeared to go back to sleep. She was almost a head and shoulder taller than Yoshi. Back in Manzanar, Yoshi was considered attractive and she wondered what they would think of Lui. The boys in California often visited and sometimes spent as much time waiting in their small home, talking with mother, than they did with her. Since she turned fifteen or so, Yoshi realized that men paused in what they were doing when she walked by. Her appearance could be a tool to get what she wanted. Yoshi had learned that early on, even before going off to Cal and its sprawling campus across the Bay in Berkeley. "A person could get lost in trying to figure you out," Starling had told her on their last day at the Presidio. She wished he had talked to her more in that tone.

"Why did you let them lock you up?"

It was Lui, who had rolled back over.

"It doesn't matter," Yoshi said.

"Don't fret, sweet one. I won't tell Madame Isobe. But I'm curious. We've heard about the camps. How they locked you up. Is it true?"

Yoshi nodded.

"Then why do you do something like this?" Lui said. She had risen to a sitting position. The blanket barely covered her nakedness. Her luminous skin was covered with welts and small cuts.

"To prove ourselves."

Lui was silent for a moment. "Prove what?"

"That we're as patriotic as the ones who sent us away."

If only it had been that easy. Maintain discipline and go with little complaint. That's what the elders said needed to be done, and pretty much everyone had agreed and followed their council. Talk of what would happen to their business and belongings was hushed into obedience, at least for the first year at Manzanar. Then they had come around with the oaths to sign—another piece of paper, another order, but this one stating that they pledged allegiance to the United States of America. When that was handed down from Mr. Ogden's office, fissures of dissent erupted, even in the Minagi household.

"What gives them the right?" Yoshi remembered her little brother asking. "Can't they see what we've done here. We prove our loyalty every day."

"Kenji," father scolded.

But the boy was up, pacing the small living area like an adult. And why wouldn't he? He was becoming a man here, behind barbed wire—growing like a weed in the desert.

"We need to stand up to them," Kenji muttered. "That's what the guys say."

The guys would be other seventeen-year-olds at school, the ones who in their old world would be thinking about college or a craft to pursue. At Manzanar, though, they did their time at the far block, at the barracks that passed for the senior high, and in the afternoon they practiced their baseball at the field down near the guard towers. Yoshi had never understood the game. It was too precise at some moments, too random at others for her to really follow. But she had to agree that it had been a good pursuit in this desolate place. On Sunday afternoons, large crowds gathered, their ranks fanning back from the foul lines. There was talk of building bleachers. Yoshi saw how even the guards in the towers, the ones with the machine guns, followed the action and nodded in approval over a good play.

"I'm going to find Toyo," Kenji said.

"No, it's almost curfew," mother said, but the boy was already out the door.

Yoshi found her sweater, the red cashmere she had bought at Nieman's in the City only a year or so before, and hurried to follow.

Outside were other teenage boys and young men. They milled around like wild dogs. All of them talked and talked until there was too much anger in the air. That's when somebody said they needed to take this up with Mr. Ogden.

"Yes, let's see Ogden," somebody answered and like that it was decided. A growing mob of young men walked down the dirt street between the barracks, bearing down upon the director's office. Yoshi hurried to stay up with them, anxious to find her brother in the dark shadows, find him and pull him away. But she knew it was already too late.

To his credit, Mr. Ogden did try to talk with the crowd. But the mob was in no mood to really listen. When several of the vocal ones began to advance upon the office, to do God knows what, Yoshi knew what was about to happen. It was one of those moments that had already slipped well out of her grasp. When the shots rang out, from the guards in the tower, she fell to the ground like everyone else. Still, she was one of the first on her feet, moving among the bodies, searching for her brother.

"I've found the way to keep you quiet," Lui said. "By asking about those camps. I'll have to tell Madame Isobe."

Downstairs they were finishing their tea when a commotion came from out in front of the theater.

"Close everything up," Madame Isobe said. "We'll go down the backstairs."

Yoshi watched as Lui reached up and pulled a wooden partition down that went flush to the floor. The small eating area and the back rooms of Madame Isobe disappeared behind the new wall.

"Lui, as soon as we're outside, you disappear until this afternoon. Go thank the monks for their great blessing."

Lui nodded.

Outside two jeeps, five soldiers in total, were waiting.

"Open it," one of them said and nodded at the towering oaken doors that marked the theater's main entrance.

Madame Isobe did as she was told.

"Nobody is allowed back in until we come out. Is that understood?"

Madame Isobe bowed low in agreement. One of the soldiers hung back to keep an eye on them.

After the other soldiers had gone in and locked the door behind them, Madame Isobe whispered to Yoshi, "Someday I must find out what they're doing."

Early in the afternoon, after the soldiers had driven away in their jeeps, Yoshi sat on the back steps, waiting for Lui to return. Madame Isobe came out and sat down next to her. In silence they looked out upon the nearly deserted street and the wide Kamo River that flowed away from them to the south.

"When I first arrived in Kyoto, I fell in love with those waters," Madame Isobe said. "I was so happy that I had come here. The man who used to run the theater had died and I was excited about what I could do, even petition the authorities to put on a few shows. They haven't approved that, but they may. They think I'm just an old woman. They don't pay any attention to me."

Yoshi almost answered her, almost telling Madame Isobe about their old family farm in the mountains south of San Jose, the way the ocean was quiet many mornings, how the sunlight lit up its surface like the same sun did now to the Kamo River.

"Good, you're learning," Madame Isobe said. "Do the same thing at the factory. Head down. Bow low. But always listening."

Madame Isobe turned to go, but before she did she said, "I probably shouldn't tell you this. But your friend, Lieutenant Starling. He's gone back to the United States. That's the chatter anyway."

"How do you know that?" Yoshi asked and as soon as the words were out of her mouth she knew she had made a mistake.

Madame Isobe's face clouded over.

"Oh, child," she said. "Don't be a *moga*."

DEALING WITH THE OLD MAN

"Starling took you girls right into the fire?" Leo heard Pa ask Taylor. "I never heard of such a thing."

The two of them were on the patio below Leo's bedroom window. It was the morning after the blowup on the Teague Fire.

"He said we had no choice."

"Then that's the fire boss's fault. You always have an escape route. That's the first rule of firefighting."

"Pa, it worked. We're OK."

"Only by the grace of God you are. The more I hear about this new fire boss, the less I like him."

"Pa."

"You forget that I know that job better than anybody," Pa said. "I did it for twenty years. For him to come into town and not even ask for help, well, it makes you wonder."

"No," Taylor said, "it just gets you worked up."

Leo reached for the fatigue-green work shirt that Starling had issued to everybody on the crew. If the two of them kept arguing, he could be out the back door before Pa noticed and lit into him too. Below his window, Pa and Taylor sat at the wooden table on the patio that was made of large red sandstone that her father had brought up from the riverbed years ago. It had rained the night before and small puddles still dotted the low spots of the gravel lane in front of their house. The main road, Route 87, lay only a few blocks from the house and ran south toward Phoenix and, in the opposite direction, up and over the Mogollon Rim to the vast hardwood forests that ran between here and Flagstaff.

On the patio below, Leo saw that the paper was spread out between his father and older sister. Pa returned to reading the front page, while Taylor glanced through the local briefs.

"Says here that the Connors kids found a tangle of rope and some kind of fabric down by the Verde River," Taylor said. "The home guard doesn't know what to make of it."

"When it comes to the Connors, I don't know who's a better liar," Pa said, without looking up. "The kids or the old man."

"Says they brought the whole mess down to the police station."

"Chief Parsons didn't seem too concerned about it last night down at the Winchester. He was more worried about what happened on the Teague Fire."

Ron Webb held up the front page. "This is what I can't figure. We've still got a war going on. That's where Neil Starling should be. Not here causing trouble."

The headlines read, 'American Bombers Attack Tokyo' and 'Allies Take Chinese Port.'

"What's your fire boss doing here when we're still sending kids off to fight Hirohito? Things may be about over in Europe, but Japan's still fighting. Your baby brother will be going over there before somebody wakes up and sends Starling's ass back where it belongs."

Out on Route 87, a truck passed by. Its wheels hissed through what was left of the moisture on the tarred road. The engine let out a low snarl as the driver shifted into a lower gear. The two of them stopped to listen to it climb the series of switchbacks that led up the escarpment that dwarfed the small town of Payson, Arizona.

"If it keeps raining like this we'll make next to nothing this summer," Taylor said.

"It'll burn," Pa said with resignation. "It always does."

Leo almost smiled. That's the old man he knew, the one who always warned that something worse was coming down the pike. From his bedroom window he could see that low clouds still clung to the ridge of the Douglas firs and Ponderosa pines. At first glance, it could have been winter. But everybody in town, deep in their bones, knew better. Summer was coming on strong and soon it would be hot and dry and there would be more big fires.

"Could be a couple of them going right now," Pa said.

"I doubt it," Taylor replied. "It's too wet for a good fire."

"Tay, don't be stupid. Get above the Rim and the wind dries things out real quick. The storm that went through last night had to pack some lightning. That's got to strike somewhere. But, of course, your Neil Starling would know all about that."

"Pa, would you forget about Starling?"

"Kind of hard to do, don't you think? I mean the government drops this guy into town, somebody with no ties to the area. He gets more support and equipment than I ever did. Just who put him in charge anyway?"

"Like you said, the government."

Pa shook his head and spat. "The same government that didn't tell us for months where Richard's carrier was. The same government that's coming after your little brother if this war goes on much longer."

Leo remembered how proud his parents had been when Richard went off to war. They kept reaching out to touch him in those days before he left for overseas, as if they couldn't believe how perfect he looked in that uniform.

Already the sun began to cut through the clouds and fill their neighborhood of clapboard houses with a golden light. God's sky. That's what Pa used to call it. The words came to Leo from out of the past. He and Pa had been sitting on the stone foundation for one of the new homes planned for out west on Route 260. The land was slated for more development if and when the war ever ended and everybody came home for good. But now they were building up for the invasion of Japan. It was supposed to happen around Halloween, with Leo probably a part of it. It was if their family was lost in a netherworld. The three of them—Pa, Taylor and him—had celebrated in style when peace had been declared in Europe a month ago. Mom had called from Phoenix, where she had been working for the past year, promising to come home soon. Pa had taken him and Taylor to the Winchester Saloon that night, where they had found most of the town tanked to the gills. The whole war should have ended then. But Japan hadn't quit. Too soon it became apparent that the Allies would have to defeat them as well, and the evenings fell back into the old routine of listening to the radio, trying to glean whatever they could from the clipped reports.

Ten days after V-E Day they got word about the Bunker Hill: Richard was dead.

Nobody could say when the war would be over, and all that was left to do was talk and sooner or later start to argue about it all. Most evenings they went their separate ways. Pa headed to the Winchester to hash things out with the other old men. Leo had taken to running at night, often taking Hunter, the family dog, with him. During the winter Taylor had been happy to be alone in the house. She took long hot baths in the guest bedroom and played the piano in the parlor with her reddish-brown hair wrapped in a towel like a Hollywood actress. But as spring changed to summer, waiting for her father and brother to come home became too lonely even for her. That's why she had joined the fire crew. That's what she had told Leo. No matter what people thought it had nothing to do with Genie deciding to join, too. That she could have another place to go, another group to belong to—that had made all the difference.

On the patio below, Taylor gathered up her breakfast plate and coffee cup, leaving her section of the paper on the table.

"Yolanda coming again today?" Leo heard her ask. God, if he hurried he could leave with her. But he still didn't have his boots on.

"It's Monday," Pa replied. "How else am I supposed to keep house and home together with your mother gone?"

By the time Leo was ready, his sister had already left for the fire station. The base camp was on the outskirts of down, a good half-mile away. Just as Leo feared, Pa heard him coming down the stairs.

"Leo, my boy."

"Yes, sir," he said.

"Come on out here. Let me take a look at you before you set sail."

Reluctantly Leo followed the voice out onto the patio. The sun had climbed higher into the morning sky. It was going to be hotter than the day before.

"Pa, I need a ride."

"We've got a few more minutes, son."

Leo sat down at the table. He couldn't believe how much older Pa looked. The war hadn't been kind to him at all.

"One of the fellas that was on the Bunker Hill wrote me the other day," his father said, almost absent-mindedly. "He told me that Richard was in the group that was to take off next. They were in the ready room below deck when the kamikazes came."

Leo was quiet. Pa had already told him this story. Richard had been in the ready room. Leo could picture him now, sitting with the twenty or so other pilots. Richard would be sipping his coffee, always eager to egg somebody on, to fuel an argument. 'Slick' they had nicknamed him. He had told them that in a letter home. His brother seemed proud of it.

When the kamikazes struck, the pilots in the ready room had been able to escape into the hallway outside. But there they were trapped. The boy who never wanted to come in from the outdoors, who loved hiking and camping, had died of suffocation.

"Four hundred and forty-six guys died on the Bunker Hill," Pa said. "That's three times as many as were killed in 1775 at the battle of Bunker Hill."

Leo nodded. Pa had told them this before, too. The past would swallow up their father. Leo could see that now, and Pa would go willingly because so much of what he had once held dear was lost to him. His oldest, his favorite child, was dead. A new tombstone in the family lot told that to the world. In actuality, Richard had been buried at sea. Wrapped in canvas, his body had been dropped over the stern as the crippled Bunker Hill zigzagged away from the combat zone. So many men had died that day in the Pacific that funeral services started at noon and didn't end until after sunset. Pa had somehow found this out, too.

After the funeral service in Payson, Mom had ushered everyone up to Richard's room. There they had prayed one last time and then selected a memento, something to remember Richard by. Leo had taken three arrowheads from atop the dresser and Taylor had selected Richard's pocket watch, the one that had belonged to Grandpa Mays. He couldn't remember what Pa had finally chosen—if anything.

"Pa, let's go," Leo said. "You said you'd drive me."

"I never should have let you join that outfit."

"Pa, don't start. I need to get to work."

"I'm serious. I never—"

"Pa, I'm almost old enough to be drafted. The way I figure it I won't need your permission soon."

He let those words linger, like a lit fuse. But, surprisingly, Pa didn't explode as he expected—at least not right away. And for the first time Leo saw that if he stayed determined and true that he could persevere in the same way youth has always overcome age—by wearing away at the situation like water across a stone.

"Well, Hotshot, or whatever the hell Starling calls your crew, it looks like you're going to be late for work this morning because I'm not driving you. Not after a cute remark like that. I wonder what your fire boss is going to say when you wander in a couple of minutes after eight. He's got strict rules about that I hear."

"Pa."

"You're right. You're old enough to be your own man. So you can walk."

"Pa?"

Leo began to argue, but he realized that his father would enjoy it too much. Besides there wasn't time.

"Thanks for nothing," Leo said.

With that he stood up and walked down the patio steps and cut across the backyard and headed for the street.

"You have a good day, son," Pa sang out. "It's nice to see you acting so independent. It makes a father proud."

That was just like him to pull the rug out from under you when you least expected it—just to teach you a lesson. But how many lessons did a person have to absorb in a lifetime?

As soon as Leo turned the corner off Main Street and was out of his father's sight, he began to run up Summit Drive. The Hotshots' fire station was located where Baseline Road dead-ended. He would tell Starling that he had already done his running for the morning and hope the fire boss would let him slide for being late.

Leo liked the name Hotshots. It had been Starling's idea to call the crew that. Or, at least, he was the one who brought the news. Only a few fire crews in the West could call themselves Shots. The rest were still a patchwork of locals and what was left of the old Civilian Conservation Corps. That's the way it had been in Payson, too, when Pa was in charge.

As Leo neared the top of Summit Drive, he heard a car idling, slowly following him, and he knew it had to be his father. The old man just rolled along, having a good laugh about the whole thing, waiting for Leo to turn around and then he would pick him up. That's all Leo had to do—turn around and acknowledge that Pa was still the one in charge, that the father knew more than the son. It was that easy, and Leo realized that he had been doing this his whole life.

But this morning, even though he was late, Leo was determined not to look back. He soon crested Summit and made the quick turn onto Baseline. There, way at the bottom of the road, where it stopped near the park and the Verde River, he saw that the crew was already out on the parade grounds. They were loading the two flatbed trucks that had been backed out of the garage.

It couldn't be eight o'clock yet. What the hell was going on? But they were all out there. There was Charlie Koch, his white-blond hair clearly visible even from this distance. The stupid C.O. never wore his fatigue cap. There were rules about that, but the conscientious objector never heeded them. And over there were Riddle and Fugery—the only other guys besides Leo left over from last year's crew. The rest were gone overseas to fight the war.

As Leo drew closer, he saw that his sister and Genie were helping load gear into the lead vehicle, Starling's truck. Yes, it was the handtools they took on a fire—the long crosscut saw and shovels and Pulaskis and brushhooks. They were being loaded into the racks that Starling had constructed for both trucks. He saw how the fire boss scrambled into the cab of the lead truck, ready to settle behind the wheel. For a moment, Starling stood on the top step, with the door open and peered around searching for somebody. Leo thought he had to be looking for him. The king in front and the prince in back, right? But then Starling slid inside and started the big rig up, its diesel engine roaring alive with a puff of black smoke.

"Son, they're heading out," Pa shouted. "What's old Neil Starling going to say about you missing this?"

But Leo refused to listen. He was running as hard as he could down the last stretch of Baseline. His sister was out front, swinging open the chain-link gate and the trucks began to lumber out in single file.

"Let them go," Pa said.

Thankfully, the caravan paused again, waiting for Taylor to close the gate behind them. That was enough time for Leo to catch up. Koch was driving the trailing truck, Starling the first. They idled there, waiting impatiently, as Leo climbed into the cab of the first truck. Starling reached out his muscular arm to pull him in. So smooth and precise was the movement that it was like they had practiced this—the last Hotshot arriving like the cavalry over the hill, joining them at the last second.

"Leo, there you are," Starling said.

"What's the hurry? We got another fire?"

Starling smiled—a flash of light along a blade—as if he had known that it would come together like this.

"Not yet. But more are coming."

"But it rained last night."

Starling chuckled as Leo tried to catch his breath. They were the only ones in the cab. He had saved this seat for him, his number two. The rest of 'A' squad, which included Taylor and Genie, was in the back, finding what comfort they could among the handtools and gear. Koch drove the other half of the crew. They had a dozen firefighters in total. This was an impressive assemblage in this time of shortages and rationing, and if anything, the ultimate tribute to Starling.

"It doesn't matter if it rained," the fire boss told him. "The fires are coming. You have to believe me about that. We're going back into the high country for the day. We're going to cut trail until we're dog-tired. After yesterday, I'm convinced it's the only way we can do business. So, Leo, you ready?"

"Yes," Leo stammered. His undershirt was soaked through with perspiration from the run.

Starling nodded. His fingertips tapped a dance on the steering wheel. "Well then, I suppose we can begin another day. Now that we're all present and accounted for."

The fire boss put the flatbed into gear and they began to parade up Baseline, heading slowly through the sleepy town, bound for the switchbacks that would take them over the Rim where the big fires were. Out the window, Leo saw his father's Studebaker Commander sedan. He had bought it before the war and Leo remembered how beautiful it had once been. Pa used to wash and wax it on the weekends. Now it stood before him grimy, sagging to one side because the front end needed work.

As they passed by his father's car, Leo was surprised by how angry Pa was, his eyes following only him. Leo tried to stare the old man down, happy with himself that this time he hadn't knuckled under. But at the last moment Leo couldn't hold Pa's gaze and had to turn away.

CURIOUS GIRL

They had a moment's rest, and Yoshi pulled the leather gloves off and briefly studied her hands. They were puffy, reddened and cracked from work. They were so unlike the way they were when she first arrived in Kyoto.

"Dove hands," mother used to say. "So smooth and white. Dove hands for my bird of a girl."

Her mother whispered such things at bedtime when Yoshi was a baby back in the family farmhouse south of San Jose, near Santa Cruz. Dove hands for my bird of a girl, my Yoshiko. That was her full name. Yoshi was only a nickname that her father had given her, a hint that he had wanted a boy to be the firstborn. Yoshiko meant the popular one and that's what her mother always called her. Her mother's voice was her earliest memory—those words and how her mother stroked the back of her head and then trailed down her spine. Her mother's fingertips felt like a moth's wings, cascading across the chubby legs to the small feet. Every touch was slightly different, but the words were the same, night after night.

Yoshi sat with the others in the warehouse on the outskirts of Kyoto, piecing together the long strips of the strange paper. The material was like nothing she had ever worked with before—thin and pebbled but so strong. The paper was produced from the *kozo* bush and they used a paste from the *konnyaku-nori*, the potato plant, as their glue. By adding a bit of water, the *konnyaku-nori* could be eaten. Perhaps, in this time of scarcity and darkness, it would be considered a delicacy. But those who stole even a thimbleful were soon discovered. Their places at the table went empty for a day or so until a new face filled the chair. No great pronouncements or second chances. They were simply not employed at the Saishi paper factory any more. That's what had happened to Lui, Madame Isobe told her. It had occurred months ago, long before Lui had led Yoshi here from the beach near Osaka. Lui had been caught eating the paste and was dismissed. Some liked to whisper that the violators were executed, but Yoshi knew that was a lie. It would take a far graver offense, like stealing into this country, for that to happen.

Around her the younger ones smoothed the seams of long paper. They were still such children. They were between the ages of twelve and sixteen, with a few older ones, like Yoshi, scattered in their midst like tall trees among the saplings. How old are you?, the little ones would ask. Where did you come from? And Yoshi would tell them that she was twenty-one and had come from the south near Okayama. She said it had been a long way to travel, especially during the war, with the trains so crowded and tickets hard to come by. That was enough. Yoshi would nod at the work, the paper on the table, and refuse to answer any more questions. The war still raged. There was work to be done.

All of them had been told not to wear hairpins to work and to keep their fingernails cleaned and trimmed. Even in the summer heat they were required to wear gloves to protect the paper. No chances could be taken. The paper must never be punctured or weakened. Such silly rules were discussed away from the Saishi warehouse, laughed at as the women and girls walked or rode their bikes home in a country that grew darker every night. Osaka had been leveled. Kobe was said to be in ruins. It seemed only a matter of time until the bombers targeted them, too.

"That's why I could work other places in town," Yoshi told Madame Isobe after her second week at the warehouse. "They're just making paper. What good is that?"

The old woman only pursed her lips and slowly shook her head.

"I'm sorry," Yoshi murmured.

"You could be like the shadows," Madame Isobe said with disappointment. "Always there, but never seen, if only you could stay quiet."

"I will, I am, it's just that nothing really happens there."

"But, Yoshi, have you ever noticed how many transports, army personnel are in the area? How the Saishi warehouse is not that far from the biggest military outpost in this region? Something important is happening there. Remember, you've only been there a few weeks."

Inside the warehouse, each day mirrored the one before. They were quiet and industrious, routinely working a twelve-hour shift. Up to six hundred pieces of the sturdy paper were glued together into long, curving sheets that seemed to stretch back to when the country was strong and confident and ready to conquer any army that stood in its path. But they had no sense of their work's destination. When the paper became too vast, longer than the table itself, overflowing the room, it was taken from them, and they began again, sitting on either side of the long wooden table, piecing together the new strips.

Even though many of them had worked at the factory for nearly two years, nobody was sure exactly why the great stretches of paper were made.

"They are our surrender papers to the Americans," one woman, an older one, said.

"No, it's a wish list to the gods," answered her friend. "And it grows longer every day."

This new stretch of paper would be done soon. That's what the experienced ones whispered, and when it was completed Yoshi was determined to discover its true purpose.

On this day, they worked through the morning and into the afternoon, once again lost in the strange rhythm of their work. Yoshi hardly noticed the passing of the hours until the men in uniform arrived.

The men reminded her of wolves and they moved to either side of the table and waved the women and girls away. The men told them to go home, treating them as if they were nothing more than servants, rather than the ones who had fashioned such a creation.

The paper was beautiful, Yoshi decided. By now the paper stretched from one end of the long table to the other and it had taken on the color of morning, a faint yellow with patches of dim white.

After ordering them to step back, the men gathered the paper to their chests, as they would a precious child. They carried it gingerly out the wide back doors to an awaiting flatbed truck. The truck's bed had been covered with white sheets to protect the paper, which was carefully folded away for its departure.

Yoshi followed them, staying in the shadows.

"To the theater then," Yoshi overheard one of the men tell another.

Theater? Her mind raced as she considered this. The only theater she knew was Madame Isobe's, The Kabuki Theater.

As the flatbed truck roared alive, the men climbed aboard with bored indifference. Yoshi backed away from the crowd and ran to her bicycle, which was stacked with the others in the alley. Before she could reconsider, she was astride it, pedaling hard up the alley, hearing the truck leave with a roar.

She swung out onto the main street and raced toward the corner. Yoshi saw that the truck was already a block ahead of her, but she pedaled hard and somehow kept it within view as it sped along the river until it pulled up in front of Madame Isobe's theater. A small crowd had gathered out front. The army must have told them to evacuate the theater again. She saw that Madame Isobe was among them.

Yoshi kept pedaling until she was around back. She ran up the outside backstairs and pushed the door open. Once more she was on the edge of the nightingale floor, the sentinel of the shogun. Below her, she heard orders barked out and heavy boots upon the stage. If she ran down the corridor the squeaking and chirping of the moving planks would alert them. Madame Isobe had never told her exactly how to move across the nightingale floor without making a sound. There had been hints and clues, but nothing told straight out. That wasn't her way.

"As you Americans would say it's as easy as one- two-three."

That's what Madame Isobe usually said, and for the first time Yoshi thought she understood. Stepping as lightly as she could, Yoshi moved onto the first plank. Nothing. The corridor remained silent. She could hear the men below her. Then she stepped two boards in front of her. Again, nothing. Now would be the test.

Stretching her right leg out in front of her, she moved hesitantly onto the space three planks away. Holding her breath she brought her body weight down upon this plank, ready to turn and run for the backstairs if there was any noise. But again she was only greeted with cherished silence.

One-two-three. She repeated the sequence, moving faster, until she reached the staircase that led to the far edge of the stage. She stole down it and moved back into the seats that lay hidden in the darkness.

A hissing sound echoed throughout the theater, a noise devoid of the melodies and grandiloquence that had once filled the grand hall. Up on stage, the men in uniform hurried about their work. When they were finished, they stepped back to watch. Way back in the blackness, kneeling among the last rows of empty seats, Yoshi watched too. Nervously she ran her hands along the edge of one of the wooden lacquered armrests. She knew she should leave before she was discovered.

But then, up on the stage, the paper began to grow. The hissing sound of compressed air filled the long panels and the paper softly crackled and rustled like an approaching storm. It was a balloon, a huge fire balloon. It looked like the photographs she had been shown at the Presidio base, what she had discussed so many times with Starling. How could she have been so stupid not to realize what she had been working on?

As the balloon filled with air, men in uniform held tight

to the long ropes that snaked over the top of the balloon and kept it from rising away from them. It was the most beautiful thing Yoshi had ever seen and, in spite of the danger, she inched out of the shadows for a better look. For a glorious moment or two, Yoshi felt as if she and the balloon were one. She felt that when it rose, ready to fly, her hopes and prayers would go with it. Together they would be borne away to a different time, a better place.

Yoshi heard the shouts. "How did you get in here?" Someone else was asking, "Who are you, girl?" And, much later, she decided that if she had run right then, she would have escaped. But the balloon would not let her go so easily. She stood in awe of it; unable to make her long legs run.

When a hand fell upon Yoshi's shoulder, she sank back to her knees, half-thinking that she could simply curl up and disappear. After all she was nothing more than a young woman who knew a bit too much. How could she be of any importance to these men? The likes of her were as plentiful as stones in the road in Japan.

They pulled Yoshi up to her feet. Their words rolled off her like a light rain. She gazed up at the huge paper balloon, whose sides were now as firm as a fattened calf. More air was being breathed into the balloon, making it almost seem alive. It slowly moved and turned like a dancer upon the stage. While men pulled hard on the ropes, others walked around the balloon, looking up at it, sometimes running a hand softly across its hide, inspecting for any blemish, leak or imperfection. But they found none. Yoshi knew that she and the others had done well by the way the men walked and stared and said so little.

Two soldiers brought her down front, near the lip of the stage.

"What are you doing in the Kabuki Theater?" demanded an older man.

His uniform had more stripes and braids than any of the others. Behind him was a younger man, who wore a white smock over his uniform.

"Isn't it obvious, Major Ito," the young one said. "She was watching us test the balloons."

The two men were so different—one old, the other young, one angry, the other almost bemused. And with both of them, their eyes were like her hands—red and tired.

"Where do you work?" Ito asked.

"At the Saishi Factory," Yoshi stammered.

"Why don't you terrify her some more," the younger man said. "She works where they make the paper for the balloons. She became curious about it, what we do with it. We knew that this would happen sooner or later."

"Doctor Takata, are you so certain about everything?" Ito said and turned to face the younger man. The attention stopped Takata in his tracks and for a moment they glared at each other.

"If you knew this was going to happen," Ito continued, "why did you not stop it? You scientists—you always have the reasons why. But they come too late for us to do anything about it all."

Takata didn't reply.

"If she was a man, I'd know how to deal with her," Ito said, seemingly to himself. "That would be an easy answer."

"But she isn't a man," Takata said, his voice now restrained and low, as if he were trying to calm an angry animal. "She is only a young one who has lost her way."

"A damn curious young one," Ito said. "Who knows where

she belongs? How she got here?"

"Look at her," Takata laughed. "She's just a frightened girl."

For the first time since she had been brought before them, Yoshi felt both men's attention fall upon her, first judging and then dismissing her.

"We've done you good work" Yoshi said, angry that she was nothing in their eyes. "Without us, you have no balloon."

Up on stage, the men paused in their inspection to peer with curiosity into the darkness below them. Who dared speak in such a defiant tone to their commanders?

Yoshi's outburst surprised them all, that she would have the courage to speak. Later, Yoshi was convinced that this was how it began between them. She remembered how Takata, the younger one, raised an eyebrow and studied her with questioning eyes.

"Indeed, you have done good work," he said, "and we thank you for it. For what you see in front of you is the most beautiful of weapons, one that will be remembered for centuries to come—"

"Centuries to come," chided Ito. "Takata, you are so believing."

"It's true," Takata replied. The men on stage once more slowed in their inspection. Like her, they hung on every word.

"Then why don't we have any confirmation?" Ito asked "Why have we heard so little, no call of alarm from the Americans?"

Ito turned to Yoshi.

"My scientist friend believes this balloon can fly across the Pacific Ocean," Ito said. "He says that it can rain down fire on the forests of western America. Not even a young girl as stupid as you could dream up such a fairy tale, could you? That a balloon could frighten so strong an enemy?"

Yoshi kept her eyes on the floor and refused to answer.

Ito laughed. "I see that you are a fool like him. The only certainty we have in our lives now is that the Americans will soon be at our shores. We must prepare everyone we can, even foolish girls like you, to fight them." He gazed about, as if he was awakening from a bad dream "But what am I doing instead? I'm here, in a theater the bombs somehow haven't found, testing paper balloons to fly across the ocean. We've grown insane in our land. What a waste."

Ito waved Takata over and the scientist reluctantly drew closer.

"Fools should be with fools," Ito proclaimed. "Takata, you seem to know so much about how this one came to be here. Somehow it makes perfect sense to your analytical mind. So, I've decided that she'll be your responsibility. Do with her what you'd like. But if she causes any more trouble, you're the one that I'll find. You're the one who answers for her now."

Yoshi had forgotten how quiet and green the countryside was. It had been almost two months since she left the submarine. Madame Isobe had kept her hidden away for far too long. Spring had blossomed into summer and she had missed so much by spending her days inside the Kabuki Theater.

As the military jeep roared ahead, Yoshi saw only random glimpses of the war. Here and there a crater pocketed the earth. In many of them, weeds had already started to grow. Up ahead a stone bridge had been bombed. It lay at an angle, looking like an old man who had gone down to the river to pray and now couldn't struggle back to his feet. The jeep swooped around oxen pulling carts, and knots of old, tired people walking, with no young ones in sight.

The jeep continued alongside the riverbank until it came to a wooden bridge that was undamaged. When the jeep blasted its horn, the people in front of them scattered like birds and they were across. On the horizon, the sky was heavy with clouds and there was little wind in the treetops. The men in uniform—the one driving and the other holding a machine gun across his lap, the muzzle pointed out toward the road—briefly talked among themselves, wondering if it would still happen. Yoshi tried to understand. They talked until Takata noticed that she was eavesdropping and he told them to stop.

"You are lucky," Takata told her. "One can only imagine what Ito would have done to you, a beautiful young woman like yourself."

He said things in a conversational tone, loud enough for the men in front to hear him, as if he was baiting them, wanting them to join the conversation. Neither of them did. On the far side of the river, the road became bumpier, and Takata allowed himself to slide slightly closer to her.

The air was humid, thick like fog in the morning. The jeep accelerated, going faster as the dirt road widened. Yet no matter how fast they went, the air never became cool enough to provide much relief. As they moved farther away from Kyoto, Yoshi began to cry. Takata and the soldiers said nothing. The tears were her only weapon. She saw that now.

"Hush," Takata said and leaned closer to her. Their shoulders touched, both of them crouched forward in their seats, talking into the calm space immediately in front of them as the road wind roared around and over them. "You will understand soon enough why I have brought you along. For months I've been saying that somebody from the factory would try to see what we were doing. But there was nobody until you. You don't know how discouraging that is for somebody in my field, in science. So, when one does show the least bit of desire, I believe that such initiative should be rewarded."

Yoshi glanced at him, but then she allowed the green land to blur again behind a veil of tears. She couldn't appear too confident—not now. Her mind was soaring out of control and she let it go, picturing the worst that could happen—that they would kill her or rape her.

As they came around a sharp bend, Takata nudged her. Yoshi saw the military base.

"Quiet now," he ordered. "We are almost there."

She stole another glance at his face, hoping to find a hint of kindness in it. He had gray eyes and black hair the color of a raven. His face sloped down to a strong jaw and a chin with a small dimple in its center. She admired how he looked ahead of them with his thin lips turned upward at the far edges in the faintest of a smile. She wanted to believe that that look held a glimmer of hope and benevolence for her.

Once more she tried to think of what it had been like before the war, before her family had been sent to Manzanar. But such images were faded and torn at the corners. Whereas a year or so ago, such visions as the waters beyond the Bay Meadows racetrack came into her head anytime she wished, they were now beginning to disappear. Such sweet memories were like mischievous little children that had grown up too fast and no longer paid any attention to their elders.

"What is your name?" Takata asked. Yoshi wished that he

had asked her that question miles ago. How much better she would have felt about being placed in his custody if the request had come earlier.

"Young lady," he asked again, leaning closer to her. "What is your name? Our Major Ito likely knows by now. He may have even said it back in Kyoto before we left, but I'm sorry. My mind has been elsewhere today. Monkey mind. That's what they call it when we try to juggle so much in our heads."

She couldn't believe it. He had actually apologized to her. The last man who had shown her any kindness had been Starling. Surprisingly, she had no difficulty remembering him, his crooked smile, his voice from the north that stretched and flattened some words almost beyond recognition.

"Yoshi," she replied.

"Yoshi," Takata repeated. "Such a peculiar name for a young woman. Named after the cherry trees? The Yoshino?"

"Yes," she lied. "Like the cherry trees."

The jeep came to a stop and the men in front scrambled out. They stood at attention, awaiting Takata's orders. The scientist remained seated, next to her.

"Yoshi," Takata said. "I still don't understand why you cry."

She glared up at him, tears still welling in her eyes.

"Because you are going to kill me. That's why you have taken me here, to this place. I know it."

Takata smiled. "I see, Yoshi. You can read minds, too. You are quite an accomplished young lady."

The men in uniform began to smirk, which infuriated Yoshi.

"Stop it," she said.

"Careful, cherry blossom," Takata replied. "You don't want to make them angry."

"Please," she began, trying to be soft and demure, the way men wanted women to be. "Please don't kill me."

"Yoshi, I don't know how such ideas float into your head," Takata said. "Perhaps if it were up to Ito, you would be shot. But I don't believe in such things. Not so soon at least. Maybe that makes me a fool, but there are better ways to conduct oneself—even in a war."

Yoshi closed her eyes and entwined her fingers, trying to keep her hands from shaking.

"It's heartening to see. I wish more had your spirit."

Yoshi reopened her eyes, first focusing on this peculiar scientist and then glancing past him to the base. They were on the far edge of it. Out in front of them were many more men in green and brown fatigues. All of them seemed busy, getting ready for something.

"Aren't the others at the factory ever curious about what happens to the things that they create?" Takata asked.

"No, sir. They make jokes and nothing more."

"But you're curious, aren't you, sweet Yoshi? You're different somehow."

Takata stepped out of the jeep.

"Come," he said. "I believe in curiosity."

Takata began to walk away and the soldier with the machine gun nodded for her to follow. Yoshi fell in behind Takata. His white smock blew back in the growing breeze as they filed past groups of soldiers. She followed him out into a vast field that seemed to stretch to the horizon. They were near the sea. She could smell the salt air and it reminded her sweetly of home.

"To bomb America without planes or missiles," Takata said. He glanced back at her. His eyes glowed with intensity. "To use something as simple as a paper balloon. It will terrify them as much as the attack on Pearl Harbor did. Once more, the Americans will have no idea of where or when we can strike."

Yoshi hurried to keep up with him.

"You and the others at the factory built a balloon of paper that can travel across the Pacific Ocean. Did you ever realize that you were creating something so magical?"

"But it's thousands of miles across the Pacific to America," Yoshi said.

"Good," Takata said, "you ask questions."

He slowed so she could fall into step beside him.

Takata pointed to the sky. "Believe it or not, there are great winds up there, high above the clouds, great winds that can carry a balloon to America in three or four days. We discovered those winds. A few of us know they are as powerful as the currents in the sea, as mighty as any of our ancient gods."

Across the muddy field, Yoshi saw balloon after balloon, easily a hundred in all, being inflated with the same urgency and precision that had been exhibited back at the theater. They needed a big enough place to test the balloons for leaks and poor seams. Yoshi realized that the Kabuki theaters were about the only places where they could do such things behind closed doors in Kyoto and throughout Japan in general. To actually launch them, though, they needed to be out in the country.

Already several balloons billowed upward and as they came to life, Yoshi saw a smile spread across Takata's face.

"My heart soars every time I see it," he said. "Maybe I'm too romantic, but I thought it important that you see it, too, my Yoshi."

As the first wave of balloons began to rise from the earth, eager to soar into the late-afternoon sky, the men held tight to their guidelines, looking back at Takata. In disbelief, Yoshi realized that the meadow was filled with soldiers, all of them awaiting his command. She watched as Takata studied the sky. Overhead it was clearing, with a breeze building out of the West. The vast meadow, which had been alive with shouts and commands, grew silent save for the crackle and restlessness of the balloons. The strange inventions reminded Yoshi of a herd of horses ready to stampede. With faint smile, Takata surveyed his kingdom one last time and then raised both of his arms into the air. As he did so, the soldiers released the first wave of balloons. Everyone briefly paused to watch them rise, prayers were mumbled, and then the men in uniform hurried to ready the next dozen or so for Takata's approval.

As the first of the fire balloons rose into the sky, the hissing sounds of the next group being inflated filled the air. But Yoshi kept her eyes on the first wave, watching them rise and run with the wind until they were just dark specks so high above them.

"That's why I brought you here," Takata said. "To see the wonder upon your face."

WOMAN IN BLUE

Osaka was ablaze again. Anyone could see that if they knew where to look. The B-29s must have arrived early because the horizon had a ragged edge to it from the flames. Up front the soldiers rode in silence as they neared the ancient city of Kyoto. Takata leaned forward, telling them something Yoshi couldn't make out. Soon afterward they turned away from the river, pulling up in front of a guard station. She could see the shadows of the low-slung buildings beyond the barbed-wire fence and more uniformed men milling about. So this is how it ends, Yoshi thought. But when the jeep stopped, the two soldiers got out without a word and left the jeep running. Takata dismissed them with a half-hearted salute and moved into the driver's seat.

"Come," he said and nodded toward the passenger seat. "I'll drive you."

Yoshi did as she was told and slid in beside him. She hung on as he put the jeep in reverse and turned it around clumsily before roaring off.

"Where should I drop you?" he asked.

"The Saishi factory—the warehouse."

"You live there?"

"No, it's just that sometimes it feels like it."

"You don't have to impress me with your devotion to the empire," he said. "Most of us grew out of that long ago."

"The factory will do, please."

Takata shrugged, "As you wish."

She didn't dare tell him the theater. That would only bring about difficult questions that would involve Madame Isobe.

The Saishi factory was a two-story structure located on Sanjo Street, where the cobbled road began to climb toward the foothills that surrounded the city. Nanzenji, the mighty wooden Buddhist temple, was only a few blocks away, situated where the street ended and the steep hills began in earnest. Yoshi realized that's why they had placed the factory here, so close to Nanzenji, in hopes that the bombers would bypass another historic shrine and give everyone time to make the paper for more fire balloons.

Takata downshifted awkwardly and the jeep trembled like a frightened animal as it struggled up the hill. In front of the factory, he swung the vehicle around so its headlights faced the building. The street was deserted. As Yoshi peered about her, the only light she saw came from down near the river and, of course, the flames much farther away near Osaka.

"What has happened here?" Takata said as he scrambled out of the jeep, leaving it running.

Something was out there—slowly swinging in the night

air above the doorway to the deserted Saishi factory. Takata stopped a few feet from the apparition. Yoshi came up alongside him. A body, a rope around its neck, hung in the Saishi doorway. Its back was to them and it swayed slightly in the shadows. Takata reached out with one hand and grasped the body above the hips and turned the face toward them.

"No," Yoshi cried out when she saw it was Lui.

The girl who had brought Yoshi to Kyoto was dressed like any of them in the Saishi warehouse—a man's work shirt, loose-fitting pantaloons and sandals. The sleeves were still rolled up past the elbows, the way Lui liked to carry herself, and Yoshi could still see a few of the scratches and wounds she had helped clean after the night at Toji Temple.

Lui's face was screwed up in a grotesque expression of terror.

"An acquaintance of yours?" Takata asked.

"No," Yoshi insisted.

"Then why do you cry?"

"It's terrible."

"She must have worked here."

"I don't know."

"I think you do, sweet Yoshi."

Yoshi nodded. "I know her face."

"What did she do wrong? What kind of trouble did she get into?"

"I don't know."

"Yes you do," Takata shouted. "Tell me. Tell me now."

Yoshi took a deep breath, uncertain of what to really say to Takata. Any good lie has a kernel of truth. Yoshi knew this and decided there was no other choice but to begin that way.

"She stole the paste from the *konnyaku-nori* plant," Yoshi

said. "What we use for the glue. She was hungry. We're all so hungry."

Takata looked at the corpse and then back to Yoshi. "But there's something more, isn't there?" he said. "She was your friend."

"No. I told you— "

"I think you knew her very well. You're not telling me everything. One doesn't cry this way over somebody they hardly know."

"I'm not used to seeing such things."

"Everyone is used to seeing such things. It's the curse that has fallen upon our land."

Takata reached into his suit coat and pulled out a small pistol.

"Maybe it's time for a traitor to join a traitor," he said.

Yoshi sank to her knees. She bowed her head in the glow of the jeep's headlights.

"The truth," Takata said. "I could impress Ito by telling him what I've done for the empire. That I've kept pace with him and his kind. That I can kill because of lies, too."

Yoshi heard a loud click. The safety was off. He was ready to shoot.

"I knew her from the street," Yoshi said. "That's where I live. Under the bridges along the river. She must live in the streets, too. One night the police were chasing me."

"Why?"

"I don't know why."

"Why!"

"Because I stole food that night. I stole from the farmers that sell across from Toji Temple. She did, too. That night they chose to chase me and she helped me escape. I don't know why.

But she led them away. She was faster than me."

"What was her name?"

"Lui."

"Lui what?"

"I don't know. I'm telling the truth. I don't know."

Yoshi kept her head down. She heard the jeep idling behind them and Takata rocking impatiently from one foot to another. When the gun went off, she rolled face-first onto the ground, feeling the cold gravel touch her forehead and waited for the pain. When none came, she slowly peered up to see Takata still standing over her. The gun was raised in the air.

"I don't know what to do with you," Takata said. "Someone so intelligent, someone so beautiful. Come, we'll decide this tomorrow."

The morning arrived in precious bits and pieces of dull light. Somehow the dawn found its way into the stone cell, where Yoshi sat on the cold floor, her head resting on her knees. Her limbs were sore, especially in the joints. Her mind felt ragged around the edges—trapped between any alertness and cherished slumber.

"We have to do something," she remembered her mother saying back in Manzanar. Her father didn't respond.

He had sat in their only comfortable chair, a small davenport that doubled as a bed. It was a gift from Mr. Ogden for the long hours Yoshi had put in. Father sat there and looked down at his hands. He was spending as much time as he could out in the fields, volunteering for extra shifts. Yoshi had been told that he usually worked alone.

In the days after Kenji was wounded, the family kept waiting for Father to once again lead them. One morning Kenji slipped out of the camp hospital and with one good arm, tried to scale the twelve-foot-high barbed wire fence. Thankfully the guards pulled him down instead of shooting him. Afterward, mother made her pronouncement. When father didn't say a word, Yoshi realized that their fortunes had fallen to her.

"The next group of recruiters is due here at the end of the week," Mr. Ogden told her later that same morning. "But your brother won't qualify, not after being designated for Tule Lake. I'm sorry, Yoshi. That's where the hard cores are sent. I had no choice."

"I wasn't thinking about my brother," Yoshi said. "I was thinking that I could volunteer."

"You?"

"Yes, as a nurse, secretary, something. I cannot get into any college right now, not that I would do that with my mother and father still here. But if I could help them somehow by joining?"

Mr. Ogden slowly shook his head. "Your mother is a resident alien. That will make it extremely difficult to be transferred out of Manzanar before the war ends, Yoshi, you know that."

"There must be something I can do."

Mr. Ogden was momentarily taken aback by her unexpected directness.

"Well, I don't know," he said and tried to busy himself with the paperwork on his desk.

"Mr. Ogden, help me. Please."

"Maybe there's something," he said. "Your Japanese is excellent. I joke that you could pass for a native."

He looked at her and Yoshi held his gaze, praying that he would continue.

"Let me talk with this new group coming here on Friday," Mr. Ogden said. "I'll speak with them personally. Underscore your special abilities."

That Friday morning she was introduced to Lieutenant Neil Starling.

At dawn the heavy wooden door groaned open and Takata was ready for her. He was freshly shaven, with a laundered suit and white smock and an air of impatience about him. In her dazed condition, Yoshi could pretend that he was one of the Shinto gods that her mother had once implored.

"On your feet," he told her. "We're going to take another trip—the two of us."

Outside they got back in the jeep and roared away from the military base. Takata drove for a long time before he was willing to acknowledge her. Near the military base, he was stern and spoke in clipped sentences, as if he was trying to impress the men around him. But as they moved away from the base, Yoshi saw the mask begin to fall away. The breeze blew back his dark hair and several times he glanced over to her, his natural curiosity creeping to the surface.

"Have you ever been to Nara?" he asked. Yoshi shook her head.

"Good," he replied. "Everyone should see Great Statue of the Buddha before they die."

He drove in silence the rest of the way, through the green countryside and the villages that were just awakening to a new day. Shopkeepers were out front, sweeping the old stone that lay between their door and the main road. Up ahead was a cluster of small hills fringed by bamboo forests. As they climbed the first hill, the road narrowed and was soon flanked by a gray-stone wall topped with prayer wheels and small canisters for candles that were sheltered from the elements.

Takata pulled the jeep over to the side and got out. From his pants pockets he took out a small white candle. He placed it in the closest metal canister and lit it. For several moments, he stood, head bowed in front of the flame and Yoshi hoped the gods would take away his anger. She hoped that he would see it in his heart to let her live.

Without a word, Takata climbed back into the jeep and they were off again. A few more minutes down the road, he turned into a small dirt lot and parked.

"Come," he said and Yoshi hurried to follow.

Soon the bamboo forests fell away to reveal the expanse of a park and there, in the distance, lay a huge temple with red columns and white steps leading up to it.

"It's Daibutsuden," Takata said without looking at her. "It houses the statue of the Great Buddha. Look up, Yoshi. Higher"

As she did so, Yoshi saw the eyes of the Buddha staring at them through huge slits in the wooden roof.

"The Great Buddha is more than sixteen meters high," Takata said, "and it is built from four hundred and thirty-seven tons of bronze and one hundred and thirty kilos of gold. I memorized those numbers when I was a boy. I believed that those eyes see all. That's why we're here. So, the Great Buddha can help me decide what to do with you."

They walked past the Nandai-mon Gate, with two fierce-looking guardian statues that towered over them.

"They were carved in the thirteenth century," Takata told her. "You couldn't find craftsmen to accomplish the task today."

Inside Yoshi stared up at the golden Buddha and Takata bowed low in reverence. What a strange man, Yoshi thought to herself. He's a scientist who pays homage to the ancient gods.

Together they moved around the base of the great statue. Except for a few monks dressed in golden robes they were alone in the largest wooden building in the world. On the far side of the Buddha, an old monk stepped out of the shadows. He and Takata bowed in greeting and the young scientist nodded at Yoshi. She felt uncomfortable as the monk first studied her and then waved Takata closer so the two of them could whisper in conversation.

"As you may have guessed, I've asked him for help in making my decision about what to do with you," Takata said when he rejoined her. "He then told me this strange story. An old tale called the 'Woman in Blue.' Many centuries ago, a tradition began in which a list of names, people who were priests or pious ones, is read here at the temple. I knew nothing of this ceremony, this woman in blue, but I'll follow the monk's advice."

Takata told her that when they did this ceremony centuries ago, a priest named Shukei was reading the list of names when a beautiful woman in blue suddenly appeared out of the darkness. Women are forbidden during such ceremonies. But she simply stood there, like a ghost, until Shukei, the priest, said, 'The Woman in Blue.'

"A scientific observation," Takata said. "Another priest could have sounded the alarm. Had her taken away. But as soon as Shukei said, 'The Woman in Blue,' she disappeared."

"They are reading the lists now, farther back in the temple. My friend, the monk, suggests that we let history decide and I've agreed. If the priest reading the list of names this morning decides you are an imposter, calls for the guards when you appear, then I'm sorry, Yoshi. The gods will have spoken and I will have no choice but to return you to Ito's care. But if the priest performing the reading is understanding, especially devout, or perhaps as tired as Shukei once was, then you will live."

Flanked by Takata and the monk, Yoshi was led deeper into the vast temple. The monk took her into a small room and began to wrap her in swathes of dark-blue cloth from her neck down to her ankles. Out beyond them she heard someone reading a list of names in a droning monotone.

"This is crazy," she whispered to the monk. "Am I to live or die depending upon an old myth? If the one reading this list happens to believe in ghosts and stories?"

The monk stopped pinning the thick cloth in place and peered up at her. He seemed to want to smile, but the pins jutting out of his month made his expression contorted, almost absurd.

"Let me escape," Yoshi said.

"It would do you no good," the monk said out of the corner of his mouth. Carefully, he took the remaining two pins from between his thin lips and continued. "They would only hunt you down. Don't you see, my dear? Every day is a blessing from the gods. They can take it away from us at any time. Let's see if you're blessed or not."

After she was wrapped in blue silk and velvet, the monk took her by the elbow and led Yoshi farther into the darkness. As her eyes adjusted, Yoshi saw that they were hidden behind a wooden pillar. On the other side, a priest was seated at a low table. He held a weathered script and the only light was a single taper with a flickering flame.

When the priest finished the page he was reading, the monk pushed her out into view. Yoshi stood as still as she could as the priest lifted his face and saw her. His mouth formed a small circle of surprise, as if he was about to call out. But then a strange calmness settled over him and his eyes returned to the long list in front of him.

"The Woman in Blue," he said in a low growl, and Yoshi felt the monk grasp her again by the elbow and lead her back to Takata.

❧

"The street is no place for you," Takata said. "Not for a Woman in Blue."

They were back in the jeep, returning to Kyoto. Takata was excited as a schoolboy about what had transpired inside the great temple. His words tumbled out as fast as the breeze that rushed past them and blew back their hair.

"You'll stay with me from now on," Takata announced. "In a few days, I'm going to Tokyo. I suspect Ito will be going there, too. He's determined to win over the generals. Turn them against me. Try to stop the flight of anymore fire balloons. You will join me in Tokyo. I'll make the necessary arrangements. But until then, you are to be with me. Someone as intelligent and as lovely as you deserves better than to lie down with thieves under the bridges of Kyoto. I will take good care of you, sweet Yoshi. The gods have decreed it."

RENDEZVOUS

As Starling drove south, out of Payson, he remembered his last day at home, before he shipped out. His duffel bag was packed and he was waiting for his uncle to take him down to the bus station in Traverse City. To kill time Starling had flipped through the world atlas that had been his father's. The book was a curiosity that bordered upon a family joke—that a man would pay half a week's wages for something so unnecessary. Didn't that prove that Samuel Starling was a bit soft in the head? After all what kind of man tried to raise a boy to be a dynamiter? Granted, that had been the family trade at one point, but where was the future in that?

In the old family atlas, the Pacific Ocean encompassed half of the world. Starling hadn't fully realized that until the morning of his departure. The Pacific was so much larger than Lake Michigan, Lake Huron and Lake Superior—the inland seas he had known as a boy. When he had enlisted, deciding there was nothing left for him at home after his father's death, Starling thought he would be sent to Europe, be one of the multitudes eager to liberate France. But, of course, that changed with the attack on Pearl Harbor, which he was somehow lucky enough to survive. Even before the day of infamy, the war had begun to shift. If he'd read the newspapers as intently as Uncle Jack he would have picked up on that. The Nazis had made a huge mistake by invading Russia. The Japs were better poised to conquer Hong Kong, Burma, and the Philippines. Yet all Starling knew that morning as he closed the atlas and hefted his duffel onto his shoulder was that the October breeze was in the poplars on the property's edge and, off in the distance, it was building over the tops of Sleeping Bear dunes and would soon bring colder weather.

A good half-hour out of Payson, Starling turned off the main road and took a narrower dirt route back into the Superstition Mountains. The sun was going down behind the jagged peaks and the wide escarpment that was the Mogollon Rim.

The fire boss drove until he saw another set of headlights flash twice—their signal. He slowed and pulled over in front of the other vehicle. It was a Plymouth Torpedo coupe. You only saw such automobiles in the bigger cities, like Phoenix, where this one had come from.

Starling got out and walked over to the driver's side. Colson was waiting for him, smoking a Chesterfield. He offered the pack to Startling, but the fire boss shook his head.

From where they stood, the village of Payson glowed like a bed of white-hot coals against the dark background of the Rim. Behind Payson, the land rose like a vast curtain. Off to the left, the lights of a stray car hugged the switchbacks that led north toward Flagstaff.

"It's a strange land, isn't it, Neil," Colson said. "Every time I drive up here from Phoenix, it never looks the same to me. Something about the way the hills build upon themselves and then just fall away to complete nothing."

Colson nodded at the Rim. "They say that lodestone can get real hot in a hurry."

"I pray that none of the devices go off up there," Starling replied. "There's so much that could burn. Ponderosa pine. Huge stands of dry firs and spruce."

Colson didn't respond to Starling's grave assessment. Instead he asked the fire boss if he had "the payload."

Starling returned to the flatbed's cab and reached under the seat. He pulled out the tangle of chords, the metal ring, and shreds of paper. This was what was left of a fire balloon he had found at their last fire. Starling had wrapped the mechanism in an old tarp he had found at the fire station. With both hands, Starling carried what was left of the Jap device over to Colson's Plymouth. Colson opened the trunk for him.

"It's all defused, right?"

"What do you think?"

"Only what I'm told, Neil."

"It's perfectly safe, sir."

Colson nodded at the open trunk and Starling set the device inside and watched his commanding chief slam the truck lid shut.

"I'd love to get my hands on one of these devices that's in better shape," Colson. "It's just pieces of a puzzle right now. Nobody's sure what an entire one looks like."

"It's only a matter of time until some civilian finds one," Starling said.

"And if and when that happens you'll need to talk to them," Colson said.

Starling looked away. Why was it always up to him?

"You could start by being more of a charmer," Colson said and exhaled out a long puff of smoke. "Hanson up in Washington state has run into similar problems. Balloons all over his territory. But the people love him. He could tell them the sky's polka-dot and they'd believe him. He's got them convinced that these damn things are put out there to measure the weather. That they're ours. But top secret, you know, so he can't tell them anymore."

"Hanson always was a good liar."

"Something you could emulate, Neil. Better than getting into it with the locals down at the local cantina."

"I'm trying," Starling said. "But these people can be so bull-headed. If I could just tell a few of them what we're up against, they'd be with me rather than against me. I know it."

"No can do, sailor. Those orders come from the White House. Maybe Mac himself for all I know. The fire balloons are top secret and they need to remain that way. End of story."

"But, sir, if I could— "

"Starling, I'm worried about you. I truly am," Colson said. "I was looking through your file the other day."

"Please don't start, sir," Starling said.

"A sweet tooth for the devil water," Colson said. "Definitely an eye for the finer things in life—wine, women and song."

"I've made some mistakes," Starling said, unable to hold Colson's gaze.

"If it wasn't for MacArthur, you could have taken up residence in the stockade by now."

"So, get me back to the Pacific. That's where I should be."

"Neil, I'd like to be in the Pacific, too. I was at Pearl myself. I'd like nothing better than to finish those damn Japs off. But we've been given this job and the only choice we have is to do it to the best of our abilities."

Starling tried to laugh. "Colson, tell me what else I'm doing wrong. Tell me quick so I can go home and get some shut-eye."

"I'll tell you something that you are doing right. Adding women to your roster was a smart move. Rosie the Riveter on the fire-line. The California crews are following your example."

"Swell."

"You should be proud of yourself."

"What I am is angry and tired," Starling said. "It's a lousy combination, sir. Now what's the bad news? You always have some. You're a regular black angel with no mercy."

Colson nodded. "Reports are coming in that a slew of new balloons are heading your way."

"How soon?"

"Matter of days. The Corsairs along the coast have taken out a few, but not nearly enough to do you any good. You need to corral 'em and keep everything under lock and key. Just like we've talked about before."

"I could really use more men," Starling said. "Qualified men."

"I can't help you there. Not yet anyway," Colson replied. "Qualified men are in short supply. You know that, Neil."

Starling nodded, suddenly reluctant to let his only contact with the outside world drive away.

"What else do you hear, Colson?"

He watched as the other man finished his cigarette and snubbed it out with the heel of his polished military boot.

"Here, you'll get a kick out of this," Colson said.

Starling watched as Colson went around to one of the Plymouth's back doors and came out holding a marquee-sized poster with both hands. Starling followed him to the front of the sedan, and Colson held the image down in front of the high beams

"Say hello to Smokey," Colson said.

Starling saw that it was a color drawing of a bear cub. It was relatively life-like but still a cartoon with wide, doe eyes and almost a human snout.

"Smokey?"

"The boys in Washington dreamed it up," Colson said eagerly. "A way to warn the public about the evils of forest fires."

"You mean like Bambi," Starling said.

"Oh hell, Neil. That was a movie. Disney doing things up to the nines. Smokey's going to be something to rally around. Mark my words, friend, he's going to be everywhere – posters, reminders before the newsreels. I probably shouldn't tell you this but guess how they're doing his voice."

Starling shrugged.

"A pencil-pusher back in D.C. talks into an empty waste basket. They tell me the echo is perfect for Smokey's growl. Doesn't that beat all? When the bosses told me that, I couldn't believe it."

Starling watched as Colson laid the poster upon the sedan's hood and carefully rolled it back up.

"Next time we visit, I'll bring you a whole bunch of these Smokey posters," Colson said. "You can paper the town with them. Soon everybody's going to know the story of Smokey the Bear. How he grew from a cub to be the one who tells people, 'Only you can prevent forest fires.' That's his shtick and Joe Q. Public is going to listen."

"If you say so, sir."

The two of them fell silent, gazing out upon the darkening land. Where Colson saw a macabre territory that didn't look the same each time he came up, Starling only saw a tinderbox ready to go up in flames.

"There's one other bit of news," Colson said.

"What? More cartoons?"

"Afraid not, Neil. I've been waiting to see if better news was coming. But so far we've heard nothing."

"What are we talking about here?"

"Your package," Colson said. "Yoshi Minagi has disappeared. As you know she made it to Kyoto, but it seems as if she's been picked up. I'm sorry, Neil."

Starling nodded.

"Our contact over there, an old woman, finally got word to us. The Kempei Tai has really been cracking down, but you knew that. We've had another operative killed. They found her body hung by the neck in the doorway where she and Yoshi worked. That's all we know right now."

"OK. Thanks for telling me."

"Figured bending a few rules won't hurt anything," Colson said. "So, what are you going to do?"

"What can I do?" Starling said. "I promised her I'd help her family. Nothing changes there."

Colson smiled. "You're a man of principle, Neil Starling. Not many of your kind left."

"Yeah, just me and your Smokey the Bear."

Colson came to attention and snapped off a salute as crisp as any at Annapolis. He returned to his gleaming Plymouth, and Starling followed the red taillights until they faded away into the shadowlands that led down to the desert and Phoenix.

Afterward, Starling gazed up at the stars, recognizing the Big Dipper and Orion and little else. He remembered how bright the stars had shone the nights he was at Manzanar. The camp was so cold and windy, but such conditions hadn't bothered Yoshi Minagi. He decided that's what he would always remember about her. She tried to appear meek and demure that first day in the director's office for her interview. But it didn't wash. Her dark eyes were on him as soon he came into that shoehorn of a room to talk with her. Down deep she was as angry and determined as the stars overhead.

TO TOKYO

Yoshi had expected that she would sit apart from Takata, perhaps even be guarded on the journey north. But when they arrived that morning at the old station across from Toji Temple, Takata nodded that she was to accompany him. They walked past the sentries that held back the rabble queuing up for second class. To the world around them, they were husband and wife, or at least a military officer and his concubine. Yoshi realized that she had fallen into an illusion, a convenience that could possibly shelter and protect all the other lies she was living.

While Takata busied himself with the bags, Yoshi stood at the end of the terminal, where the platforms led down to the tracks. She looked around everywhere, studied every face, for a glimpse of Madame Isobe. But the old woman wasn't there.

"No matter," a small voice inside of her whispered. "You'll

be safe with this one. This one called Takata."

The name warmed her lips. Already Yoshi had seen how his dark eyes came live when he studied her.

As Takata moved to rejoin her, to go together down to the train, Yoshi decided that he was all she had in the world now. She would need to do whatever was required to keep him happy and pleased with her.

In Tokyo, she was moved into Takata's apartment near the harbor. From there one could walk to the Imperial Palace and the War Ministry, where he began every day. It was almost as if Takata expected her to follow him, to be ever curious. For once they reached the capital, she was no longer locked in a room. Even though Yoshi was vigilant, she never saw any soldiers or plainclothesmen watching her. So, she did follow him in the morning. Along the way she saw the automobiles that burned charcoal because there was no more gasoline. She saw the Imperial guards with their rifles and white parade attire outside the palace. She saw the children trying to scoop golden carp out of the green-colored moat with paper cones, and for the first time in days Yoshi thought about her mother.

"There are big fish in the moat by the palace," her mother told the family. "When I was a little girl, I would go there and try to catch myself a fish. They sell paper scoops for anyone wanting to try, and my mother would buy them for my little brother and me. My brother would soon become bored, but I never did. Almost every time I would catch one."

"The trick was to be quick-quick. Look for a big one and pull the paper cone through the water as fast as you could. You only had a few chances before the paper scoop would begin to fall apart. My brother never realized that. That you had to be quick-quick. Yes, quick-quick."

Her mother had told that story again the afternoon Starling visited their barracks home in Manzanar, their embarrassingly small space with its steel-framed army cots and straw mattresses. Yoshi hadn't made up her mind yet. She hadn't accepted his invitation to go to the Presidio, to join the Military Intelligence Service. But then mother told that story again. Alongside her sat Father, with a faint Buddha smile on his face. His calloused hands were folded respectfully in his lap as if he was in church.

Afterward Yoshi had accompanied Starling to the door.

"I'll do it," she said. "But they need to be transferred from here."

Starling looked past her, to the old woman flanked by the crazy man.

"Your old home?" he asked.

"Yes, the farm. Father didn't own it. We rented the house and the two hundred acres we farmed."

"Who owns it?"

Yoshi tried to remember. "A family named Patterson, I think. They are one of the big land owners near Monterey."

Starling looked back at her parents.

"I can't make any promises," he said.

"They need to be taken care of. They can't stay here."

Starling nodded. "I'll see what I can do."

In Tokyo, Yoshi began to cook for Takata. She worried about him when he didn't return by dusk. The sky over Tokyo was never quiet at night. It was as if the smoke from the charcoal-burning automobiles was a harbinger for the nightly bombing runs. Tokyo was a city built of paper screens, bamboo frames, and tatami mats. Such materials as cotton, rayon, and the wartime sufu burned quicker than candlewicks. It hadn't taken the Americans long to determine that they could burn much of the Japanese capital to the ground, and so every night they targeted another portion of the city to carpet-bomb.

Takata's apartment consisted of two small rooms that smelled of incense and tea. It was the home of a man too busy, too much on the losing side of the war, to be concerned with seriously wooing and keeping a woman. There had been others before her. During the day, when Yoshi was alone, she often studied the row of small-framed photographs on the table near the door, trying to guess which ones were family and which ones were perhaps lovers. At night, she waited for him to come home. After hanging up his coat and slipping into his sandals, he routinely lit a stick of incense, sandalwood, in the holder by the window. Then he would come to her. His slender fingers stroked her back, steering her toward the futon. She would take one of his hands and begin kissing his fingertips.

"How are your balloons?" Yoshi whispered.

"As beautiful as any children," he replied.

Takata cradled her in one arm, dipping down as if they were dancing in a distant music hall. For a moment, she remembered the square dance and polkas at the fire hall in Capitola on Saturday nights. Her father would park their old Pontiac station wagon across the street, and the family would listen and laugh.

She arched her back as his tongue ran down from her lips, past her chin to her neck. He softly placed her upon the futon.

"The balloons? How do they go all the way across the Pacific?"

But tonight Takata was silent. His sweet mouth fell lower on her neck. He worked like a scientist. Every kiss was done with lingering patience.

He was close to telling her more. Yoshi needed only to push

him a bit further. Her fingertips brushed against his belt and she reached for his hands. She wanted them on her again. Yet, for some reason, tonight he resisted her advances.

"Who are you?" he murmured.

His head was at her waist and he peered up at her.

"There was a new security report on you today," he continued.

He rolled to one side, with one hand still resting on her hip. Even in the half-darkness, she saw how his Buddha eyes gazed upon her—unblinking and questioning.

"Why does one who grew up in the country look upon it in such a way?" he asked.

"What way?"

"Like you have never seen such country before." He gracefully sat up, his legs crossed in front of him. "Last week, near Kyoto, it seemed as if you were taking in every detail, trying so hard to memorize it. The papers on you, dear Yoshi, say you were born and raised in Okayama. I know the country-side around Okayama. We almost built a base for the balloons there. It looks a great deal like what we saw outside of Kyoto. But you searched the land with your crying eyes. It was like you had never seen such a place before."

She could never underestimate this one. He watched and listened better than any man she had ever known.

"Maybe we can kiss and love," Takata said. "Then maybe Ito is right. That it is foolish to trust anyone in such times."

Yoshi tried to be still and think—and then lie.

"My heart was breaking," she said.

"Your heart was breaking," he repeated in a harsher tone.

"Yes, my love."

He was silent, demanding to hear more. By the window, the

incense stick burned down and its soft smoke slowly drifted through the room.

"Nobody in Okayama remembered you," Takata said. "You told the ones at the Saishi factory that you had family there. But none has been found."

Yoshi realized that they listened to everything. An off-hand comment to a girl at the factory was now a part of her dossier. She would have to be careful. She closed her eyes, and tried to remember every lie she had told since coming to Japan. She reached for his hand. He allowed her to take it but gave no hint of affection in return.

"I no longer have family in Okayama," Yoshi said. "I lied."

"Why? Why do you lie?"

"Because I like to pretend that I still do. Tata, think of a time in your life when everything changed."

"Maybe there is no such time for me," Takata said.

"There is always a time like that for everyone," Yoshi said, forcing her mind back once more to the day when she left Manzanar. It still made her angry to think that her mother, such a proud woman, one who was strong enough to help her husband in the artichoke fields, was ever sent to such a place.

Manzanar meant apple orchard in Spanish. One of the girls had learned that from one of the guards and she told everyone else in camp. Manzanar had once been a fertile land. But the water, and arguably the area's soul, had been siphoned off years before to the Los Angeles Aqueduct. The authorities had no inhibition about shifting water and people away from their homeland. Their move away from the sea had driven Kenji crazy. Yoshi was convinced of that. During her training in the Presidio, she often wondered what barbed wire felt like when you grip it with all your strength in the middle of the night, when you're running from everything you hate. Does the pain somehow become more pleasant?

"You are never prepared for those times," she told Takata as she wiped a new tear away with the back of her hand. "If we have learned anything from this war, it is that things happen to you and you must accept them. We never know the whole truth. It is like a curtain of secrets and lies and riddles always hides it from us. The day my mother died I decided to leave Okayama. It doesn't matter to me that nobody remembers me there. It's not important because I forgot them long ago, too."

Yoshi was always surprised by how easy the lies came to her. She could twist what had actually happened into something far different, something that had the ring of truth.

"Where is your father? Did he serve the emperor?"

"Yes, he served the emperor, in the navy" Yoshi said, growing more confident as she felt this particular lie grow in strength. Yes, this would be a good story. "When we received the notice of his death, I barely read it. I don't know what battle, where it was. My mother died soon afterward. The neighbors said she died of a broken heart."

Takata nodded and brought his hands together, resting his chin atop slender fingertips. He could have been lost in prayer.

"Both are gone then?"

"Yes," Yoshi replied. "I am on my own. That's why I came to Kyoto."

"I see," Takata said and Yoshi knew that he would have these words investigated, too. Indeed, he would always test and probe anything she told him. The thing to do was pretend it was like a race. Her lies could extend toward the horizon, and the trick was to become so lost in what was fact and what was fiction that she remained far in front of anyone who dared pursue her.

"The report indicates that you know English."

Where had this come from? She had been so careful to speak only Japanese since the night she had come ashore near Osaka. But then Yoshi remembered the book burning in Kyoto. It was one of the few nights Madame Isobe had taken her outside the theater after they had attended the Festival of the Red Baton. A crowd had broken into an old home that belonged to a Baptist missionary with an infatuation for the classics. David Copperfield, Huckleberry Finn, Shakespeare's tragedies—the crowd had burned them all. Yoshi realized that someone must have been watching her as she drew closer to the glowing pile of books, eager to catch a glimpse of the titles before they were gone.

"The Kempei Tai believes that you can speak it," Takata said. "So, don't deny it."

"I'm not," Yoshi insisted. "But I don't know much."

"Where did you learn it? The schools in Okayama are not very good."

"My father could sew. Long before the war he would mend the suits of the Englishmen, sometimes an American, the businessmen that came through our city. He taught us the funny-sounding words. He thought he was helping us."

His fingers slowly stroked her hip again, a good sign.

"He was a tailor then."

"Yes, but he had no shop. He worked out of our home before he went into the navy."

Takata was quiet for a long time. His hand still rested on her flank.

"You become so flush when you're angry," he finally said.

"Maybe that's what keeps me warm," Yoshi said. "My anger, my madness."

"We have all grown mad," he said. "The world has done this to us."

She looked over at him. She loved how his eyes became distant and large when he daydreamed like this, when he allowed himself to be borne away from the everyday. If she could hold him there, in that faraway place, everything would be fine between them. She was sure of it.

He shook his head. "What am I doing here? With a girl like you?"

"We love the balloons," Yoshi said. "Tell me more. It makes me happy. It makes you happy."

Surprisingly, he did as she asked. Takata explained how it had taken eight years of experimentation to develop the fire balloons. He and a man named Nakoso, who had already been transferred away from Tokyo, had invented them. Takata would be transferred soon, too. He was sure of it, unless he could convince the generals of the balloons' merit.

"Perhaps that's why I'm being so reckless," he said. "Reckless with you."

"Tell me more," she said.

Yoshi kissed him on the cheek and let her lips graze his ear lobe.

"The balloons," he replied in a distant voice.

"Yes. How do they work?"

"You love them as much as I do, don't you?"

"I am in awe of them."

"They are a marvel," Takata said. "The way they soar into the sky. They rise faster than birds. Did you see that? So eager to pursue their mission."

"I close my eyes and I can still see them."

"Of course you do. You are one of the lucky ones. You have

seen them take flight. Now close your eyes again, sweet Yoshi, and I'll tell you where they go. They rise and rise from the land. Can you see them?"

"Yes," she said and closed her eyes.

His fingertips began to run down from her rib cage to her hips to the waistband of her pantaloons. Slowly he eased her work pants down from her hips.

"Soon they are high above the water," Takata said. "The Pacific Ocean that seems to go on forever. Sometimes my children become frightened, so high above this world, with so far to go. But I speak to them. You saw me the other day. How I look to them before the launch, telling them not to be afraid, to be brave, to help us defeat our enemies."

"How long do they need to fly?"

"Three days, two nights," Takata said. "Some disagree about my calculations. But I know they are correct. I have checked and rechecked many times. Professor Nakoso, my teacher, agrees with me. So, it is a dangerous journey and my children must be strong."

"They are. They are so strong," she said and turned her torso to meet his hand.

"Some know what to do, but they never act," Takata said. "But we do, don't we, Yoshi? You and I will always have courage. Now think about what you saw and I will tell you more about how it works. Remember the shroud lines that hung down from our balloon?"

The palm of his hand pushed along the curve of her lower back. "They are attached to a chord that runs to the bottom casing."

"It was round. It looked heavy."

"Yes, my love," Takata said. He paused to softly kiss her

side, his tongue running across her ribs. "The bottom casing may look formidable, but it is not that heavy. The apparatus contains an altitude device that is connected to sandbag ballasts. A dozen bags, sometimes sixteen, each filled with sand."

He slid down her torso until he had reached her waist. Yoshi's hands rested atop his head of thick black hair.

"We fill them on the beach near the launch site," he said. "If our balloon loses altitude too soon, the sandbags are dropped, like coins into a fountain, until the balloon rises back into the strong currents of winds. We drop one from each side, keeping everything in balance."

His voice was but a whisper, his fingertips light as a dove's wings.

"Remember how the housing went together? The altitude control atop the ballast and the curtain of sandbags hanging down, dangling in the breeze."

"Yes, I remember," Yoshi whispered.

"Below the sandbags usually lie three bombs—two incendiary and one fifteen-kilogram. Ito says these are pebbles being slung at a giant."

"Forget about Ito, my darling."

Takata smiled and his tongue began to work on the soft folds of skin between her legs.

"Save yourself for marriage," her mother had told her. And despite herself, Yoshi momentarily hesitated—those words returning to her from somewhere faraway. Takata sensed her reluctance and stopped to peer up at her with curiosity.

But such motherly advice had dissolved with what was left of her old world. It made no sense anymore. The only thing was to embrace what was at hand, to cherish it and to make it one's own.

With both hands, her fingertips touching the fresh stubble of his cheeks, Yoshi pulled Takata back up to her. There her lips surrendered to him once again, eager to greet him with everything that was ever held in her heart.

⌇

Afterward Yoshi tried to remember everything he had told her. Each balloon was made of four-ply paper on top and three-ply paper for the lower half. When it was inflated, each one was thirty-two point eight feet in diameter. Nineteen shroud lines hung down to the sandbag ballast and the bombs. Out there, somewhere over the vast Pacific Ocean, more were drifting toward America.

Throughout the day, the balloon would hold its course—traversing two thousand miles or more, Takata had told her. But as the sun set, the warmth from those rays dissipated and the balloon often lost altitude as the hydrogen inside the paper skin cooled. If the balloon fell below thirty thousand feet, the altimeter was activated once more and the sand ballasts were dropped. The ballast weights were three to seven pound bags hanging by metal hooks from the ring. They were released as needed throughout the night to maintain the desired altitude.

"Until now, we've only used small bombs, the incendiary ones," Takata had told her afterward as they lay there in the dark. "But I've been experimenting with chemicals, nerve gas. If I can only convince them to let us try such things."

Three days and two nights was the time calculated to cross the Pacific Ocean from west to east. By the end of the third day, the jagged edge of the North American continent could be seen, and here the hunt for them began in earnest. The binoculars and planes searched the skies for such intruders. An American Lockheed P-38 was credited with shooting down the first Japanese fire balloon over Calistoga, California, on February 23, 1945. A trio of Bell P-63 King Cobras tracked another balloon from Redwood, Oregon, to central Nevada before it was downed. A Grumman F6F Hellcat shot down nine balloons in early April 1945 over the Aleutians. But such kills were highly unusual, for the balloons drifted like the clouds. In speed and altitude, the balloons usually remained beyond the reach of detection and interception. Despite the concern spreading among the military and the scrambling of Vought Corsairs over the western U.S., less than twenty balloons had been shot down. These were capricious, ingenious weapons. All the instruments—altimeter, relief valve, ballast release, timer and fuses—were powered by a single one and one-half volt wet-cell battery.

After three days and two nights had elapsed, two incendiary bombs and a single fifteen-kilogram anti-personnel bomb were automatically released. An hour or two later, a fuse ignited the balloon's hydrogen and then shreds of paper, a twisted metal ring, all that was left, fell to the earth. That was the plan for each and every balloon. Even those that didn't work perfectly could still create havoc, chaos and fear. Any one of the balloons was capable of igniting thousands of acres of forest land. The timing fuse, even the bombs' release, were secondary considerations really. The main goal had always been to cross the wide Pacific Ocean, to arrive in America. The bombs were set to explode upon contact. Ultimately, it didn't matter if they were released from on high or if the balloon slowly lost altitude, drifting in like the morning fog. The damage could always be done.

Paper, like anything of worth, was in short supply in To-kyo in the waning years of the war. Still, Takata brought home precious slips of it. Yoshi would find it in his suit and pants pockets. She discovered it when she went through his closet. She brought the fabric up to her face to catch a scent of him when he was away. Much of the paper in those pockets was covered with numbers—mathematical doodling that she didn't understand and knew to leave alone. Occasionally she found a blank piece of paper, again nothing of consequence, something that she could close in her hand. She began to store these pieces in the inner pockets of her work pants. In a week or so, she had enough paper to begin to draw what she understood of the fire balloon.

Carefully, so the paper wouldn't move too much, she worked with a small brush and ink. The bottom quarter of the balloon reached up toward the top edges of the paper and Yoshi spent more time detailing what hung below, the intricate bomb load. From her memory of what she had seen that day in the coun-tryside and what Takata had told her, Yoshi drew the bungee shock cord that gathered together the nineteen shroud lines that ran down from the paper balloon itself. Below that was the box-like altitude control device and the metal belt of sand-bag ballasts. Tangling down slightly lower were the incendiary bombs, usually two in total, and then the larger fifteen-kilo-gram, anti-personnel bomb. It was these units that Takata said could be easily substituted with germ and gas units if he got fi-nal approval from high command. Running from the metal belt upward to the balloon itself was a sixty-four-foot fuse line. It was attached to a flash bomb on the hide of the four-ply paper of the upper sphere. The fuse line took one hour and twenty-two minutes to burn and was automatically rigged to ignite after sixty hours in the air.

Yoshi finished her sketch and gazed upon it. It was an amazing creation—simple, yet potentially so effective. She took another long look at everything she had remembered and then she scattered the pieces of paper and gathered them up one by one to hide away for what she hoped would be forever.

DRAWING IN THE DIRT

The Connors' homestead was southeast of town, hard by Snowstorm Mountain, near the juncture of the Crystal and Verde rivers. The Grapevine, Gould and Pig springs made up this watershed. Koch's Nash kicked up a roostertail of dust as it sped along the red-dirt road from Payson.

"You two are going to owe me a car wash after this outing," Koch told Taylor and Leo.

"Scrub this jalopy too hard and it'll fall apart," Leo said.

They sat three abreast in the front seat. It was Wednesday afternoon, two days after the last fire and Starling had given them the afternoon off.

"I can't figure him out." Taylor said. "He works us half to death one day and it's a vacation the next."

"Maybe Pa's right," Leo offered. "Maybe there's something slippery about the guy."

"Now hang on there a minute," Koch said, trying to keep his attention on the rutted road in front of them. "The Webbs are speaking ill about our fire boss? Especially the boy king? What's caused this shift in the wind, Leo?"

"Some things just don't add up."

"Like what?"

"Like what he did on the Teague Fire. We're putting down line one minute and the next thing you know he's pulling us off."

"It got kind of hot, didn't it? He was trying to keep his tenderfoot crew safe."

Leo shook his head. "If that's the case, why go back down into it when it's blowing even hotter. Spots everywhere. And then there's the 3-Bar."

"What about the 3-Bar?" Koch asked. "We were there."

"We missed something," Leo insisted. "Pa was talking to Tad Reals, the foreman at the 3-Bar, the other night at the Winchester. He says it was the strangest thing. Starling went back to the 3-Bar the night after we'd finished mopping up."

"Went back?"

"He borrowed a horse from Reals," Leo continued, "and rode back out, coming back with a tangle of rope and what all."

"Leo says it sounds a lot like what they found at the Connors' place," Taylor said. Her dirty blonde hair was blowing wild in the wind and she reached back with both hands to tighten the ponytail.

"That's right," Leo said. "It was a bunch of rope, a piece of metal, some cloth. That's what the sheriff said."

Koch asked, "And what happened to that bunch of what all?"

"This is where it gets interesting," Leo said. "Near as anybody can figure, Starling got it. They said he's the one who passed it along to the feds in Phoenix."

"So, you think what was found on the 3-Bar and what the Connors kids came up with goes together somehow?"

"We won't know if we don't ask."

"Where is this place?" Koch said as he squinted for a better look amid the spider's web of cracks in his windshield.

"Careful," Leo warned, "this road gets ragged pretty quick."

Soon afterward the front axle of the Nash bottomed out in a ditch that ran diagonally across the road.

"Sweet Jesus," Koch cried as he fought to control the wheel. He barely kept the Nash from hitting the earth-and rock-embankment that marked the sides of the road. He downshifted and the vehicle shuttered and slowed.

"That's it," Koch said aloud. "Nice and slow or it's going to be a long walk back to Dodge City."

Beads of perspiration had appeared on his forehead and he ran the back of his hand quickly across the area. His pumpkin-shaped face had tightened into a grimace.

"It's just a little bit farther," Taylor said to him. "Take your time."

"I hear you, ma'am," Koch said, his eyes only on the narrowing road. "Any kids that grow up out here have to be half-wolf. We sure they can talk?"

"We're going to find out," Taylor nodded. "I bet that's them."

Two figures came into view, drudging up the hill to the right. On the other side of the road was a stone-and-mud house that was below the ground as much as it was above. The two boys were carrying three pails among them.

"What are they doing?" Koch asked.

"Fetching their water," Leo said.

"So why didn't they build closer to one of those springs you were prattling on about?"

"Maybe they did," Leo said, "but the smaller ones can dry up in a drought like we have now."

"There's no figuring this country, is there?" Koch said. He stopped the Nash at the head of a dried wash that passed for a driveway. "It's about as unforgiving as the draft board."

The three of them got out and waited for the boys to come up the hill toward them. The taller of the two boys had a metal pole across his shoulders and he had draped his skinny arms over the top of it, balancing two metal pails that hung from either end. The smaller one trailed him, shifting a third bucket from one hand to the other. Much of the water had slopped out, wetting the front of his ragged jeans.

"You must be Jamie," Leo said, coming down over the embankment to take the bucket from the smaller boy.

"No, I be Jimmy," the boy replied. He didn't look happy at having visitors show up on the family doorstep.

"Here you go, partner," Koch said as he lifted the pole off the older one's shoulders.

"Don't spill any," the boy said.

"Don't worry, son. Driving out here I've gained a new appreciation for going slow."

The older boy couldn't have been older than twelve. The younger one was maybe seven. They fell into step alongside the visitors as they hefted what was left of the water down to the house.

"Going in the cistern, Jamie-boy?" Koch asked

"That's right."

"Where's it at?"

"Around the side," he said.

"What about your well?"

"It run dry," said Jimmy, the younger one. "It always does."

Jamie added, "Pa done got all the down spouts running into the cistern. Thought that would do it this time. But this summer has already run too hot. Momma keeps talking about moving."

"And Pa tells her to shut up," added Jimmy, starting to giggle.

"Ain't that the way of the world," Koch said.

"Your folks around?" Taylor asked.

"Naw," said Jamie. "Momma's working the diner. We ain't seen Pa in must be a month now. He went to Phoenix looking for work."

The two boys gazed with admiration at the three Hotshots dressed in their green fatigues and gray T-shirts.

"I wish Pa had joined the new fire crew," Jamie said. "Momma tried to talk him into it. But he didn't want to. He can be that way sometimes."

"I think he was chicken," said Jimmy.

"Why don't you shut your mouth? Pa ain't scared of anything or anybody."

"That's what you say. You don't know everything."

"Shh," Leo said, as if he was calming a pair of restless puppies. "We wanted to talk to you about what you found. What they wrote up in the paper."

"Fat lot of good it did us," Jimmy said.

"Hush," his older brother warned.

"Why should I hush?" Jimmy said. "Them men ain't coming back. They weren't going to do us no good, no how."

"What men?" Leo asked.

"They said they were from the government."

"I told you to hush," Jamie said as Leo and Taylor exchanged glances.

"Momma says it's only an eighth of a mile to Pig Springs," the older boy added, trying to change the subject. "But it sure seems farther coming back, especially when somebody's too small to really carry anything."

"You shut up," Jimmy told his brother. "I'll fight you. You know I will if you keep that up."

"And you'll get a whipping, just like last time. Just like every time."

Koch stepped between them. The younger boy's hand was already balled into a fist.

"Little man, why don't you come with me and the lovely lady here," Koch said. "Show us where the spring is and we'll carry you up another load."

Jimmy began to jump up and down. "You will," he exclaimed.

"Honest Injun," said Koch. "Just show us the way. Jamie, you put your feet up and tell your story to our kid fire boss here. When your mother comes back and sees the cistern filled, you can tell her that you and your brother did a rain dance."

Leo and Jamie watched the others pick up the pails and long pole. With the little one leading the way, they crossed the dirt road and disappeared down the far side of the hill. Only then did Leo ask, "So, what did you find?"

"What do you care?"

"Just curious. The whole town's talking about it, but nobody knows where the rig went."

"I heard it was your fire boss," Jamie replied. "That's what Momma said."

"That right?"

"It was just a lot of rope. We found it closer to the mountain. Momma was mad that we told Mr. Powers. He's the one with the big ranch over yonder. He was out riding and we gave the gear to him so he could take it into town. It seemed like the right thing to do at the time, but momma didn't think so."

"Mr. Powers gave it to Chief Parsons and Mr. Starling?" Leo asked.

"Probably so. But I betcha it was just a mess of junk by then. They didn't know how it looked when Jimmy and I found it. It was kind of pretty, really. All spread out like."

"Jamie, can you draw me a picture?"

"I ain't got no paper or pencil, sir. I only see those things in school."

Leo looked around and found a stick. "You can still draw," he said, holding it out to the boy. "Here, just do it in the dirt."

"All right, I'll try" Jamie said reluctantly. He took the stick and peered at the ground. "It was like this," and he began to draw several long lines coming down to a single point.

"Them long ones were the rope. They were all the same lengths. I didn't measure it or anything, but I'm sure they were."

"All right."

"They came down to this chunk of metal. It was in the shape of a circle. It had holes it in and I bet that it held other things. But I can't say that for sure."

Leo nodded. "What was at the other end of the lines? What did they lead up to?"

The boy pondered this, holding the stick in both hands.

"I don't rightly know. That was all tore up."

"Will you draw that for me, too?"

The boy sketched an oblong shape coming off one of the lines.

"I can't do no better, sir."

"That's fine."

"It seems to me that there had to be more to it," Jamie said. "That's me guessing again. That's what momma would said, too. But I do know it wasn't like any kind of cloth I've ever felt before."

The two of them studied the drawing in the dirt until they heard the others returning with the water. Jimmy ran out ahead, free of any obligations this time.

"Jamie-boy, you're right," Koch said. "This little pipsqueak is a real handful when he doesn't have to lug a pail around."

Leo waited as they carefully poured the cool water into the cistern and closed the lid.

"Sis, come here," he said.

Taylor came alongside him.

"This is what the boys found," he said. "What do you make of it?"

"I don't know. Maybe we should ask Pa."

"No, Sis, I'm not asking Pa," Leo said. "He'll just lecture me about how there's too many secrets in the world already and how the government holds most of them. I'm afraid this is something we'll have to figure out ourselves."

That evening Leo decided he needed to get to the bottom of things. He leashed up Hunter, the family dog, and set off for crew's base camp. Down in the Petrified Forest, where the Hotshots often practiced their woodsman skills, the government had set up a silver trailer home. It was where Starling stayed.

Leo walked through the neighborhood, but once he and his dog crossed the narrow bridge over the Crystal River, he ducked into the woods. The trails would bring him through the woods and up the back way to Starling's place. Hunter tugged hard at the leash and Leo almost unhooked him. But then he heard the hiss of ignition up ahead and saw a short burst of flame.

"Still, boy," he said, coming alongside the liver-spotted Brittany. "Quiet there. What's this all about?"

Bending low at the waist, he moved with the dog through the brush, coming up on the clearing by Starling's silver trailer. The fire boss was seated behind a foldout metal table, his back to them. An array of branches and plants lay upon the table. At one end of the table was a metal vise, and Leo watched as his fire boss put on asbestos mitts and fire goggles. Then Starling tightened a thick tuft of cheatgrass in the metal grips. Starling's short-wave radio was on and weather reports for locales throughout the West echoed in the surrounding woods.

"Hush now," Leo told the panting dog and rubbed him in the sweet spot behind the ears. "What's our Mr. Starling up to?"

After fastening the cheatgrass down tight, Starling lit a blow torch. The dog almost barked as the blue flame flared out from the metal nozzle, but the boy rubbed harder behind the dog's ears. Leo watched Starling hold the flame over the cheatgrass. As soon as it caught, Starling took up a stopwatch and monitored how long it took the material to burn. It was thirty, thirty-five seconds tops, Leo figured. Then he saw the fire boss record the result on a clipboard.

Starling was unscrewing the metal vise, dusting away the

ash, when the dog saw a squirrel scramble up one of the evergreens that rimmed the clearing. Leo reached for his collar, but it was too late. The dog bounded away from him and barked as it raced out of their hiding place.

"Who's out there?" Starling yelled.

"Just me," Leo said and stepped into the clearing. "I was out walking the damn dog and he got away from me."

Hunter bounded up to the fire boss, who impatiently reached down to pet him. Always a glutton for attention, the dog rolled over onto his back, revealing his soft belly. With a grunt of disgust, Starling dutifully took off an asbestos mitt and rubbed him a few more times.

"How long you been out there?" he asked.

"Not long," Leo replied. "Like I said, he and I were out walking. That's all."

Starling returned to his work, screwing a branch of Gambel brush into the vise.

"What's all this?" Leo asked.

"Just some work."

"What kind of work?" Leo persisted.

"You are something, aren't you, kid," Starling said. He flipped the goggles up to the top of his forehead. "Maybe there's some things you don't need to know, maybe some things that are better off kept secret."

"Me and Taylor and Koch went out to the Connors's homestead this afternoon," Leo said, cocky that he'd gotten to the fire boss. "They drew us a picture of the thing they found."

"Was it a pretty picture?" Starling asked.

"I guess you could call it an interesting picture."

"I see," Starling replied, "and you think that I know everything that happened out there. That I can just lay it out for you.

Tell you everything in one fell swoop."

"They said what they found was maybe like what you went out to retrieve at the 3-Bar."

Starling stopped what he was doing. He took off the other mitt and stacked them, one upon the other, on the table.

"I never put much credence in local gossip, son," the fire boss said.

"Maybe not," Leo replied, determined not to back down. "But I don't see where keeping everything secret has helped us much so far. We're not exactly the best crew I've ever seen."

Starling nodded briefly, in what Leo hoped was an acknowledgment. But then the fire boss fell quiet, his eyes looking at the collection of stuff on his table.

Leo decided to try again. "You know, sir, people around here aren't too happy with you or with our crew," he said.

"I'm sorry to hear that," Starling replied.

"People around here have been fighting fire for years. The new ways we have of doing things, well, they don't understand."

Starling turned toward him. "Leo, what if I told you that fires are different now?"

"Different. What can be so different about a forest fire?"

Starling looked down at the table again.

"You see all this, boy?"

"Sure, what of it?"

"It's the different types of vegetation that grow around here," the fire boss said. "All the fuel loads I could find. We know that different things burn at different speeds, right?"

"Sure."

"So, that's gotten me and some others to thinking that if you could tabulate all of this, it would help a crew on a fire.

For example," he said, holding up a branch and then a clump of cheatgrass. "Two completely different materials. Ponderosa pine and cheatgrass. If we knew exactly how fast each one burns, we'd be better prepared."

"Anybody knows that trees burn hotter than grass," Leo said.

"Careful, kid, you're beginning to sound like one of the local yokels. Of course, everybody knows that. We've been fighting fire for generations around here," Starling said, his voice growing more sarcastic. He stopped and settled himself. "There's so much that we don't know about these fires. Leo, I'm one of the first graduates of the fire generalship class in San Francisco. There were a dozen of us, handpicked from various branches of the military. As you probably heard, I'm with the navy. My specialty is explosives. Other graduates had specialties in aircraft, strategy, command. So why did they pull guys like us off the front lines? As I'm reminded all the time in this one-horse town, there's a war going on, right? Well, we're fighting our own war right here in these mountains. I've worked everything from gunpowder to dynamite. Ever seen newsreels of those Nazi rockets? The V2s?"

"What's that got to do with us?" Leo asked.

"Maybe nothing, kid. Maybe everything."

"The Connors kids said people took away what they found. That you were in on it."

"I can't talk about that."

"Why not?"

"Because it's a secret," Starling said, his voice rising. "I wish it wasn't. But it is. You and I and this whole damn town have to live with that."

The two of them stood silent for a moment, staring down at

the table covered with specimens of local vegetation and flora.

"On the last fire, some of the guys said they heard an explosion," Leo said. "Right after that the fire took off. You know what happened, don't you?"

Starling shook his head. "You must be part bulldog, kid. No quit in your bite."

He set the fire goggles on the table and turned off the blowtorch.

"Here, I've got something to show you."

The boy followed him into the trailer home where the walls were covered with topographical maps of northern Arizona, southern Utah and California. Starling found a pencil and nodded at a smaller map of their district.

"OK, the Teague Fire was here," he said and marked it with an X. "Now find me the Connors place."

Leo took the pencil and did so.

"And here's where two other smokes were reported in the last few days," Starling said and made two more crosses on the map. "See they make a line. Kind of unusual, huh?"

"Maybe, but what are you trying to tell me, sir?"

"I'm telling you as much as I can, Leo. We're up against something nobody in these parts has ever seen before. We've got to work together. It's our only way."

The boy's face folded into a mask of doubt.

"Maybe you don't want to hear this, sir," Leo said. "But I don't think it can work that way. The crew, this town, needs to know more. You can't keep everything a secret, Mr. Starling, sir. Not when it's that important to everybody in these parts."

BLOCK BY BLOCK

Beyond the apartment door much of Tokyo was in ruins. Block after block had burned due to the nightly raids. Yoshi learned that the B-29s dropped several types of bombs. There were the explosive kinds and the petrols, the ones that spit oil like she had seen that first night near Osaka. But what fascinated her the most were the electron incendiaries. When they fell they gave off an intense, bluish flame and the noise of them mimicked a human voice. From a distance, it sounded like somebody was screaming.

The first night she encountered them, she ran down to the bomb shelter as the throbbing sound grew around her. The electrons had frightened her so much that she couldn't sleep even after the all-clear sounded. But within a few nights, Yoshi had begun to anticipate them, appreciating how oddly beautiful they were. She was fascinated by the hot blasts of air that accompanied the explosions. Such fever could be felt for blocks around. It was like a fierce dragon that had come out of his lair. Such bombs were aimed at the factories, never the Imperial Palace where the emperor, the son of heaven, lived. The Americans were coming, but someone among them knew better than to level every visible landmark. The castle and the temples would be spared when possible. The new conquerors would use them to remake the country in their own image.

Increasingly, Yoshi was alone at night. Takata was putting in long hours, trying to convince the generals that the balloon program was still viable. One evening, on her way down to the shelter, as the first of the sirens pierced the evening stillness, Yoshi lingered in the open doorway. She watched the entire show from there. She never reached the shelter. After that evening, Yoshi never returned to the shelter again. Instead she slipped outside when the bombers came. Out on the street she could better witness how the bluish flames engulfed the factories blocks away.

Without Madame Isobe, there was no way to pass along the information about the fire balloons. But that didn't really matter anymore. Yoshi held her secret and let it grow and warm her on such dark nights. It soon became the treasure that only she and Takata shared.

It was strange but the prospect of death no longer frightened her, not after the hell of the internment camp. By the end of the war nothing would be as it once was. She knew that to walk amid the nightly firestorm was foolish. It was a form of suicide really, but she found it empowering somehow.

After that night when Yoshi didn't reach the shelter, she began to look forward to the darkness, when the sirens sounded and the B-29s came in low across the black waters to the east.

On the nights when Takata was home, she convinced him to stay with her as well. One missed so much by going down to the shelter, she told him. That was for cowards. It was much better to make love with the bombs falling, and if one of them should fall upon them, well, then it was fate, wasn't it?

The night had become her most trusted friend. Takata was her lover, but he was also her benefactor, the great and powerful god who had brought her to this place of nightly fire and light, the one she mined for information and comfort. At night, when the bombs fell, it was like time had been shaken to its core. That their world could be stopped, for a second or two, wasn't that novel. She had experienced such forces before. When the bombs fell, they came upon them with such fierceness and splendor, even beauty, that at such moments everything was shaken to its core. Yoshi came to love such chaos.

In the weeks since she arrived from Kyoto, Yoshi had become more convinced that random disturbances rippled though everything she remembered or ever knew. Her childhood flowed back to her in vivid detail. No longer did she long for those photographs that had been left in Starling's care. The farmhouse, the fields down to the froth-blue ocean, her family when the times had been good – such treasures rolled back to her like the movies at the old Santa Cruz Palace. In her mind they arrived as bits and pieces, never in black and white, but in color, glorious shreds of color.

It was another night when Takata didn't come home by dark. He had warned her that his presence was required in the laboratories in Yokohama, south of Tokyo. They were close to launching a new, deadlier version of the fire balloon—one with canisters of nerve gas instead of small incendiary bombs.

Yoshi walked the streets alone. She knew she should be more careful, but this fascination about the American bombs that fell upon Tokyo grew inside her. They were so much deadlier than Takata's fire balloons. Her lover could talk about his beloved inventions of paper and hope, but they were child's play when compared with the petrol and electron incendiaries that brought the torrent every evening down upon Tokyo.

As Yoshi walked this evening, the black skies were clear. Some stars, twinkling faintly, could be seen high above the world's madness. Besides artichokes, her father had grown flowers, tulips and carnations, on their family farm near Monterey. The Mother's Day harvest was expected to be the richest in years, but nobody, not her father or any of his friends, were allowed to gather the crop. After he was denied permission by the local authorities, her father attempted to plow the entire crop, flowers and his prized artichokes, under. A man from the FBI drove up in a jeep and told him to stop. If he didn't, the government would charge him with sabotage of American property and send him to jail. The final notice to evacuate came later that afternoon. There were only five days to pack and board the trains with their blacked-out windows. Soldiers with polished bayonets watched their every move. They were herded like cattle, the young and old alike, every one limited to hand luggage that was numbered and tagged by the soldiers. All of their belongings had the same number 11166. They were no longer the Minagi Family. They were number 11166. The elderly were carried on stretchers aboard the train to Bay Meadows. Worried mothers hung onto the tiny hands of their frightened children, who were dressed so nicely, like they were going to Sunday school. When the train pulled out of the Monterey Station most of them realized that the world as they knew it had changed forever.

Yoshi was near the Ginza district when she saw the sedan, idling in the shadows. She was almost upon it. Her eyes had been on the sky, her mind back in those early days of Manzanar.

"You," said a man in uniform.

Yoshi knew better than to run, but the soldier grabbed her roughly anyway. He put one arm around her neck and used the other to twist her right limb behind her.

"Bring her over," said a man in the backseat of the car. His window was down and she recognized the voice. It was Ito. He leaned out the open window. The reddish hues of the night were reflected in his spectacles, transforming his face into a hideous mask.

"Takata's concubine," he said. "If I'd had my way you would have been killed back in Kyoto. Maybe hung from the neck like your friend? The one called Lui. The lucky baton wasn't so kind for her, was it?"

Ito opened his door and the driver half-pushed her inside.

"I cannot kill you," he said. "Not while you're in Takata's keeping. But I need to understand. So many things about you confound me, young Yoshi. We've been watching you for some time. We see how you walk when the bombs come. Our friend Takata tries to hurry home every night to be with you. How sad he is when we have to send him away, like tonight. Maybe I need to understand your charms. The hold you have over him."

She tried the door. It wouldn't open.

"So pretty but so stupid," Ito said.

He was in dress uniform with gold braids that hung from the shoulders. He reached out and held her chin with his thumb and forefinger. Then he squeezed hard. Yoshi tried to push him away, but he only squeezed harder, bringing tears to her eyes.

"Sometimes I daydream about the most painful way to kill you," he said.

Ito shouted up to the driver, "Go anywhere."

The vehicle sped into the night. Down near the harbor more bombs were being dropped.

"Your Tata leaves you alone too much," Ito said. "You should tell him to stay home. To forget all the foolish trouble he makes for the rest of us. His balloons are such a waste of our time and resources."

He was next to her, reaching to undo the top button of her work shirt. She raised her hand, ready to push him away. But then she let her hand drop back into her lap.

"Good," Ito said. "You're learning."

He undid the buttons and slid his hand inside her work shirt. His stubby fingers were well-manicured, so unlike Takata's callused hands.

"Come," he said, "let's discover why our Tata covets you so."

Afterward, Yoshi sat in Takata's flat, huddled in the darkest corner. At Manzanar, there had been lines everywhere, lines for meals, laundry tubs, the latrines and communal bathrooms. About the only place they gathered as they once did was at the baseball field, which the older men had built beyond the vegetable fields. There were few bleachers, so the crowd gathered down the first- and third-base lines. They stood behind chicken wire and watched the younger boys play. Her brother had been one of the stars until his disgrace.

A knock at the door brought Yoshi around. Takata never

announced his arrival. After all, it was his apartment. He just walked in, full of breezy confidence and crazy dreams.

When the knock came again, Yoshi pushed herself farther back into the corner. She hugged her legs to her chest and closed her eyes. If it was Ito, there was nowhere she could run.

"Yoshi?" someone asked, and she recognized the hoarse voice.

Yoshi staggered to the door and opened it.

"Madame Isobe," she said, her eyes welling with tears.

"My dear Yoshi," the old lady said, "My moga, what have they done to you?"

A NIGHT OUT

"So what did our fire boss say about what the Connors kids told us?" Koch asked.

"You've got a million questions today, don't ya?" Leo said. He nodded at the half-dozen Pulaskis piled beside Koch. "You're going to be working until midnight if you keep jabbering away like this."

"What did he say?" Koch said.

"He gave me a map," Leo said. "Told me to study it."

"That sounds like Starling," Koch said. "Never a straight answer with him, is there?"

The two of them were in the backyard behind the fire station. The entire crew was scattered under the mesquite trees. This afternoon assignment was to sharpen and file every hand-tool at base camp. When they heard the loud blast of a horn around front, Leo got to his feet and everyone followed him around front. There they found a green-gray military bus idling in the gravel lot. As they walked toward it, the door opened and Starling appeared on the bottom step.

"It's ours," Starling grinned.

"What do you mean ours?" Leo said.

"Behold our new mode of transportation. No more flatbeds or you guys battling for a spot to sit in the back with the tools. This is how we're riding to fires from now on. Courtesy of the U.S. Army."

They stared at the huge bus. It was as fine a vehicle as any of them had seen in some time.

"It's all gassed up and ready to go," Starling said.

Nobody said a word. The crew continued to gaze upon the bus as if it had dropped from heaven above.

"I know," the fire boss said. "Why don't we take it for a spin?"

Where to?" Koch asked. "Do more trail work above the Rim?"

Starling tried to laugh it off. "Would I do that to you?"

"Yep," said Koch. "You sure would."

"I was thinking more like the Winchester." Starling said. "Old man Grady is willing to let the whole crew come by tonight. It's my treat. You guys have earned it."

The Hotshots stood there, unsure if they dared trust this rare display of generosity by their fire boss.

"Well, how about it?" Starling shouted.

"Yeah," Koch yelled back and the others began to shout and whistle.

"Let's go then," Starling said and he led the way onto the bus with its clean vinyl seats and well-scrubbed floor.

Once they were aboard, Leo sat down next to his sister.

Around them the crew talked excitedly.

"I don't know which is more amazing," he whispered to Taylor. "The new bus or Starling acting like a human being."

It was barely five in the afternoon and the Winchester was quiet. The owner, Grady Turner, saw the fire crew coming through the saloon style doors, and he came out from behind the bar to greet them.

Starling asked, "Mr. Grady, you got enough foodstuffs for this bunch of savages?"

"If you've got legal tender, I can feed anybody," Grady replied as he wiped his hands with a polka-dot bar rag, "We've got barbecue chicken tonight, with potatoes and baked beans."

"Let's start rolling it out," Starling said and he held up a country bankroll of bills. "Dinners all around. I've got a good crew here, Mr. Grady. You treat them right, you hear?"

"Yes, sir, Mr. Starling. I will."

The chicken was tender enough and the two waitresses, Kelly and Grady's granddaughter, Rachel, brought extras on everything. When Koch wanted some music, Kelly indulged him, first putting on Tommy Dorsey and then, of all things, Louis Armstrong.

"The Great Satchmo," Starling said as he shoveled another piece of chicken into his mouth. "Don't tell me you've got him."

The fire boss stood up and strode out to the wood-parquet dance floor. "You can't sit still when he's playing. You've got to get up and move those feet."

The trumpet music was muted and tumbled out in a hurried rush. The beat cascaded and slid, as swift as the waters of the Crystal River during the spring thaw. It was methodical one moment, a rush the next. Leo watched with the others as Starling shambled about in the middle of the dance floor—alone.

His eyes were closed and he breathed in the raging rhythms as if such sounds could sustain him for the rest of his days. For a moment, they saw Starling as he would always be remembered in these parts—the stranger who had come to town and asked too much of them, the fire boss who spoke in riddles but somehow always seemed to be telling something close to the truth.

"You better get out there and dance with him before they cart him away to the loony bin," Leo told his sister.

"I ain't going out there alone," Taylor said.

"All right then," Leo replied in disgust.

He got up and led Genie by the hand and, thankfully, Koch followed with Grady's granddaughter, as they drew ranks around their fire boss, trying to follow his lead.

The regulars had begun to file in for another night at the Winchester and they took up their regular spots at the bar and watched Starling's fire crew carry on. The Great Satchmo was singing to them now, something about the 'Heebie-Jeebie Blues.' His cherished trumpet was forgotten for the moment. As that gravelly voice of wonder rolled over them, Leo saw Starling take Taylor in his arms. He had risen from his trance and the two of them began to spin in looping circles around the dance floor. The others fell back to the perimeter. A line of bemused faces hooted and hollered as Starling and Taylor moved faster and faster. Seeing his sister in Starling's arms, Leo began to believe that things could be right again, that soon the world would turn in their favor. Before they knew it they would be able to laugh, like they had before the war had come and so much of what they treasured had disappeared.

As the song ended, the trumpet returned for a final chorus, the trombones roared to catch up, the bass coupled with the piano chugged along, and the drums held it all together. Starling led Taylor into a slow dip that ended with her head back, that blonde ponytail hanging only a foot or so off the worn parquet floor. He held her for a beat or two after the music ended. The scratchy static filled the room before it was drowned out by applause.

LISTEN TO THE RADIO

In the darkness, listening to the recordings of the American radio stations, Yoshi imagined that she was back home, hard by the sea near Santa Cruz. Takata brought her reel-to-reel tapes from the ministry. It had started as a joke, with her playing along, trying to conceal how much the music from the United States broke her heart. Takata was away more and more, and she hadn't told him what Ito had done to her.

The driver had taken them away from the harbor that evening, while Ito methodically pulled away her clothes and worked his way into her. She was forced back onto the seat and from there she closed her eyes and tried to picture her family's farm—how the mist rolled in off the ocean in the morning, how the even rows of foot-high green artichoke plants reached down to the sea, how it used to be.

When Ito was finished, the sedan slowed, the door opened

and she was back on the streets, only few a blocks from Takata's flat. The military vehicle pulled away as she was still buttoning up her work shirt.

At the ministry they listened to the American radio news and read U.S. newspapers—eager for any indication of the balloons' destruction. In its propaganda, the Japanese military told the people that bombing attacks on the United States had produced widespread damage and were a 'prelude for something big.' But so far the sleeping giant called America hadn't even acknowledged the existence of the bizarre weapon. Instead the news reports from the U.S. were becoming more enthusiastic. The Allies had been victorious in Europe. Next was Japan. The war in the Pacific was almost over. Anyone could tell it was only a matter of time.

Still, the real joy for Yoshi was found in the music. Back home she hadn't paid much attention to the radio stations from San Francisco, San Jose and Monterey. But now the music took her back to that time before the war. Once again she was at home or at college, moving like a flame to Benny Goodman's hypnotic clarinet, or silently mimicking how the DJs stretched out Tommy Dorsey's name until it became like a homage to a god. She wiped away the tears when Louis Armstrong's trumpet soared toward the heavens. To listen to such music was to fall backward into the warm pool of memory. She felt more American than she ever had in her old life. Ironically, she had to come here, back to her parents' homeland, an outcast from her own country, to truly understand who she was and how deep such emotions ran.

"You've fallen in love with him."

That's what Madame Isobe had accused her of the night before.

"I risk everything to return to Tokyo," she continued, "and how do I find you? Alone in his apartment. No guard was posted by him. You tell me you walk the streets at night. If Ito could find you, you could have found someone to help you, to get word to me."

"Not if you keep everything a secret," Yoshi snapped. "From the nightingale floor to Sorge, it's all a secret with you, isn't it? You wouldn't trust the weed in your precious garden."

With that, Madame Isobe couldn't hold Yoshi's angry gaze.

They agreed to meet the next afternoon, with Takata away once again. Together she and Madame Isobe walked in the yellow light of late afternoon in the park next to the Imperial Palace. From a distance they could have been mistaken for a grandmother and her granddaughter. But if one had drawn close enough to hear their hushed tones, an observer would have found it most curious. First, it was the older woman quietly pleading with the girl to tell her everything about these weapons. For nearly a half-hour they walked in this fashion—the older woman imploring the girl to remember her parents, even Lui. Yoshi's eyes slowly welled with tears. Once again the world asked so much of her. The old woman's words were like the wind that carried the gray dust back at Manzanar. No matter which way she turned there was no escape. A shudder ran through Yoshi's body and, for a moment, she was as sad as she had ever been.

"Child, you must have found out something," Madame Isobe said. "We're desperate now. They tell me that last round of balloons has too many people talking back in America."

"I know nothing that can help."

It was another lie. Her entire life had become a paper chain of deception and falsehoods that surprisingly pleased her in a perverse way.

"It's that man, isn't it?" Madame Isobe said.

"What are you talking about?"

"Takata."

Yoshi smiled until she saw how Madame Isobe was watching her.

"Old woman, leave me alone," Yoshi said.

But Madame Isobe refused to let her be. The next night and the one after that she fell into step beside Yoshi when she came out to survey another night of terror in the sky overhead.

"Please listen to me," Madame Isobe said. "You've gone through too much. You have to let this Takata go."

"I can't," Yoshi snapped.

"Child, don't you see?" Madame Isobe replied. "The ones back home don't know what they're fighting. Ones like your friend, Starling."

At the sound of his name, Yoshi fingered the slips of paper deep in her pockets, her puzzle drawing of the glorious fire balloon. Was Starling once again her only hope?

When her family made the move from the farmhouse to Bay Meadows and then on to Manzanar, many of the old family photographs were hidden away. That sepia tone of her parents in their new Western clothes had come with them, of course, but they weren't displayed prominently at the internment camp. The only family heirloom that father insisted be given a proper place in their new home was a wood-block print of Sado, the largest islands in the Sea of Japan, where her mother's family originated. It was snowing in the illustration and Father had once explained to her how there were no shortcuts in such artwork. Every part of the image—the black buildings, the dark-blue water, the lights' reflection on that calm surface, the snow falling softly—needed to be done with precise cuts in the old way. The wood had to be from the Izu peninsula and the ink was applied with horsehair brushes because then it went on more evenly. The paper, once it was placed against the block, was rubbed by the baren, a hard disk wrapped in a bamboo leaf.

In the days before photography became so cheap, images and ideas were rarely lightning bolts from above. That's what her father had taught her. The biggest things in a life were a culmination of small strokes and ink evenly applied. The best decisions didn't come directly from the mind or the heart. Instead they originated from that sweet spot in between. Find that balance point, he told her as a young child, and you will never lose your way for long.

"Your Takata is a most handsome man," Madame Isobe said. The old woman clung to the younger one's arm. "But his days are over. The empire will surrender soon. This world is ending. You need to let him go."

Silently, Yoshi shook her head. But deep down inside, she realized that everything had caught up with her again. Her lies couldn't stay ahead of events forever. The only thing left was to finish the job that she had been sent here to do. Make the next small cut in the wood. Apply the ink evenly. That's what her father would say.

"Come," she told the old one and they moved away from the Imperial Palace, to a grove of cherry trees in the small park that lay before it.

"These are numbered," Yoshi said, slipping the pieces of paper into Madame Isobe's hands. "Put them together and you'll see the balloon."

For a few minutes she spoke frantically about shroud lines, sand ballast, flash bombs and now chemical weapons. Madame Isobe closed her eyes, intent upon remembering every word. When she was done, the old woman opened her eyes as if coming up from a dream.

"What a marvel," she said. "Who could imagine such a thing?"

Yoshi wanted to tell her that it had been Takata, her Tata, who had conceived of such a wonder.

In the darkness, they walked hurriedly away from the Imperial Palace. From a distance, they appeared to be just two more women running home to ride out another evening under a sky of explosions and destruction.

"You have done well, my child," Madame Isobe said when they came to the place where they went their separate ways. "It will be several days until I reach a secure location to get the word out. The Kempei Tai is everywhere in this city. But I will do it."

Yoshi nodded.

"Both of us may be asked to do more," Madame Isobe added.

"There's nothing more."

"Don't be so sure, my child. A situation may present itself—some way to kill this threat at its source. Keep your eyes open for any opportunity."

"I've been invited to the Nichigeki, the music hall downtown," Takata told her that evening. "To see Kabuki."

"You should go," Yoshi replied.

But when he didn't reply, she turned toward him, surprised by how sad he appeared.

"What?" she asked. "What's wrong?"

"You don't understand, do you?"

Yoshi shook her head. "No, my darling. I don't."

Takata smiled and gazed up at the ceiling as if he could see beyond it to the darkening sky.

"We once tested the balloons at the Nichigeki," he said. "The same way we did at the Kabuki Theater in Kyoto, near where we found you."

He paused and then began again. "So, if they're reopening the Nichigeki for celebratory shows for party officials then that means they've given up on our children, the beautiful balloons."

"Then you need to go," she said.

"Go?" he replied, his eyes again finding her. "But why?"

"To show them that you'll never forget what the building was once used for, what it could be home to again."

The Kabuki faces were like something from a fever dream. The eyebrows, lips and cheekbones were highlighted by the makeup artist's dark hand. Yoshi remembered seeing a collection of horsehair brushes of various lengths with glowing varnished handles in one of the dressing rooms backstage at Madame Isobe's. The theater was supposed to be off-limits during her stay, but she had stolen below the living quarters several times during those first few weeks in Kyoto.

"It's The Story of Asagao," Takata whispered. "Do you know it?"

"No."

"No, how can that be?"

The stage before them was bathed in reddish light and a single figure moved from right to left. When it reached the lone white spotlight, the crowd burst into applause, many calling out a man's name, Kataoka

"But it's a woman, isn't it?"

Takata smiled. "You must be a country girl that knows nothing."

"Darling, don't tease."

"They are no real women acting in Kabuki. Men play all the roles."

In disbelief, Yoshi watched the figure on the stage. He had the soft look of a woman, the softness around the eyes, the hesitation before beginning. Now this one was no modern girl, no moga, and Yoshi tried to memorize every motion.

"She is carrying a ripped umbrella," Takata whispered.

"So?"

"That's an omen. Great sorrow, even death will befall her."

"Her name is Asagao?"

"Yes, my love. She cries like you used to."

Together they watched Asagao become caught up in a tale of love and intrigue. The daughter of a wealthy samurai, she falls in love with the handsome Miyagi, a young man she meets one evening down by the river while trying to catch butterflies. After her parents tell her that she is to marry someone else, Asagao becomes blind from weeping and runs away from home. For many years she wanders the countryside, singing in the taverns for handouts.

One day Miyag stops by the inn where the blind girl is singing. Broken-hearted by her song, he draws closer and recognizes her as the girl who once captivated him down by the river in the city, the one who laughed so while catching butterflies.

Without revealing his identity, Miyagi gives money and a poem about the morning glory to the innkeeper for him to pass along to Asagao. With the money, she can afford the medicine to restore her eyesight and she returns to the city.

As the show ended and the crowd applauded loudly, Yoshi brushed against Takata's shoulder. Tears filled her eyes.

"No, no," he told her, kissing her lightly on the cheek. "It is just a story after all."

But how could she tell him that it wasn't. That what they had seen that night was as true as the sun rising in the morning, the stars at night, for her.

With each passing day, Yoshi feared that she was becoming too American for any remaining task at hand. How could she remain a spy, the mistress of a government official, when a jazz note could ripple through her, a clarion call about everything that she held dear? She was afraid that someone would become curious when they saw her nodding her head along with another pell-mell beat or saw her beam when she thought of Douglas MacArthur or Franklin Roosevelt. However, nobody paid her any mind. Takata brought the tapes, several at a time, to the small apartment. She played them on the small player he had found. He did it for love and ultimately that's why she did it, too.

At night she watched the bombs fall, waited for Takata, and listened to the tapes. At some point in the evening she would feel his fingers running along the inside of her arm, his lips lightly kissing her forehead, and she would awake from the sounds of America. She would slide the earphones off and pull him down toward her. Over the last few weeks this had become their custom—to make love on the floor, by the window, under the siren call of Louis and Benny.

Tonight she listened to a tape from Bend, Oregon. Once such places as Bend, Olympia, Portland, San Francisco and Seattle had been simply names to her. But now they were like distant cousins, reminders of home, of what she could recast as home if she was ever afforded the opportunity to do so. Soon the bombing would begin and Yoshi hoped that if it became too late that Takata would stay at the ministry, safe in the bunkers they had built far beneath the ground.

The station out of Medford, Oregon, was completing its 'Tribute to the Big Bands.' Goodman's sweet clarinet was fading away when the announcer abruptly broke in with "the local news." He began with how the recent rains could bring flooding, especially to the lower stretches of the Applegate River. The local American Legion post was collecting more scrap metal for the war effort. And, finally, an unidentified object had exploded in the Mitchell Recreation Area. Six people, including four children, had been killed.

Yoshi sat up and replayed the section several times. It had to have been a fire balloon. She found the paper sleeve the tape had come in. It was dully logged, documented and dated: U.S. radio, Oregon, May 7, 1945. Somebody had listened to this tape at the ministry, or had they? The tape ended moments after the local news report. Unless somebody had paid attention throughout the long passages of music it could have been easily overlooked. There were so many tapes to go through. The Americans were playing more and more music as the war drew to an end. That's what Takata had told her.

Yoshi unraveled the tape from the spool, going further than she needed to, stretching out a length that was almost as long as her arm. She cut the end loose and held it over the candle on the floor. The tape smoldered and caught, with Yoshi turning it with her fingertips. She made certain all of it burned away to ash.

Afterward she forwarded through the next tape, this one from Astoria, frantic to snuff out any more hints of incidents. But there was nothing. With a sigh she sat back down on the floor. What if there more news reports hidden on other tapes at the ministry? Takata complained that few shared his enthusiasm for the balloons anymore—but they would if they heard that such a weapon was finally having an impact.

For a long time, her mind raced about what she could do. Outside the bombing had begun and smoke rolled in over the harbor. In time fatigue stole over her and Yoshi picked up the headphones and slid them on. All she heard was more music, the sounds building like waves, one upon the other, carrying her back to the past. Then she sensed something was wrong. Somebody was here.

"Tata," she called.

Yoshi pulled the headphones off. She told herself she had imagined it all. That it was a bad dream. But the undercurrent whispered that everything was about to change and fold back over her again.

From the embroidered pillows and futon he had given her, Yoshi glanced around the dark room and saw nothing at first. But then she could make him out. He sat in the chair in the corner, smoking a cigarette, the hot tip the only thing that revealed him.

"What is wrong?" she asked, but he didn't answer her.

"Tell me," she said, fearing the worst. Maybe somehow he had put together all the contradictions that made up her identity in this land. "Please, tell me."

Yoshi heard him rise. He moved toward the open window, the one that faced in the direction of the harbor. She could run for the door. That thought flashed through her mind. But if this was the end of her masquerade he would have others with him. They would be posted in the hall and on the street outside.

"You're scaring me, Tata."

"It's over," he said. "It's finally happened."

He turned and walked toward her. He briefly stopped to pick the headphones off the floor, moving one muff up to his ear.

"So strange," he said.

Yoshi turned off the tape player. How could she explain to him that what he heard was the future. The music was becoming louder every day.

"Tata, talk to me."

"Their melodies do stay in your head," Takata said as he tossed the headphones back onto the floor.

Even in the shadows, she saw that he was stooped over, as if he was in mourning, so unlike the proud, cocky man she had first met only a few weeks ago.

"I was right about the reopening of the Nichigeki," he said. "Ito and others above him are terminating the balloon program. They claim it hasn't shown any results. They fault my calculations. They say that we imagined that there are currents of wind in the higher elevations. That we have wasted precious resources. They will reassign the technical support to outposts throughout the island. To prepare for the American invasion."

"They have heard nothing?" Yoshi asked.

"No, they've played me for a fool. Day after day the translators are reassigned. The ones that remain aren't listening. I know it."

She walked over to him, reaching for his hand in the darkness.

"I was wondering if you heard anything?" Takata said. "When you listen to the music?"

"My English is not that good," she lied.

"Yes it is," he said. "I've seen how you smile sometimes when they talk."

He was always watching her. Yoshi knew she must never forget that.

"I'm sorry, my darling," she said. "I've heard nothing."

Takata shook his head. "I cannot accept this," he said. "I know our research is correct. That a balloon of that diameter, maintaining such an elevation, will reach North America in less than a week. I cannot believe we're heard nothing."

"What has happened to the tapes?" Yoshi asked.

He told her that crates of them remained in the translation room. He would find more help. Indeed, he had begun to listen to them at night. That's why he hadn't been home lately. The new balloons, the ones with gas bombs and others with nerve gas, were almost ready. If he could find any hint of the balloons reaching North America he could go above Ito—one last time. He could get permission to let loose the more deadly balloons.

Yoshi realized that she had to do everything she could to end this madness now.

"I'll help you," she offered.

"No, my love. It is too dangerous."

"I'll go with you at night. When the others are gone."

"If Ito found out," he began.

"I don't care."

Takata considered this. Then he smiled for the first time since he had returned home.

"Perhaps," he said. "If I can find a way to sneak you in."

Yoshi closed her eyes, feeling relieved. She began to shake, trying not to sob. She would be close to him for a few more days and if she was lucky the balloons' success would remain a secret forever.

"Yoshi, don't cry," he said, embracing her. "You mustn't blame yourself. You listened to more tapes than anybody at the ministry. And even you did not hear a word about our children."

"No, I heard nothing about them."

So many lies. Her life was built one upon the other, a house of cards.

"I didn't think it was possible, but they have been stronger than us," Takata said. "The Americans have stayed quiet. They haven't let us know and with that everything has been lost. They can babble and make crazy music. But they won't give us a word about our work."

The two of them sat there in silence until Yoshi spoke.

"When were the last balloons released?"

He studied her face, saying, "Why ask such a question? The last launch was four days ago. But like I said, it doesn't matter anymore."

"Maybe the new tapes will give us a hint," Yoshi said, praying that the right words would tumble out. "When do you receive more American papers?"

"We'll try tomorrow night," Takata said. "That may be all the time we have. There is talk of sending me to the south—permanently—by the end of the week."

"Please, lay down here with me."

"Not now, lovely one. I need to walk. My mind is so filled with hate and distrust. I even snap at you."

"I'll come with you," Yoshi said, getting to her feet.

"No, sweet one, it is cold, with more rain coming."

"It doesn't matter. I want to be with you."

Takata draped his thin trench coat over her shoulders and hand in hand they went out into the evening. He was right. It was cold out on the street. But there were no planes in the sky, only patches of fog and a faint drizzle. It was a good night to stay home, light incense and dream the dreams of the innocent and misbegotten. But this evening, she told herself, she would walk with him for as long as he wanted. Then she would betray him one final time.

CALL FROM
DISPATCH

He had wanted to take her back here, to his lair, this ridiculous silver trailer—government issue. But that had been the liquor talking or Armstrong's sweet jazz still ringing in his head, is what he told himself.

Later, when he had time to try and think things out, he remembered her sweet lips. He had kissed her right there, outside the Winchester, in the shadow of the bus that he had to somehow wheel back to the base camp.

That sweet one, Taylor, had been willing enough to let him kiss her long and slow and hard. But when he reached into the sliver of space between her blouse and jeans, his fingertips angling for the clasp of her brasserie, she had stepped back and slapped him hard across his stupid drunken mouth.

She was right. He'd had it coming and all he could do was smile as her hourglass figure disappeared in a huff into the darkness of this piss-ant town.

Colson was right, too. The alcohol was no good for him. It bore out everything in that thick dossier of his that he had tried to live down over the years, the nights in the stockade in San Francisco, the times at Lulu's, the brothel on the edge of Pearl. Why hadn't they left him in the Pacific? He knew how to conduct himself in a war zone. But back here, among the public, he was afraid to let his guard drop because this is what would happen. Then he remembered the bottle of Jim Beam back home, in the trailer, and he decided it would be bone-dry by morning.

Before Leo joined the crew, he disliked early mornings. But over the summer he discovered that he enjoyed getting up before the rest of the world, and like any reformed sinner he had little patience for those, such as his older sister, who couldn't follow his example. With Neil Starling it was hell to pay if a body was a minute late. So why even bother with distractions? Leo didn't set an alarm. He just told himself he wanted to be up at such and such hour and then he did so. He was still at the age when his body responded in such ways. If he was determined enough, able to put mind over matter, he believed the repetition would make him strong and proud.

Hunter's dark-brown eyes opened and he rolled over onto his side, ready for Leo to rub his belly. But the dog didn't show any energy. Until a few weeks ago, Hunter would have gone with Leo. Leo would have made sure of it. He'd hook up Hunter's leash and drag him out to face a new day if that's what it took. But recently he had taken more pity on the beast because of Taylor. Her schedule seemed to be growing in the opposite direction to his. She was staying up later and later, often taking Hunter with her for evening strolls. Leo sometimes heard them returning after he had gone to bed. The dog's nails clattered across the hardwood floor and the screen door slammed shut.

But he hadn't been awakened by such sounds last night. Sis, Genie, Koch, and Starling were still at the table when he left the Winchester last night.

"Did she have you up until the cows came home again?" Leo whispered, and the dog angled farther over on his side. "Yeah, she probably did," the boy said, rising to his feet. "You go to sleep. I'll fetch your breakfast later."

Leo jogged the streets in early mornings, and except for the milkman and paperboys he was the only one up. Starling had canceled training for today. The pronouncement came after they had finished their chicken dinners and everybody had made fools of themselves on the dance floor. The younger ones, like him and Riddle and Fugery, decided it was about time to leave. As the older folks rolled in, the establishment became less friendly toward them. By eight, nine for sure, the split had begun, and when Riddle talked Grady into selling him a couple of tall boys, it made perfect sense to retire to the parking lot to down the cold beer. Taylor had stayed at the table. She fit right in with that crowd. So did Koch—when he wanted to. After leaving with Riddle and Fugery, Leo hadn't gone back in. When the beer was gone, he waited for his father, who soon sauntered outside. Pa couldn't stomach the fact that the new fire boss had taken over his bar for the evening. Leo and Pa had gone home together, leaving Taylor with Starling and the others.

Leo looked up at the morning sky. The air was dead-still

and growing warmer. Perhaps there would be some clouds, a few wisps, high up, that would be gone by noon. Later in the day he knew he would become caught up with Starling's concern about the heat and what could come of it. But in the early morning, when he was by himself, running through the town where he had spent his entire life, Leo concentrated on himself. He felt the morning sunlight warm his muscles. There was usually an area or two of concern. Some mornings his lower back was a bit sore and his calves, probably from all the fire-line they had cut in recent days, were pretty tight, too. Yet during the morning run, he felt his body start to unfold and stretch out. He would think about a part of his body for a while, give it his undivided attention, and soon it would feel better. Then he would move on to the next muscle group, feeling everything fall into place as he ran through Payson toward the graveyard on the north side of town.

The United Methodist plots were on a side street, beyond the high school and the town machine shop. They had buried a coffin in Richard's memory in the Webb family plot, which was on a small knoll off to the right. Once it had been the very last row in the cemetery. In recent years they had expanded, cutting into the scrubwood and small pines to carve out another few rows before the land went upward into a steep incline. It was a good resting place. From here you could see the church steeple, and farther down, toward Route 87, the small strip of stores that had grown there like weeds in the ditch—Lucille's Diner, the B&B Market and the Winchester.

Leo came here several times a week to talk to his older brother. He still believed that Richard could hear him, that whatever happened in death didn't mean that such lines of communication were severed forever. They may be just one-way and Leo was intent on letting his brother know what was going on. Their lives, in a basic way, remained the same. But the more he talked to his brother about it, the more he realized how much everything had changed in the last few years. Some mornings he actually spoke to Richard's grave. Other mornings he just thought out the words silently in his head. The tombstone was a foot and a half high, nothing gaudy. His parents would never allow that. The inscription, just the name and dates of his life here on earth, was still sharp to the touch.

"Riddle got his draft notice the other day," Leo told his brother. "He'll head out the week after next. Fugery is keeping his word. He's going with him. They are talking about joining the Navy, like you. I wish I was going with them, but I promised Pa I wouldn't go until I'm called. I heard Pa on the phone the other night calling down to Grandpa Mays. I heard him asking if he could pull some strings on my behalf and get me as an aide to one of the generals. I don't want to do die, Rich. Nobody does, but sometimes I think Pa needs to stop trying to protect me so much. Whatever's going to happen is going to happen."

Leo looked up at the sky. It had faded from pink to bright gold. It was going to be another hot one.

"As for Taylor? She's in her own world. Nothing new there, huh? I don't know what she's thinking right now. But I can't care much about that anymore. She's got her life and I've got mine. It's been that way for some time now. You can't argue with how she's doing on the crew, though. She's holding her own real well. She's doing a good job. Anybody can see that. You'd be proud of her."

A horn sounded from down near the cemetery gate, and Leo turned to see his father's Studebaker coming toward him.

He was in a hurry and for an instant Leo thought it was good news. Maybe Japan had finally surrendered. Maybe Mom couldn't wait any longer and had come home for good. But as his father's face came into view, Leo saw it wasn't anything so sweet. His father's features were tight and angry. It was the face of the time they were trapped in. Pa so anxious that bad luck and misfortune seemed to follow him everywhere.

"The dispatcher called from Phoenix," he said out the open window. "For some god damn reason he called our house."

"Those calls go right through to the station and Starling," Leo said. "That's the way he wanted it."

"Starling's not picking up. The dispatcher can't raise him. Here, get in, son. I scribbled down the number. You've got to get back in touch with him. There's a big one brewing up on the Rim. Those were his words exactly. 'A big one brewing.'"

After putting his shoulder into the door of the silver trailer, Leo rushed in to find Starling passed out on a mattress on the floor. The fire boss was bare-chested, with a green-fatigue Army blanket twisted about his lower torso.

Leo looked around for anybody else. The scene looked like what he imagined adults did when the night was dark and the liquor was in abundance, what he had begun to believe his father was doing with women around town with Mom now gone from them for nearly a year.

But there was nobody else inside the trailer, not anymore.

Leo turned up the radio and heard the report of the Cortez Fire. It was in the hardwood forests above the Rim. This was what they had feared since the beginning of this season. It was already two thousand acres in size and spreading quickly.

Time was slipping away from them, and Leo hurried to Starling's side, eager to rouse him. As he drew closer he saw that his fire boss held a small photograph. It was cupped in his hand as if it was the most precious thing in the world.

Leo pulled it free and saw that it was of a man and a woman, a Jap couple. They were dressed in formal Western clothes. The woman was beautiful—dark hair pulled back to reveal a luminous angelic face with a small high nose and thin lips that seemed eager to say something. Even though neither of them smiled, no one could miss the joy and apprehension in their eyes.

A horn blasted outside and Leo ran to the door.

"He's here," he yelled out to his father, who sat impatiently behind the wheel of his Studebaker.

"Is he sober?" his father replied.

Leo ignored the question.

"Get Taylor," he shouted back. "You and her start rounding up the crew. Tell everybody to meet at the bus at base camp."

His father smiled in a cruel way.

"If you say so, son."

His father put the car in gear. Before he sped away, he couldn't resist a final dig.

"Your fire boss ain't worth a bucket of spit. Remember that, son. Not worth a bucket of spit."

Back inside, Leo saw that Starling still held the curious photo in his hand. Looking for a place to put it, he wedged it into the crack between the window pane and sill by the small desk—right next to the photo of a small farmhouse and the fields around it. The two seemed to go together somehow.

"Mr. Starling," he said as he shook the fire boss's shoulder. "We've got to get going. There's a big fire."

Starling's eyes blinked open. For a moment, he appeared to

be wide awake. But then the liquor rolled back over him and his face twisted into a grimace.

"Where?" he grunted.

"Above the Rim."

"Damn, will these things never let me be?"

"Sir?" Leo said, unsure of what to say.

"Where's the bottle?"

Leo began to look around.

"A bottle of the good stuff that I paid a king's ransom for at the Winchester," Starling said as he rubbed his forehead. "Good old Kentucky bourbon. What they make mint juleps out of in the sweetness of the spring."

On the far side of the mattress, Leo found a liquor bottle on its side. It had been tipped over in the night and held only a few drops.

"Give it here," Starling said when he saw it in his number two's hand. Leo reluctantly did as he was told.

"Hair of the dog, boy," Starling said and drained the last of it.

With that, Starling got to his feet. The blanket fell away and he was naked underneath. With his back to the boy, Starling set the empty bottle on the small desk, atop the maps and weather reports. With effort, he pulled on his trousers, T-shirt and button-down fire shirt.

"Let's go, kid. Back me up today. You hear?"

Leo nodded.

"I can't hear you, sailor."

"Yes, sir."

"Louder, sailor."

"Yes, sir."

"Good man," Starling said and he tried to smile as he finished buttoning his shirt.

DESTROYING
THE EVIDENCE

It was just before midnight and they stood in the shadows across the street from the Ministry of Information—a gray building whose public face had been pocketed and cratered by the nightly attacks. Even though bombs had damaged much of the entranceway, Takata told her that more floors extended below the street surface, where it was safe.

"Stay with me," Takata said, taking her by the hand, and they walked across the deserted street of rubble.

Yoshi wore a white smock, like Takata's, but the rest of her attire was a janitor's uniform—the stained trousers and work-shirt. The cleaning services were supposed to enter through the back door. The higher command came through here. Together they pulled the door open and entered the small lobby. Takata had been correct. There was only one guard on duty at this hour and he glanced at them and returned to the book he was reading. As he looked away, Takata pulled the white smock off her and coiled it tightly under his arm. Yoshi hurried for the closets on the far side of the lobby, where the mops and pails were kept. Takata walked past the guard station and up the hall. Yoshi tried the first door, but it was locked. She was pulling on the second one when the guard shouted at her.

"What are you doing?"

Yoshi kept her eyes focused on the floor, still trying the door with one hand.

"Answer me," the guard ordered. He began to come out from behind his post, eager to chastise her, when Takata re-entered the lobby.

"I need her now," Takata said, staying between Yoshi and the guard. "We have a spill on level two."

"Spill?" the guard asked. "Is this an emergency?"

"No, this one can handle it," Takata said and pulled open a closet door. Dutifully, Yoshi wheeled out the mop and pail. "But we must hurry. Come with me, now."

He had her by the elbow, leading her out of the lobby as fast as he could. Only after they went around a corner, out of the guard's view, did Takata's pace slow.

"He can be a stubborn one," Takata mumbled. "All regulation."

Yoshi took the mop handle and began to push the pail with wheels. She followed several steps behind Takata, like any lower-level employee would. Together they rode the lift down two levels and she followed him through the maze of hallways until he stopped in front of a door. He looked up and down the corridor as he fumbled with his keys. At last he opened the door and they were inside.

Takata walked around the large-sized room, turning on

the desk lamps at each of the three tables that ran horizontally from one side of the room to the other. On the tables were stacks of U.S. papers and cartons of tapes.

"Somewhere in here they have to speak of our balloons," Takata said. Yoshi didn't doubt him. So much material had been collected that she was certain another mention of those mysterious deaths in Oregon was somewhere in this room. That would be enough for Takata to keep the program going, to rearm his balloons with nerve gas and chemicals.

"We must hurry," Takata said. He pulled a small English dictionary out of one of his smock pockets. "This is where I need your help, my darling. Your English has to be better than mine."

They began at cross-purposes. He was listening for any hint of his precious balloons. She was trying to make sure that he never discovered such a revelation. Both of them put on earphones and listened to the American broadcasts, fast-forwarding through the music, hungry only for the words.

An hour after they started, Takata tapped her on the shoulder excited about something he had heard. She rewound the tape and played it for herself. Indeed, it detailed an explosion in the Sierra Nevada near Reno. Takata's eyes danced as she listened.

"It was an airplane crash," she lied to him.

"You're sure?" Takata said, looking down at his open dictionary as if the book had betrayed him. "I didn't hear anything about a plane?"

"Yes, I'm sure," Yoshi replied, but she knew that she couldn't delay such discoveries forever.

Soon afterward there was a sharp knock at the door. Takata dimmed his desk lamp and motioned for Yoshi to do the same.

Then he waved for her to hide underneath the long table.

There was another knock, harder and more urgent this time. Taking his time, Takata opened the door.

Crouching in the shadows, Yoshi saw two guards at the door and behind them Ito. Takata began to speak to the first guard, the same one who had been at the front entranceway. He talked in hushed tones and she couldn't hear. But then he and Ito began to argue in louder voices.

"What are you doing here, at this hour?" Ito asked.

"Trying to prove that my balloons have reached their target," Takata answered.

"You're impossible," Ito sneered. "Your precious project has been terminated. If I remember correctly you're scheduled to be in the south in two days. To finally do some useful work for the empire."

"I'll be there."

"You better be," Ito said, "or you'll be court-martialed. I'll make sure of that."

As the two longtime rivals continued to bicker, Yoshi carefully slid one hand down past her waistband, reaching for the small flask of petrol and the three matches that Madame Isobe had found for her on the black market only that morning. The door slammed shut and she heard Takata and Ito carry on their argument out in the hallway.

Quickly she doused her table and Takata's with the flammable fluid. The first match snapped in half. Her fingers were too nervous to hold it correctly.

Out in the hall, she heard Ito now question Takata about a janitor, somebody he had taken with him to clean up a spill.

"There's no spill," Takata said.

"That's not what you said," she heard the guard reply.

"You are just full of misinformation tonight," Ito said. "Why all the lies, Takata?"

Yoshi dropped the second match and couldn't find it in the shadows. Taking several newspapers, she wadded them into a ball. She set the empty flask atop it and successfully lit the last match. Carefully, she slid it slowly into the container's open end.

At first she worried that this one had gone out too. She leaned closer, peering into the flask, when it suddenly ignited. The blast knocked her backward and when she regained her senses Yoshi threw more American newspapers onto the fresh flames. The fire roared to life. Ribbons of bright-orange danced along the tabletops and followed the path of gasoline that she had prepared.

The door burst open and someone in the hallway yelled, "Fire." The lights in the room came on, but in the next breath they went black as the flames roared higher. Yoshi crept along the floor as gray smoke filled the room. Already the flames had reached the ceiling and now the lights in the hallway flickered several times before shorting out as well. In the resulting chaos Yoshi crawled slowly toward the door, looking for a way out.

THE LAST FIRE

The smoke from the Cortez Fire was bitter and foul, and it soon caused the crew's spit to turn coal-black. The Payson Hotshots worked into the afternoon, stopping for rations that had been parachuted into them. They shucked off their day packs to eat like hungry beggars, and some of them napped in the dirt of the fire-line. Leo saw that Taylor and Genie were exhausted. Their bodies spooned together. Genie's head rested on his sister's shoulder. But soon all of them were back on their feet, cutting more fire-line. Those were Starling's orders. They had to keep moving.

From far down the canyon came the noise of the dozers. They had methodically followed them since the predawn darkness, widening the fire-line the crews had put down. At one point, the dozers had been right behind them, spurring them on. But in the last few hours the terrain had become more rugged and their fire-line was now cut into the mountainside, not along the ridge, hoping that the dozers would be able to keep up. Despite the echoes through the forest, the kind of things that can play tricks on you, only a dozer or two seemed to be anywhere close to them now.

Leo didn't like the situation they were in. The valley felt like a trap and they were walking right into it. He reached for the new walkie-talkie on his belt, another gizmo Starling had recently procured for the crew.

"We should be closer to the ridge," Leo told the fire boss. "Why are you taking us this way?"

Starling's reply came back riddled with static.

"No can do, buddy," the fire boss said. "Orders are to stay the course. Dozers can't follow us if we go farther toward the ridge."

Leo looked behind him. There were no dozers, no more crews. Somehow they had been caught at the end of the line. Up ahead of him, Taylor and Genie had slowed. They were eavesdropping on his conversation—as worried about things as he was. It didn't take a genius to realize they were in a bad spot. The girls followed Leo's gaze as he looked at the ridge top, which was a good two hundred yards above them. Up there the winds were gusting, causing the white smoke to accelerate and be carried over the top of them.

"I don't like it," Leo told Starling.

As he spoke, he turned to peer in one direction and then the other. Eerily there wasn't much wind where they were. It felt as if their part of the world was holding its breath, waiting for something to happen.

"Just keep coming," Starling told him. He sounded as far away as the short-wave fire reports from around the West that filled the clearing outside his trailer home. "Leo, you hear me, right? Just move. Get the tail end of the line up here. We're almost out of the worst of it."

"All right," Leo replied. "Webb out."

He stood there for a moment, lost in his own thoughts, until his sister cried out, "Leo, behind you."

He turned to see a reddish glow, slightly diffused by the smoke, on the opposite side of a small ravine that stretched out below them. The various spot fires were rapidly coming together, forming a flame wall that rose only a quarter-mile away from their line. The strong wind that had been overhead now fell upon them and more of the smoke was funneled past them and toward the ridge.

"Bump up," Leo told them. "No chit-chat. Move, move, move."

Farther up the fire-line, Leo could make out the hazy outlines of the others in the thickening gray smoke and for some innocent reason he began to recite their cutting order from memory. The notion came into his head that if he could remember all their names, he could save them. Beside him, Taylor turned and looked back, and he did too. Behind them the world had fallen away. The flames had already leaped the ravine and were heading right for them.

His sister slowed to stare, and Leo shouted, "Don't look! Keep moving!"

He began to lead the caboose end of the Payson Hotshots' cutting order for the safety of the ridge. If they could reach the ridge, huddle down in the leeward side, they would be protected from the worst of the fast-approaching fire.

For a moment, they were abreast of each other and together they moved as fast as they could for safety. Taylor's eyes had grown wild with terror and Genie was already struggling to keep up. Leo calculated they had one hundred yards or so to go. Look, up there, the air was clear and the land still golden. That's what he wanted to tell them, to make them go even faster. But the path they were taking began to grow steeper with cruel intention. Leo rolled forward, onto the balls of his feet. With his arms stretched in front of him, he reached out and pulled away tufts of cheatgrass with his fingers. He was desperate to do anything that could propel him faster upward and deliver him to safety.

LETTER TO A MENTOR

1 August 1945

Professor Nakoso:

As you know, the fire-balloon program has been terminated by order of the Emperor and the top generals. I take full responsibility for this development as I believe, and always will believe, that there was nothing at fault in our design and implementation of this program. Time and time again, I've checked our calculations involving everything from materials to the wind currents and I'm as convinced of their accuracy as when we began work almost four years ago.

The fault is mine because I was not able to convince others of the program's wisdom. I've underestimated the fear that resides within most people. Whereas you and I share a fascination in invention, I was not prepared for the opposition that arises when confronted with a different idea or way of looking at the world.

As this terrible war has gone against us, I have been astounded by the madness that has taken over our land. As the Americans approach, we are training more kamikaze pilots and fukuryu divers. As you know, the later will position themselves offshore, in underwater concrete shelters, and will emerge when the landing crafts arrive. They will work like the children who have been trained to roll under tanks; able to fix their mines to the invading machines. Then everyone will be blown up together.

Our invention worked upon the mind and had the potential to create the same alarm and unrest in America that existed in the months after Pearl Harbor. These new ways are too desperate and only delay the inevitable.

By the time this reaches you, I'll be stationed in the south, at Hiroshima, assigned to working with the fukuryu divers. We have 1,200 in position, with another 2,000 ready for training.

After so many years of war, I find myself thinking of family and new beginnings. May the coming times be kind to us both.

Your student,
Kazuya Takata
Administrator, Fu-Go Project

GOOD-BYE

Light drizzle fell the morning Yoshi walked to the Tokyo Rail Station. Much of the city was hidden away, waiting for the U.S. invasion. On her last day at the balloon factory she remembered one of the older women telling them how the army had taken refuge in caves on many of the islands that dot the Pacific. They had constructed elaborate fortifications and a network of tunnels that ran far back into the mountainside. They had held off the Americans for almost two months, the woman told them. Could you believe it? Two months. Yoshi wanted to scold the woman. Why was this so important? In the end, even after two months, the army had been routed. What was the purpose in denying the inevitable? But already they were following the same course here. The homes, due to the bombing attacks and blackouts, had become caves. To each other they vowed to fight any foreigner that dared breach their borders.

They would fight them with their bare hands, rushing them in enormous packs of people, their bodies like weapons. They would do this if they were ordered.

The streets were empty as Yoshi walked north to the giant railroad station. The water seeped down the back collar of the old jacket. It had been Takata's father's. That's what he had told her. His father had been a fisherman in Kobe. The English were thick there in the years before the war. His father had traded two pearls, treasures that he had had in his possession for years, to an English-speaking sailor for the stained oilskin. Takata's father didn't mind that the jacket was soiled and extended well past his knees when he stood up. He considered it a good trade.

Soon after the English's boat set sail, the jacket tore. The seams that held the right sleeve together ruptured one morning as he pulled in his nets. No matter how many times Takata's mother stitched the seam, the jacket was never quite right again.

"Never trust the English," the father had told the son.

The wind swept up the harbor, eastward toward the ocean. Yoshi walked faster, trying to stay warm. It would have been a good day to launch more fire balloons. The strong westerly winds would have carried them far across the ocean before nightfall.

While the streets were empty, the train station was crowded. It was as if everyone who was awake in this world was here. They had decided to leave together.

Yoshi worked her way into the crowd, jostled through the front doors. At that point any progress stopped, so she edged up the marble staircase at the far end of the wide hallway. She kept her back and shoulder to the wall, sliding past the others who stood in her way. Atop the stairs were offices and a small balcony that overlooked the wide ramps that led out to the trains. The ramps swelled with people. The trains were as eager as fine horses to leave before their loads became too heavy.

For the longest time, Yoshi knelt atop the balcony, resting her chin on the cool edge of marble. She was as silly as any of them. She really thought that she could come here, in the early morning rain, and somehow find him. Takata would already be gone. He may not have even come. A man as intelligent as he, who had risen as far as a civilian could in a world of armies, would have been smarter than to be a part of this mob on this day.

But then she saw him. He was standing by himself near an empty track. He was wearing his faded trench coat. And even on this day he exuded a force. The crowds of people swept around him like a pillar in the river. They came close to him, but nobody brushed against him or bumped him despite the swelling numbers.

A train was coming into the station as Yoshi hurried back down the staircase. Even though the crowd was huge, she made good progress pushing her way through. She ignored the threats and shouts of 'stupid girl'. Once the crowd broke out of the foyer, she was able to go faster, and soon she was at the spot where Takata had been. But he was no longer there.

Yoshi spun in one place as the crowds moved past her. She looked back at the balcony, trying to gauge if she had miscalculated. But no, this was correct. This had been where he had stood.

Yoshi looked up the track. The train, the 7:15 for Kobe and ending in Hiroshima, labored into the station. That's when she felt his fingertips touch hers and lightly grasp her hand.

"Why did you come?" he asked.

"To see you."

He ran his hand lightly up her arm and Yoshi leaned into him, smelling the hint of black-market cigarettes and the sandalwood incense that he favored.

"I'll send for you," he said.

Yoshi didn't reply. One last time she betrayed him, allowing her silence to be taken for agreement.

As soon as the train stopped, the people began to stream aboard it. Yoshi heard the commotion as she remained nestled against Takata. The train stayed only a short time before it too began to grow restless. The conductors called out that they would depart soon—before the train was completely overrun.

Takata leaned down. His freshly shaven face brushed against her cheek.

"I must go," he said and he kissed her.

Reaching into his coat pocket, he pulled out a palm-sized picture framed by rough wood.

"For you," Takata said, pressing it into her hands. "You loved them as much as I did."

He joined the others who crowded onto the train. He looked back one last time and nodded at her. Then he was gone.

As the train began to leave, Yoshi searched the dark windows for another glimpse of him, but she saw nothing. Only after the entire train had pulled away from the platform and moved out into the rain did she look down at what he had given her. The small frame held a photo of a single balloon. It was almost fully inflated with several soldiers holding onto the launch lines, awaiting the command, Takata's command, to release it into the sky.

It was almost noon when Yoshi neared Takata's flat. The rain had slackened, but the sky was still gray, with more clouds approaching. Yoshi was lost in her thoughts, holding the small frame tight inside the coat pocket, when she saw the transport truck idling in the alleyway a half-block away. If the bombs of the past few months hadn't torn a hole in the brick wall, the truck would have been perfectly hidden.

Its canvas top rippled in the gusting wind and Yoshi ducked behind a pile of rubble, staying as still as she could. Only two men were with the truck. The driver was still behind the wheel and another man paced alongside. In his hands was a rifle. From the building came shouts. As she peered out, Yoshi saw several more soldiers coming out the front door. From their apartment window another yelled that she wasn't here. The girl from the balloon factory was gone.

On all fours, Yoshi crawled through the mud and puddles until she reached the corner. Only then did she scramble to her feet and begin to run.

RUNNING FOR THE RIDGE

There remains something startling, inherently memorable, about running as fast as one can. For a short time everything seems possible. A person can soar beyond the routine and briefly race into the netherworld of immediacy. One can be like the gods. The adrenaline rushes through the body, carrying it past any previous standard or expectation that it once held for itself.

That's how Leo felt in the moments after he ordered them to run for the ridge. In those initial seconds, he wasn't scared. Even though the Cortez Fire possessed a terrifying ability to leap ahead in time, to be on one side of the ravine and then amazingly on the other, he was certain that someday they would joke about this close call. Leo was easy with the situation as long as he was able to stretch his legs out and stride up the steep hill toward the wind and the sky and the expectations of safety. He was beside his sister and they easily made up the distance between themselves and the rest of the crew. Now Riddle and Fugery were within sight. He was catching them all when things began to unravel.

First his breath wouldn't come. Perhaps it was the smoke, maybe the exertion, but that experience shattered his inner tranquility. The smug confidence that he was young and could withstand the weight of anything and everything dissolved. His resolve was broken in the same off-hand way that a tall tree buffeted by decades of wind suddenly falls to the ground. What followed was the frightening realization that he was running as fast as he could and that this effort wouldn't be enough. The flames were behind him and they were closing in.

"Drop the tools," Leo shouted, and couldn't believe what he was saying.

They had never done such a thing before. Their handtools were the only weapons they had. Taylor's shovel was still in her right hand when Leo reached over and caught it. For an instant they drew close, running in unison—Leo bumping into her at the hip and shoulder but not saying a word. His hand ran down the shaft and reached her glove hand. The wood had been sanded smooth and her initials burned neatly into the white wood. Leo's hand pried open her fingers and the shovel fell behind them. Neither of them looked back.

Darker smoke rolled across the land. It covered them and then cleared, covered and cleared. They became ghosts and then human beings again. The air flared hot—dragon's breath—and the Cortez Fire crowned into the treetops. It was not only racing through the Gambel brush, the heat of it flashing on both sides of them, but the blaze had become airborne, too. It hurried past them, skipping among the treetops. It mocked their efforts to stay ahead of it. The fire was in the sky and along the ground. It was as if two hands were coming together, ready to smother them.

Forty yards away was the ridge. If they could reach that, they would survive. But the slope upward became steeper still. They dug into the slope with both hands. Hot air, smelling of sulfur and Hades, blew along the ground in advance of the towering flames, ruffling the cuffs of their pants.

Once more Starling returned to them, appearing out of the smoke. The fire boss had come down the hill and yelled above the din for them to follow him. He wanted them to go sideways across the hill—not upward toward the ridge. Drawing a flare from his web belt, he lit it. The pinkish glow burned bright through the smoke. Disbelieving, the crew slowed for a step or two. They couldn't understand what he had done—bringing fire closer to them when hell itself was reaching out to take them.

"With me," Starling shouted and he began to burn the ankle-high cheatgrass around him, pivoting in a neat circle. "Help me now," the fire boss shouted and he hacked away at the smaller ground blaze he had fostered, stamping down the low-lying flames with his hook and boots until a small circle of black burned-over area, was formed. "We'll be safe here," he shouted, but already the others had moved by him, again making for the ridge.

Leo saw that the Cunninghams, Koch, Riddle and Fugery were about to pass him. When Starling called again, the pink-hot flare still in his hand, Koch looked at him with disbelieving eyes. A look of distrust, almost repulsion, spread across his face. He seemed to shake his head as he turned toward the ridge and the remaining distance he felt he needed to run to stay alive.

Fugery, Riddle, Pierce, Anderson and Perez went with him. The dark smoke blew over them, concealing them forever from another dawn.

The cheatgrass. Suddenly, Leo realized what the fire boss was trying to tell them. It had already burned fast and quick, and they would be safe in the burned-over section.

Leo saw his sister and Genie move away, frantic for the ridge. He ran after them, ready to pull Taylor back with him, when Starling appeared alongside them. He tried to direct as many of them as he could toward the circle of black, the safety zone, that he had created.

That's how they were when the first wave of firestorm struck them. The force of it pushed Leo down and he found himself face down on the darkened ground. The cheatgrass had burned away. They might be able to survive here. With one hand he dug at the soil until he smelled the hint of roots and moisture.

Soon the fire roared over them and Leo felt somebody fall beside him. An arm slid down his back and rested on the top of his hips. He prayed it was his sister, that she had made it inside the circle, too. The heat was warm, almost sweet at first. But then the initial curtain of fire ignited the volatile gases in its path and the blaze stampeded toward the ridge. There was a brief pause, and Leo thought he heard angels, thousands of them singing. He almost got up, but the arm across his back wouldn't allow it. Somehow this one knew the worst was yet to come and soon enough the wind blew as hard as it had all day. Their bodies quivered like leaves in the fall. Frantic for oxygen, Leo dug away with both of his hands, enlarging the hole and pressing his face as far into it as he could. The searing heat drove any feeling from his back and legs. Somewhere he heard moans and cries of desperation. Somebody nearby was dying.

Ashburn was one of only five paved streets in Payson and was as close to a real main street as Payson had. There was a Main Street, of course, but it ran only for six blocks through the small downtown district, dead-ending at the new rodeo grounds to the west. Main Street, like Grace, Pine and Willow Streets, stopped at Highway 87 to the east. Only Ashburn exhibited any real character. It too showed its face downtown, running parallel to the others and coming within two blocks of the Winchester and the red-stone City Hall. But from there it swept to the north, and for a few blocks, two-story shops, and offices that were attached to modest homes, lined it. It was on Ashburn that several of the town's lawyers lived. It was also home to Doctor Dillard, the town vet, and Claiborne's Beauty Parlor.

Throughout the morning Leo had watched the cars come up Ashburn to the Summit County Hospital. They could have easily met at City Hall, but they wanted to hold their meeting here, under the same roof where Neil Starling was. Pa had told him that last night, when he, Genie and Starling, the only survivors from the Payson crew, had been brought here. The town fathers wanted to make their proclamation in the same place where the fire boss was. It didn't matter to them that he was burned across much of his back and legs. It didn't matter to them that he had almost been left in Happy Jack, the small town closest to the fire with a doctor, because initially it was thought he was too weak to be moved.

"It's a matter of principle," Pa told Leo. "I only wish we could say what needs to be said to the son of a bitch's face."

It had been three days since the Cortez Fire, and Pa was filled with more energy and fury than Leo thought he would ever see in the old man again. Pa had been there when they rose from the earth, the landscape nothing but gray hills and black tree skeletons. Overhead the sky once more showed pockets of blue and the wind hurried away from them. Pa and the other ones operating the dozers had been the first to find them after the fire had roared past. By the time they arrived, Leo was on his feet. He had tended to his sister, tearing off shreds of the burned shirt until patches of skin began to come with them. She had fallen too near the outside of Starling's circle of black. Leo would always blame himself for that. All he could do was kiss Taylor in the small of her neck, a small patch of skin that had somehow been left unscathed by the flames. When the dozers came, Taylor was taken away. Leo watched her go. She died on the way to the hospital. That's what Pa told him.

Everyone who had continued uphill for the ridge had lost the race with the flames. Their bodies were scattered across the steep rise. Shoelaces had been burned away. Helmets, gloves and a few remaining handtools littered the area. Every corpse was found in the same position—the head facing uphill, the arms outstretched in front. Shirts had dissolved on some. They were all covered with a gray dust. Except for the contorted fashion of the arms and legs and torso, they appeared to be just sleeping on a slope that had fallen completely to gray.

The man from the fire camp asked him if he knew who they were, and Leo methodically linked names with bodies as they slowly walked up the mountain. The Cunninghams. Fugery. Riddle. Pierce. Anderson. Perez. Only yards from the ridge top they found Koch. A few more feet and he would have lived. He could have scrambled down the backside of the ridge, been found, and helped out by the other crews. Only then did Leo begin to cry. The one who was sometimes mocked for being a coward, who wouldn't go to war, had run the best race of them all.

As they went from body to body, Pa placed sticks a few feet above each head.

"We're going to put crosses here," he said. "We'll make them of granite so they'll last forever."

As Leo watched the cars come up Ashburn to the hospital this morning, he tried to imagine how those crosses would look in the morning sun and decided they would shine like freshly minted coins.

After the hospital's small gravel lot was filled, the cars began to line both sides of the street. Leo's eyes followed his father's brown-colored Studebaker with the chrome bumpers. Pa's car was easy to pick out. He drove fast through town, barely slowing at the stop sign of Ashburn and Grace. It was almost as if he was begging to be stopped before he reached the hospital and the meeting there, but, of course, nobody stood in his way. Chief Parsons and Mayor Browning were already here. They were biding their time until everyone arrived. Then they could walk past the nurse's station and go right to Starling's room. It didn't matter to them that the fire boss could barely move, that he should be allowed to rest. His calculations or miscalculations would be reviewed at a later date. Somebody had to answer for the sins of the Cortez Fire, and the town had already decided that it would be him.

Leo watched his father park and walk up the hill toward the front doors of the hospital. He walked like he lived—chest out, proud, as if his upper torso was pulling his shorter legs along. When he disappeared from view, underneath the roof overhang, going into the renovated lobby, Leo rang for the nurse.

It was Mrs. Farber, the mother of Donny and David, the twins who had enlisted in the Navy days after Pearl Harbor and who were somehow still alive somewhere in the Pacific Theater.

"You sure you want to go?" Mrs. Farber asked as she came up behind Leo's wheelchair. "You being there isn't going to make one iota of difference. These people have their minds made up."

"I want to see this," Leo said.

Mrs. Farber wheeled him to the elevator. They were the only ones aboard as they slowly rode down to the first floor. When the elevator doors reopened, the hallway was crowded. A long line of men led into the cafeteria. These were the older ones who had been left in charge of the town since the war began. They glared at Leo when they felt his stocking feet bump against the backs of their legs. They disregarded Mrs. Farber's pleas of "Excuse me" and "Please clear the way." Only when they felt the push from behind did they peer back and move to one side. They saw who it was—Leo Webb, one of the survivors. First surprise spread across their faces that he would show up at such a meeting, that he looked good enough to be released from the hospital any day now. But then the surprise flared into anger, not at Leo in particular, but at his good fortune. He had somehow been lucky enough to survive when so many others from Payson had died. For that he would never be forgotten or forgiven.

Riddle's father was there. So was Fugery's. And even Perez's. In their faces, Leo caught glimpses of what their sons would have grown to be. Mrs. Faber positioned the wheelchair to one side, just inside the door. She stayed in back of the wheelchair, her hands still resting on the grips.

"I'll decide when we leave," she whispered in Leo's ear. "I don't like the looks of this."

Leo nodded, keeping his eyes straight ahead. He watched as Mayor Browning rapped his gavel, calling the meeting to order.

"This emergency session of the town elders is hereby open," the mayor said. "I would like it noted in the official minutes that we have picked Summit Hospital as our meeting place for two reasons. The hospital cafeteria is now the largest gathering place in Payson. Even so I would like it recorded that we still have more people than the room can hold, a reminder of how dire this tragedy has been to so many in our community. I cannot think of a single person in Payson who hasn't been affected by this situation."

Throughout the room many nodded their heads.

"And because of the seriousness of this situation," Browning continued, "we decided that we would meet here. First because there was more room, but just as importantly because we wanted to conduct this gathering in close proximity to the man who we feel is at fault—Neil Starling."

At the first mention of Starling's name, several men in the back raised their hands, including Leo's father.

"The chair recognizes Ron Webb," Browning said.

"I'd like you all to see what we found at Starling's trailer before the government took it away this morning," his father said. "It was stuck to one of the windows. Plain as day, so nobody can say we ransacked the place in finding it. But Grady and I think it's pretty damning. Take a look-see."

His father held the photo of Yoshi's parents aloft and then handed it to Cyril Patrick, who sat beside him.

"It's a pair of Japs," Patrick said. "A man and a woman."

"That's right," Ron Webb said. "You begin to wonder about where Starling's allegiances really lay."

"Where is that son of a bitch?" said Grady and he glared at Mrs. Farber.

Leo felt Mrs. Farber release the wheel lock with her foot.

Browning rapped his gavel several times.

"Gentlemen, we need to remain calm," he said. "I'm not going to let this proceeding dissolve into a lynch mob."

"Save that for later," a voice shouted out.

"We are here to do official work, our civic duty," Browning said. "I have here a proclamation, a letter of complaint, that I would like to see us vote on, sign and then send to the governor. It protests, in the strongest terms, Neil Starling's conduct in our town, with our fire crew."

"Read it to us, mayor."

"It's addressed to the governor and details how Neil Starling was sent to our town, over the objections of many here today. We emphasize how Payson already had many experienced firefighters, who were more than capable."

"Read it."

"All right, here's the closing, and I quote, 'In the strongest terms, we contend that Mr. Starling's inexperience, especially with large-scale conflagrations, like the one on Cortez Mountain, led to our children being put in harm's way. Our fire crew required a true leader, not somebody who mocked people's suggestions every chance he had. What happened on the Cortez could have been avoided with another fire boss in charge, one of our own. In light of that, it is our fervent hope that you, as governor, will launch a full-scale investigation of this matter. Neil Starling should be held accountable for his questionable conduct and leadership not only on this particular fire but during his entire time here in Payson."

Several in the room applauded.

"Now the next order of business would be to vote on sending this letter," Browning said. "I would like to think it would be unanimous. That would send the strongest possible signal to the governor."

Many of the men were already up on their feet. Mrs. Farber pushed Leo into the hall as the crowd began to pour out.

"It's unanimous," shouted Grady. "Now we have business to finish."

"Gentlemen," the mayor shouted, rapping his gavel.

The crowd encircled the nurse's station near the main doors. Sherrie Wilson, who had been two years ahead of Taylor in high school, manned it. Leo watched as Sherrie first refused to tell them which room was Starling's. She didn't blink when Grady leaned close to her, his face inches away from hers.

"Tell us where he is," Grady said, "or we go from room to room until we find the coward."

Sherrie replied, "He's already been discharged."

"You're lying."

"Look outside," Sherrie said.

A small group hurried through the main door. In the parking lot an ambulance, with U.S. Army emblazoned across the side, sat idling. A jeep with two MPs was parked behind it.

"It's him," somebody shouted. "They're taking him away."

As they began to cross the lot, some of the men picked up stones and pebbles. The MPs saw them and barked out orders. The ambulance shut its doors and sped off as the old men threw with all their might.

"Time to get you back upstairs," Mrs. Faber said as she spun the wheelchair around. They headed for the freight elevator at the rear of the building.

"Where did they take him?" Leo asked.

"I don't know, child. I truly don't."

From his room Leo watched the parade of cars head down Ashburn and into town. Throughout the rest of the morning and into the afternoon he waited for Mrs. Faber or somebody to bring him more news about Starling. But none came, not on that day or the remaining days that he spent in the hospital before going home.

On August 6th, the first atomic bomb was dropped on Hiroshima, killing eighty thousand people. Two days later, a second atomic bomb was dropped on Nagasaki, killing forty thousand. Soon afterward the Japanese surrendered.

The Payson fire crew was disbanded. It didn't matter because there were no more big fires, none that behaved in a strange way, as Starling used to say. Any new blazes the crews out of Flagstaff could handle. Granite crosses were erected to those who died in the Cortez Fire. The day before he was scheduled to leave, Leo drove with his father to where Taylor had died and said good-bye. Leo had joined the Navy, destined to be a member of General MacArthur's staff. After all, he was already a hero. It seemed fitting that he be with MacArthur. That's what people said. That's why strings were pulled. A special place was found for him.

When they returned late that afternoon, the sky was streaked with cirrus clouds that usually brought a smattering of rain. Pa called Yolanda, the Mexican woman who cleaned their house. He told her to meet him down at the Winchester. He did so on the downstairs phone, not caring if Leo heard.

That evening Leo walked down to the Crystal River. At the water's edge, he tore up the topographical map Starling had given him into small pieces. They had all been fools to believe in this stranger and his ideas about fighting fire.

He held the map fragments aloft in both hands and watched as the evening breeze scattered them across the water.

THE END OF SUMMER

As they crested the last in the series of hills on their way to Payson, they saw the gaudy red and luminous yellow of the Ferris wheel above the houses and businesses that ran along Ashburn Street.

"Neil, why can't you let this slide?" Colson said as he eased his foot off the accelerator.

"I forgot it was Rodeo Days," Starling said. "The crew was going to march in the parade once upon a time."

"Why don't we come back when it's dark?" Colson asked. "That's only a few hours off."

"Because it's like I told you," Starling said, focusing on his driver for the first time in many miles. "The cemetery closes at eight. That's what the woman on the phone told me."

"You didn't tell her who you were, did ya?"

Starling smiled. "What if I did?"

"Then they'll have a welcoming committee waiting for us bigger than that lynch mob that tried to have at you the last time. You don't remember much about that day, do you? You being all doped up, but Neil they would have killed you if they'd gotten their hands on you."

"I remember," Startling replied. His eyes grew distant again, recalling nightmares of light and darkness only he had witnessed.

"If you remember everything so well, what are we doing back in this piss-ant town?"

"It's like I told you. It's the proper thing to do."

They cruised through the small downtown, past the streets thick with people from the Winchester Saloon.

"You couldn't save everyone," Colson offered. "You did the best job you could. More of them could have listened."

"They wouldn't listen because they didn't trust me. I was the man with too many secrets."

"You saved Taylor Webb's brother. You saved Genie Holahan."

"And the rest are gone."

"That's right, Neil. It's like any battle. Afterward some are gone."

Starling had studied the preliminary fire report during his month-long convalescence at the military hospital in Phoenix. No longer would such tragedies and near-misses be allowed to fade into legend, worn ragged at the edges by the retelling among the locals. Instead his actions and decisions would remain open for second-guessing by anyone who wished to pull the bound report down from a shelf in the years to come. The report hailed his "remarkable knowledge of fire behavior." But a few lines later, it detailed how "few in his command heeded his orders."

When Starling dreamed of the Cortez Fire, it never returned to him as a complete story. Instead it rolled out in a jumble of moments and glimpses. He remembered waving the others toward him, trying to tell them that his 'escape fire' burning in the cheatgrass, would soon die down to nothing. "We'll be safe in the black," he shouted, and saw how that had registered on the boy's face and nobody else's.

Since the crew had formed in mid-May, that's the way it had been. The king in front and the prince in back. If he could save the prince, then everyone else should have been saved, too. That conviction made little sense upon reflection, but literally in the heat of the moment that's what his mind had seized upon.

As the fire roared over them, the accompanying blast of hot air drove the two of them, as well as Genie Holahan, into the small ring of burned-over cheatgrass. The same force propelled Taylor Webb too far to one side to be saved. That's what the fire boss determined from rereading the preliminary fire report and studying the map of that slope. On one level, it made perfect sense. On another, it was maddeningly arbitrary.

"It's the next right up here," Starling told Colson.

"I don't know how you talked me into this milk run," the older man grumbled.

"Because you know if you hadn't done it, I would have found somebody else who would," Starling said with an edge in his voice. "I would have driven myself if I'd had to."

"You're in no condition to drive anywhere."

"Tell that to the brass, Col. They think I'm fit enough to ship out. I'll be in the Presidio by next week. Then I have some unattended business."

Colson pulled around the next corner and began to accelerate across the open range below the Rim.

"How'd you know their family plot was out here?" Colson asked.

"I followed the kid one day. That's how I discovered the older brother had been on the Bunker Hill."

"You heard about the kid, right? Your old number two?"

"How couldn't I?" Starling said.

"You've got to wonder how many strings were pulled in this town to get him on Mac's staff. The kid goes from basic training to Tokyo. Gets there in time to see the surrender papers signed aboard the Missouri. Unconditional surrender. If anybody should have been there it's you Neil."

"Col, don't roll it out like I should be bent out of shape about the kid. He landed in a sweet-smelling patch. I hope he makes the best of it."

Colson drove beneath the arched red-stone gateway and followed Starling's directions to the last rows of headstones.

When the car stopped, Starling opened the door, and in measured movements, he went around to the Plymouth Coupe's trunk. Colson already had it open for him, and Starling gathered up the bouquet of red roses in both hands, like he was picking up a baby.

His feet, where they had been burned, still hurt the most. The fire boss half-expected Colson to offer to help, and was relieved when he let him be. Gingerly, Starling made his way to Taylor Webb's grave. It was next to her older brother's and was adorned with fresh-cut roses, carnations, daisies, and black-eyed Susans. Starling set his bouquet atop the small pile.

The headstone was white marble. It had just her name and time on this earth. He leaned the bouquet against the headstone and ran his fingertips along the fresh indentations in the cool stone.

"I'm sorry," he whispered.

INSIDE DAI ICHI

By midmorning, the expanse between the U.S. Embassy in Tokyo and Dai Ichi, a mile away, had grown quiet. Far down the street, policemen posted at every corner turned the lights to green, and then bowed as the 1941 black Cadillac exited the embassy grounds and passed by them. Everyone on the streets stopped and bowed too, as the Cadillac, rarely surpassing thirty miles per hour, slowly drove past. The great man who sat in the backseat, his head slightly raised, sunglasses shading his eyes, rarely turned his head and seemed oblivious to all that adored him.

"Best show in the occupied territory, ain't it, kid?" said McCeney.

"It must be," Leo replied, "because every morning I'm up here with you."

The two of them stood atop Dai Ichi, the headquarters for

the Allied occupation of Japan. It was a six-story building, one of the few tall structures to survive the systematic bombing of Tokyo. On one side, it overlooked the Imperial Plaza—the former parade grounds of the mikado's guards and the network of streets leading back toward the embassy. On the other side, it faced the moat with the goldfish ponds that surrounded the emperor's palace. Such symbolism, that there was a new chief in charge, hadn't been lost on the Japanese. Soon after General Douglas MacArthur moved in, the building became known as Dai Ichi, Japanese for 'Number One'.

Two white-helmeted MPs on motorcycles preceded the general's Cadillac.

"I can't believe the old man won't let them go any faster," McCeney said as the Cadillac drew closer to them.

"Admit it, there's another reason you watch," Leo said. "To see if anybody takes a run at him."

"You've got a real sense for the melodramatic, kid," McCeney said.

"I went to him last week with an intelligence report about how the communists were going to chuck grenades at his car some morning. Paulie and I pushed him to add more security. At least a guard or two. Some show of force."

McCeney glanced at Leo. "And he didn't want to hear it, right?"

"The only thing he agreed to was an officer riding in the front seat next to the driver. On our own we added a jeep with more bodyguards, but they have to stay back so the general doesn't see them."

Both of them gazed at the jeep, just now coming into view, a block and a half behind the Cadillac.

"A lot of good that's going to do if something happens," McCeney said.

"No kidding. But the general keeps saying that as long as you don't show any fear the Japs will respect you."

McCeney nodded knowingly. "When we flew in here, the first day, the old man said the same thing. Hardly any security at all. Eichelberger was seeing bogeymen everywhere. Rumor had it kamikazes were going to dive-bomb the field after we arrived. The whole world is holding its breath. On the flight in, Mac's napping. Can you believe it? Napping. When we land, the newsmen run over, everybody's rushing the plane and our Supreme Commander comes down the ramp as poised as a debutante at the spring ball. Even paused two steps down the gangway, puffing that god awful pipe of his, so the newsboys could get his best side. Maybe he's right. Maybe if you don't show any fear, nobody will dare cross you."

The Cadillac pulled up in front of Dai Ichi and the Japanese on the street below stopped chattering and grew deferential. Even though they were cordoned off so far to one side they could hardly catch a glimpse of the general as he walked past, they waited, and then bowed en masse. More MPs in formation twirled their rifles and MacArthur gave the assembled throng, American and Japanese, an exaggerated salute and then followed the white line painted on the sidewalk into the building.

"He wants to see you this morning," McCeney said.

"I figured that."

"What's this all about?"

"Yoshi's digging in her heels about testifying at the tribunal."

McCeney shook his head. "I still don't understand why we didn't line up all those sons of bitches, the general and admirals in charge, and shoot them the day we arrived."

Leo turned and looked at the older man. "I may be the tenderfoot in these parts, but I already know that's not how General Douglas MacArthur does things. He wants a show. Something they can write about in the history books."

"You're a quick study, kid. No wonder the old man likes you."

Majestic and regal were the words that came to mind when Leo came in contact with the old man. MacArthur had a large jaw which jutted out, and a high forehead. These characteristics could have been unattractive in a lesser person, but with the general such flaws flowed together to make him appear larger than life. Part of it was his reputation. He was a man who made big promises, such as vowing to return to Manila, and time after time he made good on such pronouncements. But it was also how he carried himself. The man was from aristocracy and walked with his chin slightly in the air, always a bit proud, always confident. Such good breeding carried to his personal grooming. His nails were always well manicured. That jaw was cleanly shaven—never a nick on him. The skin, even around his eyes and mouth, was still tight, amazing for a man of his age. Except for a few brown spots, his skin glowed like fine marble. Even though he was still very much alive, MacArthur was in a way already immortalized, simply by how he carried himself day after day.

It was just the two of them in the general's office. MacArthur reached for his trademark corncob pipe, one of a half-dozen that lined a small rack at the front edge of his desk. As Leo sat down, MacArthur placed the pipe in his mouth and drew a box of matches out of his top drawer. His office barely fit two people. As Supreme Commander for the Allied Powers he could have commandeered one of the large rooms on the top floor of Dai Ichi. But again that wasn't his way. The larger rooms went to his appointment secretary and his inner cadre, those who were trying to make his transformation of Japan work.

Smoke from the general's pipe curled up above their heads. Below them Japanese children were playing a sandlot game of baseball and MacArthur paused to watch them, nodding his head when one of them stroked a solid line drive into the outfield.

"They tell me that they played ball in the camps as well," the general said. "Manzanar, Topaz, Gila Bend—they all had outstanding teams."

MacArthur took another puff of his pipe.

"When you see one of those tykes hit like that, like DiMaggio himself, it helps you believe that all of this is going to work."

"Sir, it will," Leo said.

The general turned back toward him. "You're supposed to say that, Webb."

"Maybe so, sir. But I believe it."

"Why? Tell me about your optimism for our mission here."

"Remember that order you gave a few weeks ago? The one saying that any American caught striking a Japanese would be jailed?

"Indeed. There were many in my command who vehemently disagreed with me about that order."

"An old woman, that friend of Yoshi's, said that when she

heard that order she knew that the war was really over. One side was finally acting like human beings."

MacArthur chuckled and stood up. With his pipe in hand, he slowly paced the room.

"I hope we don't have to put Yoshi on the stand," he said. "But she knows so much about this world. The way it used to be. She's a marvel, an unsurpassed enterprise in espionage."

Leo nodded.

"I was reviewing your file the other day," the general said. "That unfortunate fire. So many good people killed, including your sister."

"She was as good as any of us by the end," Leo said. "I'm not just saying that because she was my sister. I'm saying it because it's true."

"And I believe you. It's there in the records. She was a very good firefighter, and you did an excellent job as assistant foreman. Forgive me, but I had my doubts when you first arrived here. Yours was a true political appointment, truth be told. But you've accounted yourself well. You seem to be a man comfortable among resourceful personnel of any gender or race."

"Well," Leo began.

"It's all right," the general said. "I'm leading you down the garden path a bit, son. The reality is that I wish more of my men possessed your open heart. I've driven so many of them for so long that I worry about what kind of man we are sending home. The memories of what we've done, had to do, can be simply overwhelming sometimes."

"Yes, sir."

"But then I come upon somebody like you. Yes, our Yoshi may be as American as apple pie and the game of baseball those children are playing. We know that. Everybody in this office knows it. But I grow concerned that others could look upon the two of you and draw a different conclusion."

"It's fine, sir," Leo said. "I can take it."

"I hope so, Webb."

MacArthur sat down again behind his small desk and tapped the ash from his pipe into a crystal ashtray.

"I can't tell you how much the addition of a young man like yourself has meant to me and the staff," he said as he set the pipe back in the rack with the others. "You bring an innocence that we have lost. You can see an attractive young woman of Japanese descent and not immediately dismiss her as the enemy. Well, it gives me hope."

"Yoshi did as much as anybody to secure an unconditional surrender," Leo said. "At least that's what I hear."

A thin smile crossed the general's face.

"She certainly did," MacArthur said. "More than many of us realize. She went to extraordinary lengths."

CANDLES IN
THE WINDOW

Yoshi stood at the launch's rail as they returned to Tokyo harbor. She was returning from another briefing, this time aboard the Renegade. As they drew closer to shore, she tried to imagine where the gun emplacements had been. She searched the hills that swept up from the water for the sights that Leo had described. A vast armada was anchored near the entrance to the harbor. Row upon row of steel-gray battleships and destroyers made her wonder how the war had gone on as long as it had. The hills leading down to the water seemed innocent enough. They were not so different from the ones back home on the road between Monterey and Santa Cruz. Farther away from the water, there were dark patches, places that had been leveled and burned.

To Yoshi, they were like ravaged cells, areas of a huge body that had been wracked by cancer or gangrene. Still, the more she gazed upon the land, in the twilight of this mid-November day, she was reminded once more how resilient the world could be. For more than five years, the war had torn away at the corners of the planet and everything in between. But even with all that had been done, the world was still turning. Things would heal if they gave the process half a chance.

Unlike the general populace, Yoshi was given a military briefing about the bombings of Hiroshima and Nagasaki. One of MacArthur's aides, a man named McCeney, told her about the operation. Afterward she had no doubt that Takata, her Tata, was gone. Yoshi realized there, in the briefing room at Dai Ichi, that if she didn't find someone new she would lose her mind. For a few moments, she considered McCeney. But he talked too fast and was too full of himself. He had been with MacArthur's command since the beginning and was more than willing to tell you about it.

She asked about Neil Starling. McCeney was non-committal.

"He could be discharged by now," McCeney said. Yoshi suspected he was lying.

"How can I get word to him?"

Had he kept his promise, she wondered. Had he helped her family?

"I'll look into it, check with the old man," McCeney said. "But the way things are now, everything breaking up after the war, old Neil could be on the far side of the moon for all I know."

In a hurry to change the subject, McCeney told her about the detail MacArthur had sent to Hiroshima. A kid fresh from America had been a part of it. He told the story like it was the punch line to a joke.

"Can you believe it?" McCeney chuckled. "The kid's fresh off the boat and the old man sends him along, too. He'd already stood drop-jawed through the surrender ceremony. The boy's fallen through the rabbit hole. He's doesn't know which end's up."

"What's his name?" Yoshi asked.

"Oh, hell, I forgot," McCeney said. "Leo something."

"I'd like to meet him when he returns," Yoshi said.

"You would? Why?"

"To have an eyewitness account of the site. It's important to me. To hear from somebody who has been there."

"All right," McCeney said. "When he comes in, you can help debrief him. Ask all the questions you want."

Yoshi nodded. "Thank you," she said.

That's how it began between her and Leo. That's how desperate she had become for somebody in her life.

The launch powered up another swell, lingering atop it for a moment or two, and then it plunged into the next trough. There, as they climbed the back of the next wave, Yoshi saw Leo among a half-dozen others in military khaki. He shielded his eyes from the late-day sun and followed the launch all the way into land. When the launch reached the brand new pontoon dock, Leo was the first alongside. He wasn't exactly a handsome boy. He was more enthusiastic and happy than anything. He caught one of the lines and quickly tied it off. Then he held out his hand, half-pulling Yoshi ashore and into his arms.

He drove the jeep away from the water and up into what was left of the city. Soon they stopped in front of a two-story, brick building with a corrugated tin roof. Candles sparkled in the windows, reminding Yoshi of Christmas back home in California.

Inside Madame Isobe had dinner waiting for them. A small table with a single candle stood in the middle of the main room. The air smelled of smoke and ginger and fish. From the kitchen Madame Isobe brought out a large elliptical bowl with dragons and warriors etched with gold leaf around the sides. A large silver spoon was already on the table for serving the contents—fish chunks, shrimp, and scallops that swam in a thin ginger sauce.

"You're not the only one working hard," Leo told Yoshi as they sat down. "McCeney's called another meeting for our group tonight. It's going to be catch-while-catch-can until this tribunal gets done."

"How did it go today?" Yoshi asked.

"Seemed fine to me, but what the hell do I know, right?" Leo said as he ladled a generous portion onto her plate and then his. "They say it will be over in another couple of days. Then we can get back to normal."

With his mouth half-full he smiled. How Yoshi wanted to be carried aloft by his innocence. He was such a boy still.

"Back to normal," she repeated.

After they finished, Leo left for Dai Ichi. Yoshi and Madame Isobe walked him to the door and waved as he drove toward the six-story building, the lighted sentinel of Allied Command. Not only was it the only building left standing for blocks around, but it was the only one fully lighted at night. It glowed like a distant dream in the darkness of this conquered land.

"He's a fine one," Madame Isobe said.

"Yes," Yoshi agreed. "He's good for me."

"But what about the other one? Starling?"

Yoshi tried to smile. "Nobody knows where he's gone. He's nowhere close to here. That's all I'm sure of. I would know it if he was."

Madame Isobe nodded and turned to go back inside.

"I'm worried about this tribunal," Yoshi said. "They're going to force me to testify. McCeney may deny it, but I can feel it coming. To accomplish what they want I will need to talk."

"There are other ways, child."

"I don't see how."

"And you're worried about what Leo will do if all is told? If there are no more secrets."

"Nobody has a heart that big, Madame Isobe. To accept everything I've done. All the lies I've told since I came to this country."

Yoshi followed Madame Isobe back into the small foyer. There she watched as the old woman lit more candles, including the one beneath the small photo Takata had given her. In the dancing light, the fire balloon seemed ready to rise again. It moved and pulsated like it had back at the Kabuki Theater on that day that seemed to be a lifetime ago.

"I'm going to take a walk," Yoshi said.

"Please be careful, child. You know how I worry."

"I'll be fine."

Only a few blocks from home the cries of "Give me chocolate?" began. Yoshi found them cute, almost reassuring. It was so amazing that the concerns of the world could be distilled down to something so basic—a hunger for sweets.

"Give me chocolate?" the voice repeated and two young boys stepped into the street, blocking her way.

They couldn't have been more than ten years of age. But

they had the faces of old men. The shortest of the two wore only a pair of ragged shorts. The older one smoked a cigarette and wore canvas shorts and a shirt missing many of its buttons. They were both barefoot.

"You got chocolate?" the older one asked, holding out his hand.

Yoshi burrowed through her pockets and found a few sticks of chewing gum.

"Gum?" she asked and the street children eagerly nodded their heads.

Yoshi held the sticks out to them and the oldest one snatched them away. She watched as they tore the paper off and shoved the gum into their mouths.

"What's going on down here?" an adult voice, an American, shouted out.

The three of them turned to see a soldier with a kerosene lantern walking toward them. When Yoshi looked back, the boys had disappeared. She saw no trace of them in the shadows.

"Ma'am?" the soldier said, coming closer.

"Yes, sir. I'm with Allied command."

"What are you doing here, ma'am?"

For a moment, Yoshi almost told him it was none of his business. If he had any problem he could take it up with Mc-Ceney at Dai Ichi. But the soldier had a decent face with a bit of a dimple. A lock of dark hair fell across his forehead where he had shoved his helmet back. He was the kind who would listen. But then she didn't go ahead. Why would he be interested in her troubles? Undoubtedly, he had enough of his own.

"I was out walking," Yoshi said. "I got a bit far from home."

"A bit," the soldier chuckled. "We'll have somebody drive

you back home. If you go around unescorted somebody will mistake you for a panpan."

"I'm no whore. Anybody who propositions me is in for a hard time."

"I can see that," said the soldier. "Still, it wouldn't be good for you to stay here. Now where can I drop you?"

~

The soldier grew more nervous as they pulled up in front of the U.S. Embassy.

"You sure, ma'am?" he said. "This is the general's posting."

"I know where I am," Yoshi replied.

The jeep stopped and Yoshi got out.

"It's OK," she told the soldier. "There's no need for you to wait."

Visibly relieved, the soldier saluted and sped off.

At the front door, MacArthur's wife, Jean, answered her knock.

"Miss Yoshi," she said. "Is he expecting you?"

"No, ma'am. But I need to speak with him."

Mrs. MacArthur directed her toward a wicker chair in a room where colorful drapes hung from the ceiling and Japanese paper umbrellas were fanned in half-open pinwheels against the far wall. Once Yoshi was settled, the general's wife returned with a tray with two small cups of green tea.

"He'll be down shortly," Jean said. "Please, warm yourself up with this. The weather has been so awful lately. It's becoming winter far too early for my bones."

Upstairs Yoshi heard shouts and laughter, and soon a boy

of eleven or twelve, with his mother's dark hair, shot through the room, heading for the breakfast table. Trailing him was General MacAthur.

"Please pardon that torpedo," he said, smiling. "If our enemies had such a weapon they surely would have hung me in the Imperial Plaza, as Tokyo Rose vowed they would."

Yoshi stood up and shook his outstretched hand. "General MacArthur," she began. "I apologize for barging in uninvited, but I need to talk with you, sir."

"About the tribunal, isn't it?"

"Yes, sir, I don't think I can go through with it."

The general nodded. "It will be difficult. I'll be honest about that. But I'm afraid if you don't testify Yoshi, some big fish are going to slip the hook."

"I'm afraid about Leo, sir. He won't understand everything I've done."

"I see," the general said. "Here, bring your tea and follow me. You need to fully understand the gravity of the situation, what's at stake."

The two of them retired to MacArthur's study and Yoshi watched as the general spread a map of North America across his desk. Red stars were speckled across the western half of it.

"We need to have their entire command, the ones who originated this operation, dealt with," MacArthur said. "You know what operation I'm talking about, right?"

"The fire balloons."

"Every red star on this map indicates a place where a fire balloon landed in our country."

"They must be in the hundreds," Yoshi said.

"More than three hundred," the general said. "People died, like those on Leo Webb's crew, and thousands of acres were burned. Those weapons were peculiar, even beautiful, as you've told us, but it's time to close this chapter. I need your help to hold the necessary people accountable."

"How was this kept a secret in the United States?"

"We were fortunate," MacArthur told her. "I cannot think of a more thankless job than that posting—trying to keep secret that the heavens will bring a red rain upon the land. You're not fighting a real enemy then. You're fighting ghosts and half-truths, and that's the position I put those poor men in. I believe you knew one of those I sent home to keep this all a secret."

"Neil Starling."

MacArthur said. "He's the one who spirited you out of Manzanar, isn't he?"

"Yes, he was."

The general nodded. "He directed one of the fire crews. McCeney couldn't tell you that because so much of this information remains classified. We ordered Starling to keep this weapon, the ramifications of it, from those in his outfit. We asked him to lead, but never tell. Perhaps an impossible situation. Starling was a good man. I probably asked too much of him. I may ask too much of you now."

"Where is Starling now?"

The general peered down at the map and ran his large hand across its surface, as if it was within his power to reorganize the armies of the world.

"From what I understand, he's not doing well."

"But where is he?"

"At the Presidio, in San Francisco. This will be his last posting. I've decided to accelerate the process for his discharge. From what I hear, he's not much of a military man anymore."

"My parents?"

"He promised to help them, didn't he?"

Yoshi nodded.

"I don't know if that's within his power anymore," the general said. "I don't know if it's within anybody's power right now. I'm afraid that I don't have an answer for you about them yet. They are no longer at Manzanar. Nobody is at Manzanar. The internment camps were officially closed some months ago. As I told you, your brother is in the army and has done very well for himself. I was able to grease the skids enough for that to happen. But as for your parents? I'm sorry. I don't have any word. Not yet."

CRIMES OF WAR

It could have been something out of the movies. The klieg lights bathed the dark, walnut-toned paneling. The newsreel and still photographers were afforded lofty perches to record the entire scene. Their lenses panned one end of the room to the other, first taking in the side where the defendants sat small and stone-faced, then the other side where the judges, twenty of them, representing the victorious nations, were seated. The main floor was filled with U.S. servicemen. They wore khaki uniforms and served as pages and translators. Other Americans, seemingly every available MP in Tokyo, moved about the throng. Their polished white helmets reflected the white light back to the onlookers.

"It's so bright," Leo told McCeney.

"That's the way the old man wanted it," McCeney whispered. They both wore their best dress uniforms. "This used to be the Imperial Army Officers School. MacArthur ordered the Japs to renovate it for the trial. Kind of fitting, don't you think?"

Leo wasn't sure what to make of it. The gallery sat only five hundred or so. Outside a bigger crowd clamored to get inside. McCeney told him it had cost two hundred thousand dollars easy to refurbish the auditorium. It now had air conditioning and central heating, as if this trial could last for years, when everyone expected it to be over in a week or so.

"I saw the newsreels of Nuremberg," Leo said.

"This will be the same," McCeney said, "except that the defense can answer back. MacArthur somehow didn't feel it was sporting that they couldn't argue a bit."

Below them the swirl of activity settled down and the first gavel was sounded. The prosecutors, all Americans, stood by their long mahogany table. They appeared confident and at ease. Leo looked again for Yoshi, but he didn't see her anywhere. He couldn't quite imagine her here—having something to say that would impact any of this.

The main charge was that the Japanese had conducted an eighteen-year-long 'common plan' to wage aggressive war; and that this common plan not only extended far into Asia but was just as effective and threatening close to home. The prosecutors spoke in English, the basic language of the trial, and as they did so, Leo watched the Japanese generals and high command, looking in their faces for any flicker of recognition.

The American prosecutors began to call one Japanese officer after another to the stand. With the help of their lawyers, as specific charges were read aloud, the Japanese either pleaded guilty or said nothing. To Leo, what now transpired had all the predictability of a calf-branding back home in Arizona. It seemed only a matter of time before the show was over and they would go home. But then a taller man, his chest and shoulders decorated with ribbons and medals, walked confidently to the witness box. On his face was a scowl of contempt.

"Who's that?" Leo asked. He hated how the words came out. He sounded like a boy at a horse auction or ballgame, where nothing could be understood without questioning the adults or consulting some piece of paper.

"His name is Ito," McCeney said. "He was in charge of the home front. He's one reason why I'm happy we dropped the bomb. He had a hellstorm waiting for us if we'd tried to invade in a conventional sense. He had everyone down to women and children ready to fight us. He wanted to go toe-to-toe until the last one was standing."

They watched as Ito stood ramrod straight—the charges being read to him. He listened until the prosecutors were finished. Then he sat down and turned his attention to one of the Japanese lawyers.

"It's Kenzo," McCeney said. "He's supposed to be the best lawyer the Japs have."

Kenzo began to speak in English, with little trace of an accent, and his words transformed the room. For the first time in the proceedings, somebody for the defense dared speak the language of the victors. Leo saw how Ito's dark eyes glowed.

"If it would please the court," Kenzo said, "Major Ito would desire to hear how the charges against him were determined. As you know, he never left the mainland. He was in charge of the defense of Japan. To include him in this so-called conspiracy to carry out a common plan of warfare seems quite far-fetched."

Back at the prosecutors' bench, the half-dozen American lawyers huddled until one of them stepped forward to address the three rows of judges. These judges represented the Allied countries. They were from the United States, Australia, Soviet Union, Korea, China and India.

"Benson will stop this crap," McCeney whispered.

The gallery listened as the prosecution's top lawyer argued eloquently for several minutes that nobody could differentiate among those in the Japanese command.

"To say where one man's jurisdiction ended and another's began is impossible to ascertain," Benson said. "For in these proceedings, we must view the Japanese command in its entirety. That is the only way to truly understand and fathom the evil that they have carried out over the last two decades."

"That should do it," McCeney said confidently.

But it didn't. Leo saw that one of the international judges, a small man with black hair and a dark complexion, stirred to life. He sat in the middle of the second row of judges. His nameplate read Radhavinod Pal. He was the one from India.

"The defense raises an interesting question," he said in a voice that sounded half-mocking, half-serious. "Is defense at home as evil as aggression abroad?"

"I can assure the court that it is," Benson retorted. "Crimes against humanity do not become more permissible when the particular locale changes."

"That may be," Pal answered. "But to truly know such insight, it would seem to me that we need to know how these specific charges were brought against Major Ito. Crimes from the battlefront can be better documented. But how do we know first-hand of these crimes against this person. There was no battle in Japan proper. Some could say that the only real crime on this soil occurred when the United States of America dropped its bombs on Hiroshima and Nagasaki."

The mention of those two cities brought ripples of consternation through the crowd, followed by a rapping of the gavel.

Benson turned toward the prosecutors' table. He was met with confused faces. The lead attorney for the Allied Command stepped back in front of the judges.

"Very well," he said. "If Major Ito would step down. I'd like to call Miss Yoshi Minagi, a member of our intelligence sector."

With that a louder ripple of noise spread throughout the crowd.

Yoshi was dressed in a khaki, military-style dress and the gallery quieted as she walked to the dais in front of the judges. Ito sat down with his lawyer at the table.

"Do you know the defendant?" Benson asked.

Yoshi nodded.

"You'll need to speak for your comments to be recorded by the court stenographer," Benson advised her.

"Yes," Yoshi began in a soft voice. "Yes, I do."

"Could you please briefly chronicle the crimes the defendant committed in the last four months of the war. That accurately indicates the period of time that you were in this country, correct?"

Yoshi started to nod again, but then added, "Yes. I've been here for that amount of time."

She told the tribunal about the war Ito and those in his command waged on the home front. Under his direction Japanese schoolchildren were taught to strap small bombs to their chests, ready to roll under Allied tanks. Old women were instructed on how to load and shoot a rifle. Ito wanted the Japanese population to fight to the last person and those that refused were tortured or killed. Yoshi told them about the insanity that existed in Tokyo before the Americans arrived. As she spoke, Ito rubbed his hands together, staring at her, as if his presence could force her into silence.

When Yoshi finished, the room erupted again. It was as if the crowd had been taken to the depths of war's madness and now fought upward for light, for normalcy. Leo watched as Ito leaned over and conferred with his lawyer.

"Thank you, Miss Minagi," Judge Pal said.

"They're going to call me back," Yoshi said, "I just know it."

"It's over, child," replied Madame Isobe.

"No, it's not. I just have this feeling. Did you see how Ito was staring at me? Like he'd like to strangle me with his bare hands?"

Yoshi and Madame Isobe huddled on a wooden bench in a courtyard outside the busy courtroom. The trial had broken for recess after her testimony.

"I should leave right now," Yoshi whispered. "I'm crazy for staying here. Where's Leo? As soon as he comes, we're leaving, understand?"

"Yoshi, you're talking like a crazy woman. Hush, everything's almost over. See, here he comes now."

As the man in uniform drew closer, they saw it wasn't Leo, but another fresh American face in dress whites.

"Ma'am?"

"Yes," Yoshi said in a resigned voice.

"They're calling you back. The Jap lawyer has a few more questions and that Judge Pal is letting him ask them."

Yoshi nodded and exchanged looks with the stunned Madame Isobe.

"One last question, Miss Minagi," Kenzo said as he rose to stand next to Benson. "One wonders how this woman comes by her information. Could she please characterize her relationship with another from the high command? A Doctor Takata, who unfortunately was among the casualties at Hiroshima."

Benson protested. "This isn't appropriate. This has nothing to do with her testimony."

"No, I would argue it has everything to do with her words, what weight they carry," Kenzo argued. "For it was through Takata that she found herself so close to the high command. The court needs to hear how this came to be."

"May I?" Pal interrupted and once more the room grew silent. "I do not doubt this woman's testimony. She has been direct and credible. But the defense raises an interesting question. That's why I thought it important to pursue this. How was this information obtained? This Takata—I've heard of him. We have evidence of a particular weapon he designed—the fire balloon. Very interesting, potentially very deadly. So, I too find myself curious. How does this woman find herself in a position to know so much? It is her decision if she wants to further discuss this Dr. Takata. But if she decides not to, her words become weak. Accusations and little more."

All eyes fell on Yoshi. Her head was bowed and her hands tightly folded in her lap. Silently, Leo urged her to simply stand down from the witness chair, walk away from these men and their crazy notions of honor and revenge. But instead Yoshi raised her head and stared straight at Ito with defiance.

"As you well know, Major Ito," she said, "Dr. Takata was my

lover."

Everything fell into bedlam. From the judges to the gallery the room began to buzz about the revelation. The gavel was rapped several times, but was ineffective in bringing the grand scene back to order.

Leo sat in his seat and stared down at his hands folded in his lap. His eyes began to well up. God, he couldn't let anyone see him like this. God, no. Once more he felt as if everything he had believed in had been taken from him. It was like the fires, the red rain that fell upon his land. It had forced him to the ground, and when he did stand again his world was disfigured beyond recognition. Everyone he had ever trusted—his parents, sister, Starling—had let him down. None of them was strong enough to withstand the chaos let loose in the world.

Beside him was McCeney, the older man who was unsure of what to say. Finally, McCeney stood and briefly clasped his shoulder. He said he was heading down. Left unspoken was whether Leo wanted to join him. Leo shook his head and stayed in the spectator's gallery, unable to raise his eyes.

That's why she hadn't wanted to testify. She knew what the repercussions would be. She knew all along that it would destroy what they had, the future they believed in. She knew all along that he didn't have a big enough heart to forgive all of this.

It was a trick question. Kenji was the first one in the family to see through it back in Manzanar. Now, years later, here in Japan, after being exposed in the bright lights of the trial, Yoshi realized why her little brother had been so angry.

Question 27 of the loyalty questionnaire had read, "Are you willing to serve in the armed forces of the United States on combat duty, whenever ordered?"

Kenji had written yes. He was determined to get out of Manzanar and in doing so perhaps help the family, too.

But it was the next question—No. 28—that had him scratching his head and then crumbling the questionnaire at the edges with his long fingers. All of the family was in the one-room barracks flat, intent on doing the right thing.

"Will you swear unqualified allegiance to the United States of America and faithfully defend the United States from any or all attack by foreign or domestic forces, and foreswear any form of allegiance or obedience to the Japanese emperor, to any other foreign government, power or institution?

Yoshi had watched him begin to write yes. But then he stopped and looked at her. Everyone in the family had a questionnaire in front of them.

"But if I say yes," Kenji began.

"Then it means you once were loyal to the emperor," Father said, now crest-fallen.

"But you cannot say no," mother told them. "That would prove disloyalty."

"It's all a stupid game," Kenji said, throwing down the government-issue pencil. "Who do they think we are. Idiots? We're Americans. How are we supposed to answer this? What do they want from us?"

The next day the buzz around Manzanar was "no, no." That was the only way to answer questions 27 and 28 and still retain any self-dignity. Yoshi tried to explain this to Mr. Ogden. How could you ask people raised as Americans such things?

"Just tell them to say, 'Yes,'" he cautioned. "It's only a piece of paper."

"Not to them," Yoshi said in a low voice. "Not to me."

As she waited in the hallway outside the trial room for Leo, those old words of protest—no, no—kept coming back to her. That's what she should have told General MacArthur and the lawyers. Simply no, no.

She had been a fool to think that a boy as innocent as Leo would be able to see through the parade of hateful words and war slogans. Eventually, the truth would come out and one couldn't say 'that was me then and this is me now'. That only came across as an excuse, another lie.

McCeney came striding down the hallway toward her. As usual, he was all smiles and carried himself in that important, crisp, hurried way.

"Thank you," he said. "I know that wasn't easy."

You have no idea, Yoshi thought as she returned his salute.

"The old man will be happy," McCeney continued. "Ito will be going to prison for a long time."

Ito? She hadn't thought about him since she stepped down from the stand.

"Where's Leo?" she asked.

"He's coming along," McCeney said and glanced about them. The hallway was filled with clumps of people in uniform, but none came any closer. They were giving her, Takata's woman in blue, plenty of distance.

"Is he okay?"

McCeney refused to look her in the eye.

"To be honest, he's a little shocked. But he'll come around. You'll see."

McCeney continued to gaze about, eager to move on.

"Here he comes now," he said and briefly gestured toward

the end of the long hallway. "I'll leave you two alone. Let me know if you need anything."

McCeney nodded in Leo's direction.

"Thanks again," McCeney said and broke off another quick salute for her. He was gone before Yoshi could return it this time.

Leo wouldn't look her in the face.

"Good job," he said in a low voice. His eyes were focused on his polished dress shoes.

"Thank you," Yoshi half whispered and reached for his hand. He drew back.

"You all right?" she asked.

"Yeah, sure," Leo said, trying to put a good face on it all.

"Madame Isobe has cooked up a good dinner for tonight. Another seafood stew."

Leo seemed to flinch. "No, not now," he said. "I need to be back at the barracks tonight."

She wanted to just hold him and repeat to him over and over again that they could move past this. But Yoshi saw that to him it would be just another one of her lies. Whatever had held them together was broken. She knew that in her heart. In dealing with Ito, she had once again risked everything that she loved.

"Leo, we can— "

"Why didn't you tell me?" Leo said. She saw that he was on the verge of tears.

"How could I? Look at what it's done to you. Please, I love— "

"No," Leo interrupted. His voice briefly echoed down the hallway and heads turned toward them. That only embarrassed Leo even more.

"No," he hissed in a lower voice that somehow held more power. Then he walked away from her, almost assuming the same hurried style that carried somebody like McCeney through the war.

"Good-bye," Yoshi whispered, but he was already out of earshot.

Yoshi looked around and saw that she was once again alone. She began to walk faster up the dark corridor beyond the tribunal's klieg lights. As she approached those who were clustered outside, they stepped back until her path seemed to extend all the way to Dai Ichi and to the last man that she needed to see in Japan.

⟿

"I can have you on a transport back tonight," MacArthur said, "if that's truly what you want."

Yes, sir," Yoshi replied. "Yes, it is."

She slumped forward in the chair across from his deck. In her heart she believed that if she curled up tight enough she could make herself disappear.

"But it's a long way," MacArthur continued in a calm voice. "You have no idea what you'll be returning to. Please, let me make some more calls. Find out as much as we can from this end."

"No, I want to go," Yoshi said and looked up at him. "Now."

MacArthur nodded his head and began to pace. It was late afternoon and Yoshi wasn't sure how she could hold on once the darkness came.

"I fear I asked too much of you," MacArthur said. "I ask too much of everyone."

"Yes, you do," Yoshi said defiantly before closing her eyes, anxious to disappear once and for all.

Lui, Takata and now Leo. Her memories of them came flooding back, and Yoshi saw that she had bungled the job as badly as MacArthur or any other commander in this damned war. She had tried to help them all with her lies, but she hadn't allowed for how fickled the world really was or how eager it was to strike at the ones who are very brave or very gentle.

"Yoshi, you're trembling."

MacArthur was behind her and when she opened her eyes to his voice, she saw his row of pipes at the front of his desk. They stood like little soldiers—so prim and proper.

Without thinking, Yoshi brought her hand back, as if to find the general's. But when his fingers touched her shoulder, her arm snapped forward, sending the row of pipes tumbling to the floor.

Her scream of anguish brought MacArthur's secretary in from the outer office. He could have been Leo, another prim and proper soldier boy dressed in creased khaki.

"It's all right," MacArthur said.

"Sir?"

"Please leave us," the general said and the door closed.

MacArthur dropped to one knee beside her chair.

"Yoshi," he said, his sweet voice whispering in her ear. "Find something in your mind to hold onto, something bright and good and filled with hope. It's the only way. Find the happiness. I assure you, there is still some there. The world cannot drive every last bit of it from us."

In her mind, Yoshi saw the old family farmhouse—

golden and regal in the setting sun.

"I can have you stateside by tomorrow if that's truly what you want."

"Yes, please, sir," Yoshi said as she sat up.

"But be careful," MacArthur said, still on one knee. "Your mental state isn't the best—"

"I'll be fine," Yoshi interrupted. "Just fine."

LOOKING FOR HOME

When the plane landed in San Francisco, the city was shrouded in fog. They had flown through the night from Pearl, with Yoshi sitting on a small jump seat by a portal window. The fog began to burn away as she rode the military bus, the only woman on it, through the gates of the Presidio. Eucalyptus trees, with their peeling bark, ran in neat rows along either side of the street. Red-tiled roofed buildings of whitewash clapboard led away at right angles and the air smelled of the sea and hope. With her one suitcase, she got off at the administration building and went inside.

"There's nobody by the name of Starling here, not in this building, ma'am," the private said. "That's not to say he's not on the base for we have thousands stationed at the Presidio at the present moment, with more being processed through every day.

"I was told he was here."

"But no company or regiment, posting?"

"No. Could you please look?" Yoshi asked.

The private had the impatient air of youth about him.

"That's going to take a while, ma'am. I've got a laundry list of things already to do this morning. Why don't you try back? Maybe tomorrow?"

"I'll wait."

"Suit yourself," the boy replied, intent on putting her in her place.

Yoshi made herself comfortable as she could on a marble bench beneath a clock with black Roman numerals. From here she could keep an eye on the private. Time passed slowly and he worked with his back to her. Her stomach rumbled with hunger and she was so tired. Outside she could hear the base coming alive. Once more she felt as if she was struggling against the tide of everything. The world was turning back upon itself, changing once more, and she couldn't help thinking that if she didn't find Neil Starling soon she never would. The chance to start again, to forgive, would be lost in the hurly-burly whirl of this new world, intent upon reinventing itself.

It was early afternoon by the time the private spoke to her again. He had glanced over several times throughout the morning to see if she was still there. He had gone as far as to eat an early lunch at his desk.

"A month ago, Lieutenant Neil Starling was in the quartermaster's office," he said. "But he's not there anymore. You might think about if you really want to find this guy or not. I mean according to his record, he's been in and out of the stockade several times. Public drunkenness. Disorderly conduct."

"Where is he?" Yoshi said.

"Ma'am, I don't rightly know. His file ends at the motor pool. But that doesn't mean anything, really. The paperwork here is at least two weeks old, near as I can tell. That's where they put him to keep him out of trouble."

"Where is the motor pool?"

"At the other end of the base, ma'am. I can see about getting you a ride."

"No, just tell me where it is."

After getting directions, Yoshi set out, walking as fast as she could with her small wicker suitcase across the base. The motor pool appeared as an afterthought after the rows of officers' homes and regal dining rooms and barracks. The warehouse-style building seemed deserted and the front door was indeed locked. But when Yoshi heard the revving of a single engine, she walked around to the rear of the building and saw a man on tiptoe working on the guts of a car. At first she thought it was Starling. Rather she could pretend it was him. As she drew closer she saw that he was too wide in the hips and not nearly tall enough. When she said hello the second time, the man who turned toward her had a flush round face and a generous smile.

"What can I do for you, darling?" he asked, wiping his greasy hands on a rag he pulled from the back pocket of his overalls.

"I'm looking for Neil Starling. Do you know him?"

"Sure do. He and I have been known to share a bottle of dago red now and again."

"Do you know where I can find him?"

The mechanic shook his head. "Now that's a tougher question to answer, my dear. First off, who are you?"

"I'm a friend of his."

"That so," he said. "I'm Hal Palmer, his best buddy on this base. I don't remember him ever talking about a beauty like you."

"I was told that he was last posted here."

She didn't mention that she had gotten this information from MacArthur—the Supreme Commander of the Pacific.

"That's right," Palmer said. "The key word in what you said being last. Old Neil was discharged a couple of weeks ago, an honorable discharge. I don't know how he landed that after all the trouble he got into around here over the past few months. You name it—booze, whores, pardon my French."

"So he's not here?"

"Afraid not, ma'am. He drove off a week ago Sunday in a powder-blue Hudson convertible. As beautiful a car as you'll ever see, and I should know. I helped the son of a bitch—I'm sorry, hon—fix it up after-hours. Not that being a Good Samaritan did me any good with that old boy. My car's over there," he said and nodded at an Oldsmobile sedan. "It needs a fair amount of work itself. I could have used a bit of help with it. But Neil was in a big hurry, so he couldn't stick around. It seems he couldn't do the proper thing much anymore."

"Do you know where he went?"

"No, ma'am," Palmer said. "To be honest, I don't think too well of old Neil right now. All he said was that he was going to drive that new car of his off into the sunset. Those were his words exactly. Drive off into the sunset."

Yoshi looked down at the ground and felt as if she was about to fall apart. First Takata, then Leo and now Starling had fallen out of her life. Around her the world marched on—matching up and eager to forget about the past and its heartbreak. Somehow she had been caught on the wrong side of the river, not knowing where or how to cross.

"Hang on, darling," Palmer said as he came over to her. He wrapped the rag around one hand and draped that arm around her shoulder, steadying her toward a bench outside the roll-up garage door. "Sit down here. It's going to be OK. You can take old Hal's word on that. Trust me."

"I thought I'd find him here," Yoshi said.

"I know, I know," Palmer said as he stroked her back. "I wish I could help you. I know I'll hear from him, but who knows when. That damn Neil."

The mechanic looked up at the clock on the wall. Except for them, the garage was empty.

"I know what," he said. "Let me buy you an early dinner. If I'd known a fresh face like you was coming for him I would have grabbed old Neil and held him down until you arrived."

Yoshi rummaged in her purse for a tissue.

"He didn't say anything about where he was going?"

"The way he talked the last few days, where wasn't he going?" Palmer replied. "I mean at one point he was heading down the coast to L.A., the next he was going up north. Next minute he was going east, straight on through to New York or Boston. Places he knew nothing about, but somehow couldn't wait to see. He kept babbling that he had to help somebody. Why couldn't he help me with that car? Well, Neil couldn't really address the situation at hand, could he?"

Palmer gazed about the garage. The gleaming forms of several cars were hidden by the lengthening shadows of the afternoon. Almost to himself, he said, "I started early this morning, so I'm due an early slide. Not that there's anybody around to tell me any different these days."

He turned back to Yoshi. "Let me buy you dinner. It's the

least I can do."

Without waiting for her response, Palmer picked up her suitcase and carried it over to his car. He wiped his hands once more with the rag and slammed the hood shut.

"Give me a minute to wash up, will ya?" he said. "We'll have some fun. Sometimes that's all you can do, you know? Make the best of a situation."

Yoshi decided that Hal Palmer was a decent enough looking fella. He was a bit overweight, but another one that she could lose herself in. Another lie was ready to be told.

Palmer drove her to the Tenderloin section of San Francisco. They parked on the street and he put his arm around her and steered Yoshi through the crowded sidewalk to an Italian restaurant. Inside it was almost as frantic and noisy as out on the street. They sat at a small table near the bar. Just beyond them was the kitchen and they watched as the orange flames from the charcoal grill leapt into the air when their steaks were placed on it. In quick order, the rib-eyes arrived at their table with sides of spaghetti, garlic bread and salad. Palmer drank wine, more dago red, and at his insistence she did, too. Between them, they soon finished the bottle and Palmer ordered another.

"It's over, isn't it?" Yoshi said.

"What's that, darling?"

"The war."

He nodded. "No kidding. What's that FDR said way back when? We have nothing to fear but fear itself? That may be more true now than it was after Pearl."

"Why?"

"You know, Miss Yoshi. You tell me."

She sighed and replied. "Because everything's changed. Anything you tried to hang on to disappeared. Gone. Kaput."

"The girl's a poet," Palmer said and took her hand in his, raising it to his lips. "A beautiful, beautiful poet."

After dinner he drove her to his uncle's place. It was an upstairs flat south of the city, a block from the beach.

"He's moved down past San Jose, to Big Sur country," Palmer said. "He can't stand all the people beginning to fill this city up. Calls it another goddamn Gold Rush. I'm going to buy this place from him once I'm out of the army, get a job, start putting two and two together."

After that he mercifully stopped talking and began to kiss her, there, in the living room. He was so full of energy and intent that she couldn't comprehend such power. How could he possess such desire, such innocence, in these times? Yoshi let him sweep over her—drowning her soul in his loving attention. As he worked away, she imagined that it would be the same if she simply walked down to the beach and strode out into the fierce waves of the Pacific. His love pounded like those waters, again and again, as she stretched out for him there, on his uncle's couch, in the darkness, with the stars barely showing themselves outside because of the evening fog's early arrival.

In the morning, he was gone. A note explained that he had the early shift back at the motor pool. He left a number, begging for her to call. Breakfast—half a grapefruit, orange juice and coffee—had been placed on the small table in the half-kitchen adjacent to the living room. Yoshi's mouth felt full of cotton and her head ached. She looked through his cupboards until she found some aspirin, then sat down to study the sea. Outside the light blue waters were calm and the fog was lifting from the beach. Her suitcase still stood inside the front door, where they had left it the night before. She showered, and changed into an old dress, nothing fancy, and flats. She hungered to be unadorned. She wanted to fade into the background for as long as it would take to find anything of value.

After the shower, Yoshi sat again by the window. Her hair was wet. She sipped Palmer's black coffee (no cream to be found) and stared out at the Pacific Ocean.

She couldn't believe that she had slept with him, that she had become so desperate for anything passing for love or affection. If she was back in Tokyo, she knew what the boys on the street would call her. Panpan. A whore. She had become so adept at twisting the truth she wasn't sure where her life stopped and the deception began anymore.

She found a new pack of cigarettes, Pall Malls, atop the bureau in the bedroom. All of the furniture was second-hand, with several coats of chipping paint. Last night he had said he couldn't wait until he was out of the army. He had less than three months now. After that he would buy new furniture for the place—more of his big plans. The apartment wasn't bad. It just needed some sprucing up. She remembered him saying that.

Deliberately she stripped away the cellophane skin to the cigarettes and crumbled it in her hand, listening to the crackling sounds it made. Not that long ago she would have been happy with a man like Hal Palmer. Now she couldn't stand the thought of seeing him again. It was as if the world had been revealed to her and Yoshi didn't care about how it used to be.

Could you still forgive if you knew all the secrets of your world? Once upon a time, Yoshi would have said yes, a thousand times yes, to such a question. Secrets were born to be revealed. That's what she used to believe.

As the morning light burned away the fog, she realized that she had been truly cursed. Her lot was memory and nothing more. Her better nature, the angels that tried to watch over her, chattered in low voices, telling her to move ahead, live life as she once had. Embrace, perhaps even treasure, a man like Palmer, somebody who would take care of her. She lit one of his cigarettes, trying to convince herself of such wisdom. But it was no use. She set the cigarette down on the saucer and watched the light gray smoke curl upward toward the ceiling.

By noon she still hadn't called Palmer. Instead her first and only call was to the local taxi company, requesting a cab to the bus terminal below Market Street. When she arrived, the saleslady advised her to come back in two hours. There was a direct to Santa Cruz then. But Yoshi didn't want to wait and instead bought a ticket on the local through San Jose that left in a half-hour. When the bus pulled into its berth, Yoshi was the first in line, handing her suitcase to the driver and stepping aboard. She sat two-thirds of the way back and nodded as an old lady took the seat across the aisle from her. The elderly one had a book with her, a weathered family Bible, as well as knitting needles and several balls of yarn. The lady's face crinkled into a lopsided smile. She seemed eager to start up a conversation. Instead, Yoshi turned back to the window and rested her forehead against the cool glass.

Minutes before they were scheduled to depart, she saw Hal Palmer hurrying through the crowd toward them. Immediately Yoshi ducked down. She put her head close to her knees and prayed. She prayed with all her heart that Palmer wouldn't find her, that she would be allowed to leave and somehow start again.

The driver put the bus into reverse. Above her head Yoshi heard the palm of a hand strike the glass—hard and frantic. The driver honked his horn. They began to pull out, but then the bus jerked to a halt. The horn blasted again before they were finally away.

Minutes went by. The bus was moving faster and faster. Still, Yoshi waited, quiet as death. She kept her head down, hidden from view, until the blood began to pound in her temples. When she did rise, they were already outside the city. On the left was cobalt-blue San Francisco Bay. Outside Yoshi's window were the straw-colored hills near Bay Meadows racetrack and rows upon rows of orchards.

"He wasn't bad looking," the old lady said.

Yoshi tried to smile.

"He really wanted to find you. He even tried to get on the bus, but the driver wasn't having any of it. Damn near ran the poor fool over."

By late afternoon they began to climb into the Santa Cruz Mountains above San Jose. The land was dry and hot. There hadn't been much snow this winter. That's what the old lady told her. Yoshi nodded politely and closed her eyes. She wanted to be lulled asleep by the sound of the tires and the road ahead of her. She thought she heard the whistle of a train, thin and lost in the distance. Still, when Yoshi opened her eyes she saw nothing but a clear blue sky and the black asphalt road that was taking her home, to the beginning. She was unsure of what she would find there. Kenji had joined the U.S. Army, a member of the 442nd Division—one of the most decorated units in U.S.

military history. MacArthur had helped get him out of the Tule Lake Prison. Unfortunately, the 442nd was still in Germany as part of the occupation, and Kenji hadn't heard from mother and father since Manzanar closed months ago.

The whine of the engine slowly calmed her mind and Yoshi nodded off once more. She dreamed that she was in San Francisco—the big city of her youth. In her vision, the sidewalks were crowded with people rushing toward something to be cherished and loved, and she was moving against them. Every now and then she recognized a face. General MacArthur or McCeney or Hal Palmer. But none of them paid her any mind. She was a ghost in a world hurrying to be reborn.

It was dusk when she awoke. At first she feared that they had already reached Santa Cruz and nobody had been courteous enough to awaken her. As she came around, Yoshi saw that the bus was empty. They were pulled over to the side of the highway, with cars lined up in front of them.

"I figured I'd let you sleep," the driver said when she stepped down from the bus. "It looks like we'll be here a spell."

"Why's that?" Yoshi said.

"Brush fire up ahead. We're a half-mile or so away. Some of the others went to take a look. That old lady was leading the way. But it seems to me that if you've seen one fire you've seen them all."

"I'm going to walk up and join them."

"Get on back once it's over, hon. I plan on moving out as soon as I can."

Yoshi nodded and began to walk up the shoulder of the highway. Light-gray smoke rode the dying breeze and the fire came down to them from the left. It wanted to cross the highway and run into a small ravine of good-sized pines and brush.

A crowd had gathered up ahead to watch a rag-tag bunch trying to control the blaze.

The crew was disorganized and spent more time yelling at each other than actually working the fire. Still, there was one who calmly went about his business. He stood atop the rise closest to the bystanders and the highway. He directed the others along the ridge, trying to contain the fire's leading flank. He didn't have a radio. Instead he moved the others into position with arm motions and distinct commands that echoed across to those watching the fire.

He left the most difficult stretch, between the hill and the road, for himself. Through the smoke, Yoshi watched him share a canteen of water with another man. Shucking his helmet for a moment, he poured water over his brownish-red hair. It was slightly longer than she remembered. The other man must have said something, cracked a joke, because the fire boss's face briefly broke into that crooked smile she would never forget.

Yoshi moved past the others and began to walk downhill, toward the fire-line.

"Hey, lady, where you going?" somebody cried. "Come back."

But she didn't pay them any mind.

In the small valley below, Yoshi reached a makeshift camp. Small piles of equipment—boxes of fire shirts and trousers and cap helmets—were littered across the ground, and shovels were stuck into the earth in groups of three.

"What the hell do you want? You lost or something?"

It was a young kid, maybe seventeen. He reminded her of Leo when they first met. He was impulsive and frantic back then. She watched as this one grabbed a canteen and drained it, with a few frantic gulps.

"You shouldn't drink all your water," Yoshi said. "Not at once"

"Thanks, sister. When I need your precious advice I'll be sure to ask."

"Johnson, where you at?"

The voice came from up toward the smoke.

"Johnson," it repeated.

"Damn it," the boy said and he began to run back toward the fire-line.

Farther up the hill, appearing out of the gray smoke, came the fire boss. After waving Johnson past, he saw her and came down the hill to shoo her away. The right side of his face was purple with scars. She guessed they came from that fire that had killed so many, including Leo's sister. As he drew closer, Yoshi peered into smoke and twilight. She held her breath as the lines came together and she saw that it indeed was Neil Starling.

"Well, I'll be," he said with a smile. "You've come back."

"Are they all right?"

"What do you think?"

"You said you'd take care of them. Get them out of Manzanar."

"You'll find them down the road apiece. We're working to get them back into your old house."

Yoshi shook her head in disbelief.

"I finally got through to Tokyo last week, before my discharge," Startling said. "But McCeney wouldn't do me any favors. He was concerned about the tribunal."

"The tribunal," Yoshi repeated.

"He was worried that you wouldn't go through with it."

"I shouldn't have."

"You never know that at the time," Starling told her. "You just do the best you can."

"But why?" Yoshi began. "Of everywhere you could have gone?"

Starling shrugged. "You see, I used to have this photo, a nice enough picture of a beautiful farmhouse hugging the Pacific. I just couldn't get it out of my head. I found your father working at a farm nearby. He and your mother were living in a hovel in town. That didn't seem right to me, so I raised a ruckus. It landed me in some trouble, but I figured it was worth it."

"They're back home?"

"Almost, Yoshi. And in coming down here so much the last couple of months, in being derelict of my duties at the Presidio, I grew to appreciate this part of the world. This local crew needed some help. So, here I am. And you want to know something? Right now we could use as much help as we can get."

"You mean me?"

"Why not? You finally got here."

"I don't know anything about fighting fire," she said.

"If I can land you on the coast of Japan with a son of a bitch like Butch Allen breathing down my neck, I can teach you to fight fire," Starling said. "First thing we need to do is get you in some better duds. At least you had the sense to wear flats."

He undid the buttons that ran down the back of Yoshi's dress, and she stepped out of the calico, not caring about the people back on the road. She pulled her arms through the long-sleeve fire shirt and stepped into the green-fatigue pants. Side by side the two of them walked up to the fire-line.

Closer to the flames, he showed her how to dig and throw the dirt at the dancing light. As Yoshi worked, she remembered a story her father had once told her. He read it in one of the

English books he bought to prepare her and k
nia public school. It was a story about how
fire and held it for their own, until a man na
stole the elixir from the heavens and brought the flames down
to earth. Here, mankind used fire to cook, warm himself and
make the weapons and tools to rule the world. But as with any
blessing, there comes a time when the magic grows too strong.
Then those who have the courage to act as gods step forward
and save the rest.

By dusk their work was done. The firebreak that Starling
had supervised appeared to be wide and sound enough to do
the job. They gathered with the others to watch. All of them
were silent as the yellow-orange flames hit the fire-line several
times. Yoshi saw how Starling's eyes watched the embers float
into the sky. Had the embers decided to ride across the land
again, Starling stood ready to command his meager forces into
action.

As darkness fell they saw that they had been fortunate.
The embers, flickering above their heads, were as harmless as
victory parade confetti. They witnessed the fire take one last
run at the line before dying down, and eventually coming to an
end.

EPILOGUE

August, 10, 1988

This would be her last trip back to Washington. Earlier that afternoon, in the White House Rose Garden, President Reagan had signed HR 442 into law. The new legislation provided twenty thousand dollars to each surviving internee from the camps and established a multibillion-dollar education fund for their descendants.

When one remembered the harsh winds that blew down the eastern slope of the Sierra Nevada or considered how many had forever lost their homes and businesses, it should have been more. But as Yoshi picked up the pen with the White House seal, one of twenty-two the President had used to sign the bill into law, she knew that the federal government had already moved on. This is where the story of the Japanese internment camps would end.

Yoshi slipped the pen inside her handbag. This was one memento she was determined not to lose. Inside the bathroom, the water in the shower came to a halt. Her husband would be ready soon. Unlike most marriages, she was routinely the first one dressed and ready to go. Tonight Yoshi wore her black Bill Blass. She adorned it with a dark red shawl that Madame Isobe had given her shortly before her death.

Yoshi slid open the glass door and stepped out onto the hotel balcony. It had a magnificent view of Rock Creek Parkway, with its bridges of concrete surrounded by the low-lying apartment buildings of white marble, yellow limestone and red brick. Washington was such a curious town, she thought. One had to wait a long time to catch any glimmer of a soul, but Yoshi liked to think that she had been afforded a glimpse during the years when the legislation had been in committee, subject to the injustices of backroom wheeling and dealing on Capitol Hill.

The heat and humidity rose up from the ravine below her. She wouldn't need the shawl tonight, but she would wear it anyway as a talisman of the past and everything that had led up to this evening's celebration. The Omni Shoreham was built on the side of the tree-lined ravine that overlooked a ribbon of black asphalt. The Potomac River was a short cab ride away and beyond that was the airport, where they would fly out tomorrow morning.

"You ready?"

"Yes, dear," Yoshi replied and stepped back into the suite.

"What were you doing out there?"

"Just looking around. Waiting for you."

At such moments, the years fell away. In his eyes and in his smile, she saw him as he had once been—the young man who had done his best with what the world had dealt him. He was still solidly built. In fact, he hadn't retired from the local fire crew until ten years ago. But age was catching up to them. This final trip back to the nation's capital had been complicated by the grandchildren. Sasha and Cloe were sick and it would have been better for everyone if Grandma Yoshi had stayed home to help out. But Yoshi chose to come because the past needed to be honored and accomplishment needed to be celebrated. That was something she was determined to teach her grandchildren.

"That was damn decent of Senator Inouye's people to give us a tour of the Capitol," her husband said as they headed for the door.

"Yes," she replied. She resisted repeating her favorite line from a lobbyist about life on Capitol Hill—'You spend your time sitting on marble benches, waiting for people in suits to come out and lie to you'.

She straightened his bowtie and let her hands briefly settle on his shoulders.

"You look good in a tux," she said.

Downstairs, outside the ballroom, a crowd of people waited to enter. They recognized a few faces but were soon swept along with the multitudes.

"I find it heard to believe that all of these people had something to do with the law," Neil said.

"Hush," Yoshi replied.

"But it's true, hon."

As they made their way inside, they found themselves eavesdropping on a heated conversation behind them.

"So, I told him that you cannot keep everything hush-hush forever," one voice said.

"There are a lot of skeletons in the closet, especially in this town," replied another. "You know that, Chuck."

Yoshi turned back to see two men in their early thirties. They wore the ubiquitous dark suits—the foot soldiers for anything of consequence that happened in Washington.

"But I do know, sooner or later, the secrets come out," Chuck told his friend. "You know that, Ben. Somebody always spills the beans."

"And what's wrong with that?" Ben replied. "Isn't the truth supposed to set us free? Somebody famous said that, right?"

"Yeah, it's in the Bible, Ben."

"You see, I knew it was somebody famous."

"But between the last Senate hearing and what the Post had yesterday, I'm just plain worn out, Ben. Maybe we don't need to know every secret."

Ben laughed. "You know it doesn't work that way, Chuck. Nobody can keep a secret in this town. Never have, never will."

Neil took Yoshi by the hand and led her to their table near the front dais. Around them, the room momentarily grew quiet. The President had arrived and the Marine Corps band began to play "Hail to the Chief."

As everyone turned toward the door, Yoshi's husband leaned close and whispered in her ear. "If they only knew the stories you could tell, hon," he said. "God, they wouldn't believe it."

(From the National Archives)

WAR DEPARTMENT
Bureau of Public Relations
Press Branch
Tel. – RE 6700
Brs. 3425 and 4860
FOR RELEASE SATURDAY A.M., FEBRUARY 9, 1946
JOINT ARMY-NAVY RELEASE
A REPORT ON JAPANESE FIRE BALLOONS

A total of one hundred and ninety one paper balloons and three rubberized-silk balloons, all of Japanese origin, were found in the United States, Canada, Alaska, Mexico, and the Pacific Ocean area during the period from November 1944, to February 1946. In addition to the one hundred and ninety-four balloons, there were eighty-nine recoveries of small fragments of paper or other balloon parts, too incomplete to be classed as a balloon recovered. In all two hundred and eighty-three separate recoveries of balloon material were made, the findings ranging from small pieces of paper to a few almost intact balloons. Also, thirty-two bombs (or bomb fragments), which had been dropped by balloons on the North American continent, were found, and four hundred and seven reports of the sighting of one or more balloons in the air were received.

The balloons were launched in the early morning or early evening, when surface winds were low, by one of two methods. When the wind velocity was two miles per hour or less, the inflated and loaded balloon was held with doubled ropes passed through the loops at the equator of the envelope. One end of each holding rope was released simultaneously, permitting the balloon to rise free. When the wind velocity was greater, up to ten miles per hour, a different method was used. First, the ballast-dropping apparatus and load were placed on a stand several feet off the ground. The envelope was then filled upwind from the stand and loaded equatorially with sand ballast in special containers designed to open when pulled from below. The balloon was then walked into position.

The Japanese expected that information on damage caused by the balloons would be available from normal press channels and radio broadcasts. However, after the first mention of the original balloons was found, the press and radio of the United States and Canada maintained a very complete voluntary censorship at the request of the Army and Navy through the Office of Censorship, and thus denied the Japanese information as to the number of balloons arriving and the landing points.

The impact of that joint order was that the Japanese military ended the fire-balloon program of their own volition.

Acknowledgements

The party was in Washington, D.C., during the time that the Monica Lewinsky scandal rocked the Clinton White House. Until that point, I'd thought it inevitable, perhaps even good for the world that all secrets eventually come out. Now I wasn't so sure, and I was telling a friend about my change of heart when somebody nearby overhead me.

"Do you know about the best-kept secret of World War II?" this stranger asked.

Of course, we had no idea what he was talking about.

"The Japanese fire balloons," said the stranger. He said he worked at the Smithsonian Institution. He told us about these most curious Japanese war machines, and how the Roosevelt administration kept them secret from the American public. Having heard no word of their success, the Japanese ended the program because they thought their calculations, even the fire balloons themselves, were somehow flawed.

This stray fact of history stuck with me because I had fought forest fires in my mid-twenties. I knew first-hand how dangerous, mercurial and hypnotic coming face-to-face with a major forest fire can be. So began a tale that focused on the improbable link between war-time Japan and forest fires in the American West.

Now, one cannot draw close to the flames without others to show you the way. In that task I am indebted to Fred Schoeffler and the Payson Hotshots. Theirs is a far different world than many of us know. They were generous with their time and knowledge, and always kept an eye out for this tenderfoot from the East.

I need to thank John McKelvey, Hugh Thompson, Sue Husari, Lynn Biddison, and Dick Henry. They belong to a select group within the U.S. Forest Service often referred to by their peers as the "fire gods." They took the time to explain to me how large-scale forest fires gather force and need to be fought.

John Katsu was exiled to an internment camp with his family as a teenager. His insights of that ordeal were invaluable. Hal Fuller told me about growing up a generation ago in the Southwest. The good people at the Smithsonian were always there when I was perplexed by how the Japanese fire balloon actually worked. In addition, John Taylor and Will Mahoney of the National Archives were there to answer my questions about Japanese fire balloons and spying during World War II. At several crucial junctures, I would have been lost without Howard Mansfield's sense of American history.

I have relied on the prior labor of several excellent writers. Stephen Pyne's **Fire in America** remains the historical authority on this subject. In addition, Steve was generous with his time, often agreeing to meet with me when I was in the Phoenix area. Of course, there is Norman Maclean's landmark work, **Young Men and Fire** and his son John's **Fire on the Mountain**. Other useful books were: **Embracing Defeat: Japan in the Wake of World War II** by John W. Dower; **American Caesar** by William Manchester; **Japan's World War II Balloon Bomb Attacks on North America** by Robert C. Mikesh; **A Spy in Their Midst: The World War II Struggle of a Japanese-American Hero** by Richard Sakakida and Wayne S. Kiyosaki; **A Boy Called H: A Childhood in Wartime Japan** by Kappa Senoh; **Manzanar** by John Armor and Peter Wright, with photographs by Ansel Adams and commentary by John Hersey; **Nisei Voices: Japanese American Students of the 1930s–Then and Now** edited by Joyce Hirohata and Paul T. Hirohata; and **Printed to Perfection: Twentieth-century Japanese Prints from the Robert O. Muller Collection**, general editor Amy Reigle Newland.

Ethan Kline, Gary Brozek, Rafe Sagalyn, and Andrew Blauner were insightful readers and patient friends from the beginning of this often serpentine project. Alma Katsu, Elwood Reid, Carolyn Doty, Nick Delbanco, Oakley Hall, Colson Whitehead and Wendi Kaufman stepped up when I lost my way; and I wouldn't have gotten very far without the support of David Everett and the Johns Hopkins University Writing Program. And, in the end, Shana Yarborough and the great folks at Writer's Lair Books made sure this novel found a home in the world.

Tim Wendel
Vienna, Virginia

Author's Biography

Tim Wendel is the author of a half-dozen books, including **Castro's Curveball: A Novel**; and **The New Face of Baseball: The One-Hundred-Year Rise and Triumph of Latino's Favorite Pastime**, which was named Top History Book for 2004 by the Latino Literary Awards. His stories have appeared in *Gargoyle* and *The Potomac Review*, and his articles in *The New York Times, Esquire, GQ, Washingtonian* and *USA Today*, where he is on the Forum's op-ed Board of Contributors.

Wendel received a Master's Degree in Writing from Johns Hopkins University, and has worked on both coasts, covering everything from the Olympics to the America's Cup. He lives in northern Virginia with his wife and their two children. More of his stories can be found at www.timwendel.com.

Reading Group Guide

RED
RAIN

A novel by

Tim Wendel

A Conversation
with the Author of
Red Rain

How did the Japanese come to use paper balloons as a weapon?

Faced with dwindling resources, paper was one of the few materials that the Japanese could produce in large amounts. Once it was determined that the jet stream could carry the balloons (33 feet in diameter and made of several layers of paper) across the Pacific Ocean in approximately three days, they were rigged with 11-pound incendiary and sometimes 33-pound, high-explosive bombs. The Japanese Imperial command knew that fire balloons made of paper paled in comparison to other weapons being used by this point in World War II. Still, their goal was to generate the level of hysteria, especially along the U.S. west coast, that occurred after Pearl Harbor. In that way, the Japanese hoped to avoid an unconditional surrender to the Allies.

What historical significance do the fire balloons have?

The fire balloons would seem to be nothing more than a curious footnote to World War II. But in the aftermath of 9/11, they demonstrate how any country can be threatened by even the most primitive weapon. In addition, every threat doesn't need to be confronted by highly publicized direct measures. The struggle against the fire balloons was done behind the scenes by highly capable people. The Japanese abandoned the campaign because they thought, erroneously, that the balloons weren't reaching the U.S. In fact, if the Japanese had persevered and equipped the balloons with germ warfare (for example), the threat would have been far more dire.

Describe the typical flight of a balloon.

The Japanese decided the best time to launch was in the early morning, especially after the passing of a high-pressure front. Windy days often made filling the balloon with the necessary hydrogen gas too difficult. In fact, weather conditions were only conducive for launches three to five days a week. After launch, a combination of pressure vents and sand ballasts kept the balloon between 30,000 and 40,000 feet, for approximately three days and two nights. By that time, usually the balloon had reached North America, and either settled to earth or had a time fuse ignite the hydrogen, causing the bombs to fall.

Where did the fire balloons land?

With their flight path governed by the prevailing westerly

winds, the fire balloons were a difficult weapon to aim precisely. Most of the confirmed sightings were in the western U.S. and Canada, especially in the Pacific Northwest. The fire balloons fell on most of the western states and in one incident carried as far east as outside of Detroit, Michigan.

WHY DIDN'T THE JAPANESE WORKERS ASSEMBLING THE FIRE BALLOONS REALIZE OR KNOW MORE ABOUT WHAT THEY WERE PRODUCING?

Most of the workers in the initial stages weren't in the military. While there were rumors about what the vast streams of paper were used for, the balloons were routinely taken away from the women and young girls working on them as soon as they were completed. Few of these workers ever saw the balloons fully inflated and certainly not equipped with weapons. The project was top secret in Japan and only military personnel were present when the fire balloons were launched.

HOW EXTENSIVE WAS THE ALLIES' SPY NETWORK IN THE PACIFIC THEATER?

While it wasn't nearly as extensive as the Allies' effort in Europe against Nazi Germany, spies had been used successfully in the recapture of the Philippines. There were discussions within the Pentagon and General Douglas MacArthur's command about duplicating the effort in the Pacific in anticipation of the invasion of Japan, which was expected to take months. Of course, that changed with the decision to drop the atomic bomb on Hiroshima and Nagasaki in early August 1945.

Why were the Japanese-Americans who were interned in Manzanar and the other camps so eager to volunteer for the U.S. war movement?

First and foremost, they saw themselves as Americans and didn't understand why the federal government treated them so abysmally during this time. "Let us prove that we are the stuff of which the best citizens are made," said one Japanese-American high school student on the eve of World War II. By volunteering to serve in the armed forces, they hoped to demonstrate how loyal they were to their new homeland. Despite being interned in camps like Manzanar, Japanese-Americans were allowed to serve in the military, and thousands enlisted. The 100th Battalion and 442nd Regimental Combat Team out of Camp Shelby, Mississippi, were largely composed of Japanese-Americans and "fought with great distinction in Italy and France," according to **Manzanar**, a book by John Armor and Peter Wright, with photographs by Ansel Adams. The 100th Battalion and 442nd Regimental Combat Team won 18,143 individual decorations for valor in battle during World War II, including one Congressional Medal of Honor and almost 10,000 Purple Hearts.

What was the Conservation Civilian Corps or CCC?

The CCC was a federal work program started by the Roosevelt Administration. Besides fighting forest fires, they built bridges and roads and planted 2.5 billion trees between 1933 and 1942. At its height, the CCC employed 3.5 million men, and remains one of the most extensive public works programs in U.S. history. However, in the battle against the Japanese fire balloons, the administration decided new fire-fighting crews were needed. This was done, in large part, to help keep the balloons secret from the general public.

WHAT IS YOUR BACKGROUND IN FIGHTING FOREST FIRES?

I served on a Hot Shot crew, an elite 20-person firefighting unit, in the early 1980s. The crew was located in Payson, Arizona, where the 'home front' story for **Red Rain** takes place. My summer in Payson was one of the most intense and spiritual times in my life. I learned a great deal about teamwork and coming together under pressure. Away from a fire, those of us on the crew debated everything from our favorite movies to politics. But when we were on a fire-line, we trusted each other, often with our lives. If one of our squad leaders said to move in this direction or do this job, we did it—no questions asked. Since that summer, I've often written about forest fires, including covering the Yellowstone fires for *The Washington Post*.

Questions & Topics
For Discussion

1. During World War II, the United States made a conscious decision to keep the Japanese fire balloons a secret. What were the positive and negative ramifications of that decision? In general, what can be the positive and negative ramifications of keeping anything secret?

2. The first of more than nine thousand bomb-bearing fire balloons wasn't released until November 3, 1944. By this point, Allies had the upper hand in Europe and increasingly in the Pacific theater. The fire balloons were considered a last-ditch effort to retaliate against the United States. Some historians even called the use of man's oldest air vehicle pathetic or generally useless. But what if the Japanese had been able to employ the fire balloons earlier in the war? Perhaps even have launched such weapons from other points in the Pacific? Would that have made a difference in how the war in the Pacific ended?

3. Throughout the story, Yoshi seemed to be constantly searching for affection. Do you agree or disagree? What do you think was the source of this need?

4.   In 1942, people of Japanese descent living in California and the western parts of Washington, Oregon and Arizona were incarcerated. One of the major internment camps was Manzanar, which was located near the California and Nevada border. Despite being removed from the general U.S. population, many Japanese-Americans volunteered for military or other jobs in the war effort. Is that surprising? Would it happen today?

5.   The Roosevelt administration and General MacArthur's command decided the best way to fight the fire balloons was by keeping them secret from the general public. They didn't want to alarm U.S. residents, especially along the West Coast. In the end, the measure appeared to work as the Japanese military ended the fire balloon campaign because they didn't think it was very successful. Would such an approach work today?

6.   What was the basis of the tension between Leo and his father?

7.   Was the fact that the fire balloons were kept secret in any way responsible for the death of those who died in the Cortez fire?

8. The United States was severely devastated by the attack on Pearl Harbor and by the attacks which occurred on 9-11. Compare and contrast the American responses toward people living in America who subsequently became viewed with suspicion. Were these the proper responses?

9. Do you feel having a female (Yoshi) rather than a male protagonist added to or detracted from the story?